Alimar's Quest

by

Mark and Josie McKinney

DREW,
I HOPE YOU ENJOY OUR BOOK.
IT IS NICE TO RECONNECT WITH
FRIENDS FROM MY CHILDHOOD.

Mark McY—
Josie

First published by Dog Ear Publishing
4010 W. 86th Street, Ste H
Indianapolis, IN 46268
www.dogearpublishing.net

dog ear
PUBLISHING

ISBN: 978-160844-503-5

Printed in the United States of America

Dedication and Acknowledgements:

This book is dedicated, in loving memory, to David Warren McKinney. His passion for the art of literature and his dream of writing a novel "one day" gave us the motivation and desire to take the time to make ours a reality. Since you weren't given the time, this book is for you Dad.

This book could not have been written without the support of our entire family. Most importantly, our sons were a huge part of making it the story it became. Johnathan, our youngest, created every fantastical creature in the book. From the docile yegoxen to the nasty nocturnals, he gave us detailed specifications on every one. He was also our top motivator with his daily question of "How much did you write today?"

Tyler, our oldest, is a very talented artist who is currently creating custom tattoos we never would have known could be done. Some of the incredible work he has shown us reminded us of our story. We asked him to take the time to draw a few simple illustrations. Once we saw them, we begged him for more. What you see is what we got. If we have our way, you will see twice as many in the future books!

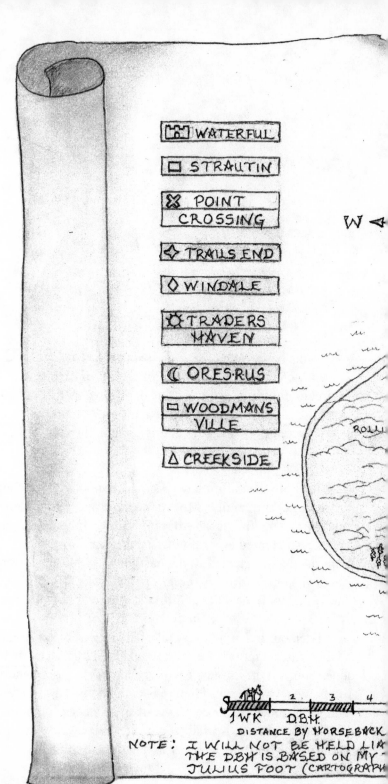

WATERFUL

STRAUTIN

POINT CROSSING

TRAILS END

WINDALE

TRADERS HAVEN

ORES·R·US

WOODMANS VILLE

CREEKSIDE

W ◄

ROLL

1WK D.B.H.

DISTANCE BY HORSEBACK

NOTE: I WILL NOT BE HELD LIA
THE D.B.H IS BASED ON MY
JULIUS FOOT (CARTOGRAPH

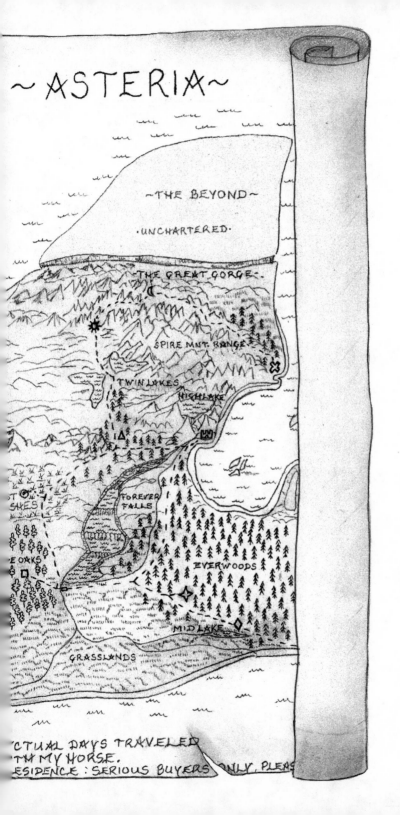

Prologue
Recurring

The battle raged on around the two men who fought back to back with a practiced ease. The slightly taller of the two had wavy brown hair that shone like copper in the waning light of the day. His hazel eyes were lit with intelligence and determination. Blood ran down his face from an ugly gash above one eye, and he had another even deeper cut on his shield arm.

The hazel eyed man was obviously tired, but fought on. His bow was on his back, and his sword, armor and shield were smeared in blood. His companion's face was hidden from view. His golden hair was barely visible as was a blood caked sword held in a well muscled arm.

They battled atop a grassy knoll that would have been a beautiful, peaceful vantage point to look out over the valley on any other day. While it was a cloudless day, no one present would call it beautiful or peaceful. Each foe that approached the pair was dispatched with proficiency.

It was a savage battle with steel clashing and men grunting with the effort of wielding sword and shield. Many combatants on both sides had fallen until the battlefield was littered with bodies and the ground soaked with blood.

As yet another undead creature approached, the hazel eyed man was forced to step over a fallen comrade. As always, he was aware of his companion's movements behind him. The two worked hard to keep their backs towards one another and never let an enemy get passed them to the space between.

As he blocked the creatures thrust, his front foot found purchase on the back of one of the littered bodies. He rammed his sword straight through the creature's torso. It shuddered as he pulled it free. Had this been a man, he would've fallen dead. Instead, it only cost the creature a moment's pause. The hazel eyed man used that pause to sever its head. Only then did the creature fall to join the carpet of bodies.

As he stepped back to close the gap between him and his companion, he felt movement under his feet. Glancing down he saw that one body was trying to rise. He quickly severed its head too and readied himself as the next foe approached. Yet another head rolled passed him as his companion dispatched one as well.

The smell of sweat, fear and blood was thick in the air. As the sun touched the horizon, the constant press of combatants eased. The two men knew that they were on the winning side of the battle for now, but only one death could end it all.

The moment of that death was now approaching. A figure moved with frightening grace through the field of bodies. The figure was clad all in black. Equally black was his hair. Even his eyes seemed unnaturally dark in his pale face. He was The Dark Lord. No man had been able to stand before him this day. He had slaughtered them all.

His army was made up of men and undead. The men who followed him looked to be an unsavory lot. The undead obviously had no choice in the matter. His staff sent tendrils of power across the knoll. It wove its way through his undead creatures giving them some sort of artificial life force. The tendrils also skimmed the ground, where the newly dead lay. Every body the power touched that still had its head, rose and fought for him.

Boys not yet of age to join in the fighting for the King-dom beheaded the bodies of all who had fallen with sharp-ened axes. They worked diligently to reach the bodies before the magic. Those they couldn't reach in time rose from the ground and joined in the fight anew. Even those that wore the colors or crest of the kingdom rose to fight on the opposing side.

As the Dark Lord fought through the sea of bodies, the hazel eyed man began battling his way towards him. The blood on his armor and shield did not hide the noble crest of the King. Destiny called and would be answered this day. Even through the blood and sweat, grim determination was etched onto his face.

The hazel eyes of the King locked on the Dark Lord just as the Dark Lord's eyes locked on his. Men and creatures on both sides continued to fall away between them until they stood framed in the light of the setting sun. They both under-stood that, for one of them, this would be the final battle.

The noise of the fighting around them faded until it was as if they stood on this blood soaked knoll alone. They looked at one another, not with hatred, but with wary accep-tance. Both knew they could not deny their fates. With a slight nod and a sigh from both men, the fight began.

Steel and magic along with sheer force of will were the weapons used. Both men held their ground for several min-utes. Sword struck staff. Sparks of magic seemed to grow brighter as the sun dipped further down below the horizon. Suddenly, the King struck with such force it seemed the staff would shatter. The force of the blow almost knocked the Dark Lord to his knees. The Dark Lord's eyes grew cold as he straightened. Magic shot from his staff hitting his opponent with a searing blast.

The King fell to his knees and felt his heart sputter in his chest. He knew this was the end for him, but could not let this be the end of all that was good. He could not let Hell on

Earth be the future for his people. With his last ounce of strength, he thrust his sword.

The Dark Lord had thought it was over. He had seen the life fading from his opponent's eyes and was already raising his staff in victory. A shout was on his lips when he realized something was wrong. He was shocked to see a spark of life return to the King.

Death had been his companion for many years. He had thought it was on his side. The blow from the King came too fast for him to defend himself. The blade struck home and the victory cry on his lips died with him. Both men fell to the ground simultaneously, one dead and one dying.

The sounds of battle returned to the ears of the dying King. He had killed the Dark Lord, but knew that his heart was soon to beat its last beat. As he lay there dying, he couldn't help but wonder if this was a true victory for his people. He struggled for every breath hoping his friend would make it to his side before it was too late.

As the magic of the Dark Lord faded from his staff, the undead fell like marionettes whose strings have been cut. The men that were left in the Dark Lord's army were quickly outnumbered and began to flee as the soldiers of the Kingdom began to cheer. The King was glad there would be no more death this day. The cold numbness of his own death was spreading through him.

His relief was great when he saw his friend finally kneel beside him. His fair-haired friend had distress and anguish marring his usually happy face. The King looked fiercely into the clear blue eyes of his companion. He took the man's hand and spoke his last words, "Louis, take my child. Take him, and protect him. I trust you above all others. For Asteria's sake, I pray this ends here, but if it does not you must see he is ready."

The boy awoke. Gasping for air as if he had been in the battle himself, he shook off the last remnants of sleep. What did this mean? He had never before seen the end of the battle in his recurring dream. The face that had always been hidden to him in the dream had finally been revealed.

A chill went through him as he pushed off his covers. Not from the cold of the morning, but the implications of the final piece of the dream. He quickly dressed and went to find his uncle. He needed the answers to questions he had been asking for years. It was obvious to him, now, that his uncle had the answers he needed.

Chapter 1

The Truth

Alimar was nearing the end of his fourteenth year. He had lived with his aunt and uncle his whole life. They lived far from any cities or towns and very few other families lived nearby. Winter had just ended and while the morning was cool, spring was in the air.

Alimar's room was on the second floor of their modest, but comfortable home. His aunt and uncle's bedroom and one spare room were the only rooms upstairs. As Alimar dashed down the stairs, he didn't see his aunt. He figured she must be starting to get the dirt turned for this year's garden, or maybe sleeping in a little since it was still very early.

At the bottom of the stairs was a small living room that held a large fireplace. The furniture was unmistakably hand carved and well cared for. The kitchen took up the bulk of the main floor with a large wooden table sitting between the two rooms. Alimar rushed through the kitchen door out onto a small covered porch.

Even though they were far from any towns and cities, they lived just off a main road travelers frequented. His uncle ran the messenger delivery service between two major cities. Couriers would drop off messages and packages from the south, picking up any that were headed back that way. The riders would come from the north and do the same.

His uncle also provided travelers on long round trip journeys with a fresh horse while boarding theirs. Long trips could be hard on a horse if the rider was in a hurry. This way they could make better time, and still have a healthy horse when they finally made it back home.

They also had a small garden, but mostly just for their own needs. Occasionally Alimar's aunt would sell her herbal remedies or a little of their produce during the growing season to the travelers.

While Alimar helped with the horses and the tending of his aunts herbs and garden, he was not often able to interact with the people that came through. It seemed as though he was always given chores that would keep him out of the way when his uncle saw visitors coming down their rocky lane.

He often wondered who they were and where they were going. He wished, sometimes he could go too. He yearned for some sort of adventure or excitement in his life.

His life was simple and safe. He found it rather dull, but was careful not to complain to his aunt and uncle. They had always treated him as if he were their own. They had no other children. He had always secretly thought if they would have had children of their own, they would not have wanted him. There was nothing special about him, after all.

Alimar thought of himself as average. He felt he had average looks, and average smarts. He was tall and gangly, always growing out of his clothes as soon as his aunt made more that fit him. His brown hair grew too fast and always seemed to hang in his eyes. It had just enough waviness to be unruly. His eyes seemed to be confused about what color they were. Some days they were clearly blue, but other days they hinted at hazel or grey. His feet were too big always causing him to stumble about awkwardly. His aunt said he just hadn't grown into them yet.

He knew where to find his uncle. His uncle had a routine that he rarely deviated from. Alimar struck out towards the stables. His stride was long and sure. As he had expected, his uncle was busy grooming the horses that would go out today.

As soon as he saw his uncle, his step faltered. His uncle, though getting on in years, was a strong, proud man. He stood tall. The muscles on his arms working as he brushed the horse's mane and tail. His grey flecked hair still gleamed golden in the morning sunlight.

As he caught sight of Alimar coming towards him, his mouth began turning upward in a smile of greeting, then faded as his blue eyes focused on Alimar's grim expression. Alimar looked into the blue eyes that he had seen just minutes ago in his dream. Though older, Uncle Louis was unmistakably the man he had finally seen at the end of it.

His uncle spoke first, "You've had that dream again then, haven't you? What did you see this time to give you that sullen look?" Concern deepened the lines on his brow.

Alimar opened his mouth to tell his Uncle Louis the new end to his dream, and realized that it would change everything. He wasn't sure yet how things would change, but change was coming. He suddenly wished he had just gotten busy with his chores and not rushed to his uncle with this. He realized he was afraid to know what this meant.

"Uncle Louis, it is my dream I came to speak of. I realize now it can wait. I will get to my chores and we can speak of this at a less busy time." Alimar turned to go, but felt his uncle's hand gently take his shoulder to turn him back to face him. His uncle didn't speak, but waited for Alimar as though he understood the gravity of the situation.

"Why do these dreams plague me so? Why do I have them so much more often as I get older? It is almost every night now." Alimar avoided getting to the truth of it by asking the questions he had been asking for years.

His uncle's expression said he knew Alimar was holding back. "I know this isn't easy. I know you want answers that I haven't been able to give you. The time for those answers may be sooner than I had hoped. For now, you have to tell me what you saw. What was different that has you so disturbed?"

Alimar knew that there was no point in arguing. His uncle had always been direct and to the point. He had come to expect nothing less of Alimar. He shook his brown mane sadly. "Uncle, I saw the final battle. It was more real than ever. It had no feeling of a dream this time. It was as real as if I had actually been there. More importantly, I saw you. You are the man that fought back to back with the King. You went to him as he died. He called you by name. He told you to take his son." His voice wavered and grew so quiet he was almost whispering at the end.

Fear crossed his Uncle Louis's face like a ghost in the fog. Then it cleared, leaving sadness behind that Alimar had seen from a distance when his uncle hadn't known he was observing him. He had never seen this sadness up close. It made Alimar's chest feel tight.

"Alimar, I have dreaded this day. I hoped it was still far off if ever it did come. I knew when you started having the dream more frequently that we were running out of time. I am not done teaching you. You are but a boy, a strong and capable boy, but a boy none the less. How can the time be now? It can not be so."

His uncle's voice was almost as quiet as Alimar's had been. He shook with frustration. He looked at Alimar. Alimar was very still. The color had drained from his face. His uncle realized that he was making the situation worse for Alimar and worked to get control of his emotions. He stood up straight and continued. His voice growing strong and clear again.

"All of these years I have avoided your questions and put you off. Now it is time for you to know. It happened just like in your dream, Alimar. It was the most awful experience in my entire life.

We were waiting there on the top of that beautiful hill. We could hear the enemy approaching. Suddenly the wind changed direction and the smell was so bad the men around us began to gag.

As the army came through the trees we could see the undead. They were in all stages of rot. From the newly dead that must have climbed out of their graves to join the army as they approached our position, to the dead that were almost completely skeletons.

We realized quickly when the fighting started that we would have to take off the heads of the undead to put them down. We soon found out that applied to our own dead as well. Men were fighting the enemy one minute and the next having to fight their friends, comrades and even their kin.

Soon our young squires were forced to pitch in or we would have been overrun. They were only there to carry our gear, care for our horses, and bring us what we needed from time to time. They were too young to have had to do what had to be done. Soon we had all of them beheading the fallen. They had to sever heads of men they had known. Many cried at first, but eventually became numb due to the shock of it.

I was fighting back to back with the King. We had gained the upper hand. I did not see the Dark Lord at first. I felt the King move away from me as I continued fighting. By the time I could turn to see what was happening, the King and the Dark Lord were locked in battle. I started fighting my way towards them.

When the undead all suddenly dropped to the ground, I turned in joy to your father sure that it meant that he had killed the Dark Lord. Then I saw him lying in a pool of his own blood right next to the man he had still managed to kill. At first I thought he was already gone. He wasn't, but by the time I reached the King he nearly was.

He had fought to hang on long enough to ask me to take his son. To protect him and train him in case it wasn't over. Unfortunately, it isn't over. Your dreams told me it wasn't, but I had hoped I was wrong. Now I know the truth of it and so must you.

I took you. I hid you. I raised you as my own far from the world we came from. You are the son the King spoke of Alimar, and now your quest must begin."

Chapter 2

Pride and Acceptance

Before Alimar could ask any other questions his aunt came across the yard towards them. Both man and boy stopped talking to watch her approach. The look on her face was one of distress.

Her hair was dark brown, almost black. She was a petite woman, but far from fragile. She had streaks of gray that ran through her hair. Even with the gray hair and the lines around her eyes that crinkled when she laughed, she still seemed almost youthful.

She smiled often and usually had a bounce to her step that most grown women lost. She stayed active and fit tending her garden and collecting herbs in the forest. This day she had no bounce and her distress showed all of her years.

"Louis, I could see it on your face all the way from the kitchen window. It can't be. He is not ready. I am not ready to lose him." To the surprise of all three, Aunt Jana threw her arms around Alimar and began to weep.

Alimar was astonished. His aunt had always been the strongest woman he had ever met. She had always been kind, but firm with him. He knew she had affection for him, but the love and grief that poured from her now made him realize just how blind he had been.

He looked over his shoulder at his uncle whose eyes glistened with the same emotions. They loved him. He had been so childish and foolish. He was special. He was their family. Strength and pride rushed through him.

"Alimar just look at you. At this moment you look so much like your father. He would have been so proud. I see now what I have tried so hard to ignore. You will be just fine. You are our King."

His uncle spoke these words and did something Alimar had never thought to see his uncle do. He knelt. He knelt in front of Alimar. Alimar turned to his aunt as she shifted away from him. Tears still streamed down her face, but they were now tears of pride and acceptance. She too knelt at Alimar's feet.

Louis had spent his entire life in the service of his Kingdom. When the King had asked Louis to take his child, Louis had done it without a second thought. He would give his life to protect this young King. He hadn't even consulted his wife. When Jana saw the baby in Louis's arms all those years ago her eyes went wide.

She had also been in the service of the King. That is how she and Louis had met. She had been a young herbologist with a touch of magic. At a very young age she had been recognized as a great healer and maker of herbal remedies and was invited to live and work at the castle. She, like Louis, was a very loyal subject.

Louis had explained what had happened quickly, as he stood holding their new King, and she hadn't asked a single question or made so much as a single protest. She had just started packing. It had been simple at first to care for the baby. She was too busy to think too much about it with all the work of it.

Somewhere along the way Alimar became more than a job they had to do. He became this little person that looked to them for everything. As he grew so did their love for him grow, but always they remembered he was their King.

The Kingdom was a very traditional one. Even very close friends and advisors treated the royal family with great respect. What Alimar didn't understand yet is that in all the years they had been raising him, they had been warring inside. To teach a child to be respectful when all of your training tells you to grovel to him, it had not been easy.

Finally, now he knew. It was a relief and a joy to finally let down the walls they had built around the truth of Alimar being the King. To kneel before him was an honor but he didn't understand that.

Alimar shook his head in disbelief. His thoughts were in turmoil. This couldn't be happening. He was a regular boy of fourteen. He mucked out horse stalls and ran through the forest. He was no King.

"What are you doing? Get up, both of you. This is not right. You shouldn't kneel to me. Please get up. I need to know what is happening." He dropped to his knees shaking with distress. He grabbed them both and hugged them fiercely. While they had raised him well, nothing could have prepared him for this.

The three got slowly to their feet. Louis spoke first, "Alimar, what you have to understand now is that it has been very difficult for us to raise you as a normal boy when you are anything but. Understand that we love you like our own in our hearts, but you are our King. Hiding it all these years has been very difficult.

We don't know when we will see you again. While that makes us feel very protective and insecure as parents, we have known this day was coming from the moment we took you. You would always have to resume your rightful place in the Kingdom one way or the other.

We even thought a long time about whether to raise you as our son or not. We didn't for two reasons. First, we needed to be reminded that, while we cared for you, you didn't truly belong to us. Also, we wanted you to realize, even if it was just on a basic level, that you were not meant for this place.

So before you went, we had to show our respect in the most profound way possible. As much as it is a shock to you, you are the King of all that you see, and of everyone you meet. Remember that and you will figure out the rest."

Alimar's aunt, realizing he was in shock and needed some kind of normalcy even if just for a little while, took his hand and started leading him towards the house. Her practical side kicked in as it always had in times of great change. "Come on you two. Let's get some breakfast in our bellies and get this all cleared up."

Alimar trailed behind his aunt and his uncle followed. No one spoke. They entered the kitchen and Alimar's aunt led him to a chair. She then went about pulling ingredients out to put together some breakfast. Once Louis came in she spoke again.

"Louis, it's time he hears all of it. Start from the beginning. Alimar, you just try to take it all in and wait till the end to ask questions."

Alimar watched his uncle as he joined him at the table. Suddenly it felt as if this were the last meal they may have together. He wished his uncle wouldn't speak. He wished for his simple life. It no longer seemed dull. He didn't wish for anything but for things to go back to normal.

There was one thing he had already learned, though. No matter what happened next, his life would never be normal again. Then his uncle, with a sigh, began from the beginning.

Chapter 3

Kilian and Alana

"I will go, and you can't stop me. I am older than him by over a year. Just because I am a girl doesn't mean I will pick a husband and stay here for the rest of my days content in the kitchen.

No offense Momma, but that just isn't for me. If Kilian gets to go off adventuring then so do I. If you make me stay here I will just run away the first chance I get. At least this way Kilian and I can look after each other. "

Kilian grunted at this, but didn't speak as Alana glared at him. Alana was tall and curved. She was also strong and muscled. She had insisted on training with her brother. Their father had indulged her. She dressed more like a boy than a girl, but no one would make the mistake of thinking she was a boy. At seventeen years, she was more woman than girl. Besides her womanly curves, she had long brown hair that gleamed red in the sun. Her green eyes were like emeralds.

Many men had bid for her favors. She was not interested in any of them. She had other plans for herself. She had always known she was different than most girls and had no interest in changing that. Her parents had thought she would grow out of her tomboy ways, but they were both realizing how wrong they had been.

Kilian's hair was the red Alana's hinted at being. It was straight and well-kept. While her eyes sparkled like emeralds, his eyes were a subtler hazel. He was handsome and tall like his sister. At sixteen he still had very little facial hair, much to his dismay, but otherwise he was quickly growing into the man he would become. Muscles rippled on his arms and under his shirt.

He glanced at their parents with humor on his face. What had they expected to happen? He had always known that when this day came, it would come for both of them. His parents just hadn't wanted to see it.

"Alana, what you ask is not acceptable. Men traditionally leave home to find their true path. Some return home, some don't. A woman just doesn't go off like that. I let you train like a man and now I see what a mistake it was. The world can be a hard and frightening place. There are places Kilian will have to go that you should and could not."

Her father spoke in his most stern voice. Somehow it never had worked on Alana. Her mother had always said that it was because he spoiled her too much. He had always told both of the children stories of great adventure while they were growing up. He had never even thought that the stories should be reserved for only Kilian.

Kilian had started off hunting with his father with a small blowgun. He was soon making easy kills of small game like rabbits and pheasants. As he grew stronger his father taught him to use a bow. He excelled at that as well and was soon hunting larger game.

Until just the last couple of years Alana had always been stronger and faster than Kilian. She had taken up his blowgun when Kilian had switched to the bow. Kilian told her she should get a bow too, but after trying it a couple of times decided she liked the blowgun better.

They lived far enough from town that the two had been close growing up and had stayed that way. They weren't just siblings, they were best of friends. They spent most of every day growing up in the forest tracking, hunting and playing. The fact that Kilian had gotten taller and stronger than Alana, just made her work that much harder to prove she was equal in every way to him.

" Well, Da, now that you put it that way I am not so sure I want to go myself." Kilian, always trying to lighten the mood, said with sarcasm.

Their father looked at both of them with frustration on his face. He had light brown eyes and strawberry blond hair that he had his wife keep cropped close to his head. He was tall and muscled in a wiry thin way. "Oh the both of you could drive a man early to his grave. " He looked to his wife. "Ily, can you help me explain to these two why Alana can't go off with Kilian?"

Alana and Kilian both looked at their mother. She was the perfect country wife. She wore her thick red hair in a long braid down her back. Her eyes were green, but a soft green that was a cross between the colors of her children's eyes. She was not as tall but just as curvy as her daughter. She had thickened slightly over the years, but was still fit.

She seemed to enjoy her life and did spend much of her time in the kitchen. She was a quiet woman. She didn't always have a lot to say and let their father do most of the disciplining.

"I have listened to this argument that I think we all knew was coming. I am content with the choices I made with my life. I will not force those choices on my daughter. She is capable and you have helped her be so by allowing her to train alongside her brother. I am not happy with this, Davin, but we can not stop it now."

The stunned silence that followed spoke volumes about what a long speech that was for her. Not one of the other three family members would have thought this would be her response.

"Well, I guess I'm just a bit outnumbered now aren't I? I guess we all have some hard thinking to do about this. I for one need some air." They all watched as Davin left the house.

"I always knew this day would come." Ily looked sadly at both of her children. "Keep each other safe from harm. That is all I can ask." She got up and went into the kitchen with her back turned. They could hear her sniffling. She was hiding her tears from them.

Kilian and Alana looked at each other sadly. Their mother obviously needed some time to herself. They knew that if she wanted to talk any more on the subject she would rather come to them about it when she was ready.

"Ma, we're going outside to practice. Everything is going to be alright. You'll see. We will take care of each other. We always have." Kilian spoke in his most serious tone.

Kilian and Alana both got up from the table. They walked sedately out the back door. As soon as Kilian stepped into the sunlight, he turned to Alana with a sparkle in his eye and his wicked grin back on his face. "Keep up slow poke."

The race was on. He dashed through the yard with Alana right on his heels. Around the yard and through a gap in the trees they ran. Alana's hair streamed behind her like copper ribbons in the sun. Their laughter floated through the trees.

Their father shook his head as he heard them from the other side of the house, but couldn't stop the smile from forming. He understood the bond that Alana and Kilian had formed. He had always known it would be hardest on Alana when Kilian left. As their father, it was his duty to teach his son to protect himself and prepare him for the world and its dangers.

Davin was a hunter. He spent his time in the woods. He hunted and trapped and used everything he caught. He used or traded the fur, his family ate the meat and if he had extra he would trade that too.

He had naturally taught his children to hunt. Part of those lessons included only killing when it was necessary. He firmly believed that you only killed for food or self defense, never for sport. It was not something to be taken lightly.

He had always admired Alana. Her desire to train with Kilian had, at first, seemed like a lark. Then as the years past, he couldn't think of any good reasons why she should not continue. They lived in the forest. She might need to protect herself from danger.

He blamed himself for her desire, no, determination to go with her brother. He felt as if his heart could not hold up to losing both of them. He just couldn't see a way to keep Alana from going.

Kilian and Alana returned to the back yard. They were breathing hard, but not tired in the least. "I would have beaten you had I had more room to pass on the end of the trail." Alana threw out as Kilian went into the shed to retrieve their practice swords.

"Delude yourself if you'd like. You do have another excuse." He tossed her sword to her has he jumped out of the shed with his up and ready. "You've got shorter legs." He finished with a grin.

Alana shrieked in feigned anger. Then a matching grin lit on her face. The swordplay began. Alana had great speed and agility and used it to equal Kilian who was bigger and stronger.

Their father had joined their mother in the kitchen. He stood behind Ily and wrapped his thick arms around her in a comforting embrace. They stood at the window watching the well matched sparring.

"I needed you with me today. We're going to lose them both." Davin said sadly.

Ily took his large callused hand in hers. "Better they are together. Better that than Alana slinking off by herself in the middle of the night. You know as well as I she would do it. She is so headstrong. I don't like it any more than you do, but there is nothing to be done."

She turned into his chest and they hugged quietly as shouts, laughter and stinging remarks floated in through the window. Kilian and Alana sparred on with the tirelessness of youth. Davin kissed his wife softly.

"Well, I have a trip to town to make then. I better get going. I may be late returning. Don't keep dinner for me." He kissed her once more before breaking the embrace. He went through the front door as not to disturb his grown children. He went to the stables and saddled up his old horse. He rode off towards town with sad acceptance on his face.

Chapter 4

Gifts

The morning sun woke Alana. She had not seen her father for the rest of the day after their disagreement. When she had asked her mother about his absence at lunch, she had just said he had needed to take a trip to town for a few things. Alana had spent the rest of the day grumpy and out of sorts. She wanted this whole thing resolved.

The Kenney Family lived in a cabin Davin had built. Ily had been a merchant's daughter. When Davin had first seen her he had fallen instantly and madly in love. They spoke from time to time and she seemed fond of him too. He had wanted to court her, but had nothing to offer. He was a hunter who lived wherever the game took him.

So, he had found this piece of land on the edge of the most abundant forest in this half of the Kingdom. He had started cutting trees and building a cabin. He had gone months before making it back to town.

When he saw Ily again she looked terribly sad. He asked her what was wrong and found out that she was to be married, but she was not fond of the match her father had made for her. He took her aside and told her of his efforts to build a cabin and his desire to court her.

He asked her if she could talk her father into waiting on the wedding. He would come speak to her father himself once he could show he had something to offer. She said she would find a way to delay and admitted to having feelings for Davin in return. Elatedly, he returned to building his cabin.

Twice more he found time or need to go to town. Both times Ily was waiting for him. She was getting a little desperate for his proposal to her father. She was running out of excuses why she couldn't wed. Her father was growing impatient with her delays on his match for her.

Finally, the third time he went to town she begged Davin to talk to her father. He was insisting on setting a date for her to marry the match he had arranged for her. Davin made an appointment with her father. It wasn't unusual. If he had good quality furs to sell, he would do the same. Ily's father dealt in many items the townsfolk might need including furs for coats and blankets.

When Rand, Ily's father, realized that Davin was asking for his daughters hand instead of trying to sell him furs, he grew quite angry. Davin calmed him by professing his devotion to Ily and offering to take him to the cabin he had almost completed for their marriage home.

Rand finally relented with the agreement that if he felt it wasn't good enough for his daughter, Davin would leave town and not come back until she was wed to another. Davin felt that Rand was an honest businessman and would make an honest assessment of the home Davin was offering. He only hoped it was good enough. They set out together the next day. Ily watched as they rode out of town with hope and desperation on her face.

When Rand and Davin arrived at the site, Rand seemed unimpressed. They dismounted and Davin showed him all he had completed and explained the work he still had to do. Rand listened respectfully then asked for a timeline.

Rand offered him a deal upon hearing his reply. If Davin could finish the home in half the time he had said, then he could marry Ily. If he didn't, Ily would marry the other man and move away.

Davin didn't see a choice in the matter and sent his regards for Ily with her father. He got right to work knowing he would have no time to spare. He worked night and day, sometimes going without food or sleep till he just couldn't anymore.

On the last day, Davin heard horses approaching. He turned and, seeing Ily and both her parents riding up, shook his head in despair. Even at the pace he had been working, he still needed at least another week to finish.

All three dismounted and walked through the cabin. Davin was so tired and forlorn that he couldn't even follow along. When the three reemerged, Ily and her mother both had tears glistening in their eyes.

Rand looked stern and unreadable. Then he spoke, "Davin, I gave you an impossible timeline. You have made remarkable progress. You have proven your dedication to my daughter. You have my blessing."

Davin finished the home that they lived in to this day. He and Ily had been married and were very happy. The home was all logs. Even the eating table was made of logs. It was all one level with the original construction including a beautiful bedroom for the newly married couple that overlooked the forest.

When Alana had been born, Davin had added her room onto the far side of the house and then had added one more when Kilian had come along. The fireplace was in the kitchen and acted as both heat source as well as cook top. Morning sun poured in to the kitchen making it the favorite spot for the whole family.

Ily had taken to her new home and life with ease. She made breakfast each morning and baked throughout the day. This day was no exception. She had meat sizzling on the fire, and biscuits in a pan.

The smell of breakfast lured Alana to the kitchen. The scene was so like yesterday that she hesitated in the doorway. She didn't want to argue with her father. She just had to go with Kilian. She put her chin up and entered the kitchen. Kilian was already at the table with Davin.

As she sat down and faced her father, she realized that something was different. He looked at her as if he had a secret. He didn't look angry. He looked... mischievous. She sat in silence as her mother put breakfast on the table. She wasn't sure how to bring up the subject of her leaving with her father acting so strange.

Their mother joined them at the table and they dished up and began to eat in silence. Suddenly, Alana realized this may be the last breakfast they had together as a family. She looked at Kilian and saw in his eyes the same thought.

Their parents had given them a good life. She felt bad over fighting so hard to leave them. She just knew she would never be happy staying.

"Da, please understand..."

"Alana, just eat your breakfast for now. Then I have something to show you and we can talk then. "

Puzzled, Alana went back to her breakfast. They continued eating in silence. Both Alana and Kilian started helping their mother clear the table while their father went into the yard. Alana gave Kilian a questioning look. He just shrugged. Neither one of them knew what their father was up to.

Their mother finally shooed them both out of the house. Their father stood in the yard, arms crossed, with a sack and a box at his feet. He looked at both of his children. With a lump in his throat he turned to Kilian.

"Son, we have been planning for this day for some time, haven't we? You always were determined to go off and be a soldier. Your skill in the forest and with the bow never held your interest beyond helping put dinner on the table. You always wanted to pick up your practice sword every chance you got.

I knew it would be hard to see you heading out on your own, but I knew it was coming. I had time to prepare. I did some trading and called in a favor or two and had a couple of things made for you."

From the sack he took out a sword and scabbard. They were nothing fancy, but they were well made and crafted especially for Kilian. Kilian took them from his father and with a whisper of steel drew the sword out of the scabbard. The steel shone bright. He tested the balance and weight of it, and then swung it whistling through the air. He slid it home and opened his mouth to thank his father.

"Wait, I've got one more thing for you now."

Out of the box he removed some heavy leather armor. It had also been made for Kilian. He traded sword for armor so Kilian could try it on. It fit him perfectly and made him look more grown up than ever. He took the sword back from his father and slung it across his chest so it rested with the hilt just over his shoulder.

"You shouldn't have, Da. You're going to be working twice as hard around here. These must have taken some precious trades. I guess I should just say thank you. Grumbling won't change what you did, and I can't say I am not happy to have these. Thanks Da."

Kilian hugged his father tight. He saw the look on Alana's face. She tried to smile, but she was too hurt. He didn't know what to do. As he let go of his father, he saw that he wasn't done yet.

Turning to Alana, their father spoke. "And you, my beautiful headstrong girl. Since I was in complete denial that you would leave us, I did not prepare as I did with Kilian. Now that I see there is to be no stopping you, I did the best I could with a quick trip to town. I couldn't have anything made special for you with only a day, but I did find something I think will do the job."

Out of the box he pulled out a second leather armor. This one was not custom made, so it had several straps that could be tightened or loosened to fit. It was also much softer that Kilian's so it would mold to various shapes easier. Alana slipped it on with wonder in her eyes. With the help of both her father and Kilian she got it adjusted to fit.

She watched with damp eyes as her father pulled a second sword and scabbard out of the bag. It was light and made to fit a smaller man. The balance, when her father gave it to her, wasn't quite as right as Kilian's was for him. It was the best she had ever had, though.

"Da, thank you so much! Does this mean I have your blessing then?" Alana got right to the point as usual.

Her father pulled her into his arms for a hug with a chuckle. "You are a wonder. We will miss you dearly. One thing is for certain. The two of you together will be safer and stronger than either of you alone. You have our blessing."

Both Kilian and Alana ran into the house to show their mother what their father had given them. They then began to prepare to leave the safety and comfort of their home in trade for the unknown.

Chapter 5

History

"There is one thing you have to understand, Alimar." His Uncle Louis started out. "Everything that happened to your father, and his before him, was foretold. These dreams you have been having are part of that foretelling.

I don't know exactly how long your father had to prepare after his last dream. I do know that the one you have had now showing the end of your father's life, has happened much earlier for you than your father's did.

The fact that you are not even fifteen yet concerns me greatly. I thought you would at least reach manhood before this time began. You see, now that you have had your final dream, you must go start your quest."

"I don't think I understand. What quest must I start?" Alimar didn't feel like he was getting any real answers. In fact, he was thinking of many more questions.

"You must leave here, and right away. Events are in motion that neither one of us can predict or control. Your preparations must begin because somewhere out there, your enemy, whoever that may be, has begun his preparations.

"Uncle, I don't have any enemies. I am just a farm boy, or at least have been so far. How could I have an enemy?" Alimar said in alarm.

"You can no longer afford to be naïve, Alimar! Dark times are here for you. The comforts and protection we have given you are no good to you now.

Let me explain more of what I know. Somewhere back in your family's history, two brothers were born. They were twins, but looked nothing alike. The first born was fair and a good child. The second, but by only minutes you understand, was dark through and through.

The King naturally groomed the oldest to take the throne when the time came, practically ignoring the second born. The younger grew bitter and discontent. He had some magical abilities and began practicing Necromancy in secret.

A trusted teller came to see the King. She told him she could see a great tragedy. Either she was unclear of what exactly would happen, or I just don't know the whole story. One thing is sure. She told the King he must put his younger son to death immediately if the tragedy was to be avoided.

The King was a confident, strong King. He was sure she was wrong. He didn't listen. While his younger son did not take after him, and was even a little odd, he was still his son. He surely posed no threat to the Kingdom.

Only weeks later, the King was dead. He had been poisoned, but no one knew who was responsible. The teller returned and asked to speak to the firstborn prince. She told him of her earlier visit and the warning she had given his father. She told him that she had no doubt that his brother was responsible for his father's death.

Children sometimes see things in other children, especially siblings that adults fail to see. The older twin knew his brother better than his father had. He believed the teller and asked her what to do. She told him to see to his brother's death before his brother saw to his.

The older prince was afraid of his brother. He had not yet been crowned and wasn't sure how to go about having his brother killed. He went to his father's most trusted advisor, told him the whole story, and asked him for advice.

The advisor was a careful man. He felt that having the young price killed would have gone against the King's wishes. Instead, he helped the prince have his brother banished from the Kingdom.

I don't know much else. What I do know is sketchy at best. Years passed and the new King was married and had a son. An army approached and without warning attacked the King's castle. It was the younger twin's army. Much of the army was made up of undead and evil creatures. The King and his army fought and the King was able to defeat his brother and kill him.

At some point later the teller returned. She warned the King that the threat wasn't over. She told him that his brother had had a son also, and that as long as a descendant lived from both brothers, the conflict would continue through the generations.

He tried to find the son of his brother, but was unsuccessful. He warned his son before his death. Eventually, his son took the throne and a battle took place that I don't know the outcome.

Down through the generations it has come to pass, just as the teller foretold. Your father had his battle. If the Dark Lord hadn't had a son, you would not have had the dreams and the chain would finally be broken. Once the dreams started, I knew that the Dark Lord also had a son.

You had only just been born. Most of the Kingdom was unaware of your birth. The King was determined to defeat the Dark Lord before he made the formal announcement. Then he died and I took you away as he wished. Your mother was devastated but knew she could not raise you and keep you safe. She went into hiding herself soon after we left and I know not what became of her.

So, your quest must begin. Years ago, if the dreams hadn't started, you would have gone back to the castle to start your training and schooling to take over the throne. Instead, I had to keep you hidden. The Dark Lord had many followers that would have surely done you harm if they could have found you.

Your quest will not be easy. Your father gave each of his most trusted advisors one of his most prized possessions. Not one of them knew the others item or hiding place. I can only start you on the trail your father has left for you. The more items you retrieve, the more danger of discovery you will be in.

Your father did this for two reasons. One, when the time came, you would have to go through vigorous tests to find the items he left for you and that would give you the strength you will need to meet your foe in battle.

Second, it would build your character and make you ready to take your place on the throne, with all the proof of your heritage and rightful place as King to show those that will challenge you. The caretaker for the throne will have to be totally sure it is you. There will be those that will not want you to come into power.

This is the last advice I will be able to offer you for some time. Be weary of all you meet. Keep your guard up, but take help when you are sure it safe.

I can not go with you although I wish I could and have pondered on it for some time. I am very recognizable in many parts of the Kingdom. Your father and I were almost always together. If I am with you, you will be recognized much more quickly. To keep you safe, I must let you go without me.

I am going to leave you to think on the things I have told you. I could tell by the frequency of your dreams as of late that the time was drawing near for you to have to leave us. Knowing it would take some time for him to get here, I sent for Fogerden who will travel with you.

I must go out and let him know the time has come. He has spent this last fortnight waiting to see if he was indeed needed. He is one of the ones you can count as a friend. He was a man your father trusted with his life. You can trust him with yours as well.

I know you have questions, but I have told you all I know. You will learn more as you progress. Go now and pack your things. Fogerden will not be long, and he will want to set out without delay."

With that Alimar was left to his chaotic thoughts. Having so many new things to digest at once was difficult. He decided the only thing to do was get packed and figure it all out as he went.

Chapter 6

Fogerden

Alimar hugged his aunt fiercely. He knew it may be a long time before he saw her again, if ever. He knew he could not take anything for granted now. Fogerden sat astride his horse ready to set out, just as Alimar's uncle had warned.

Fogerden was much older than Louis. His face was lined with age. He had obviously spent most of his life out in the elements. His face and hands looked like the tanned hides they sold in town for making coats and blankets.

Alimar turned to his uncle. He didn't know what to say. He had packed up enough clothing and gear to last several days at a time. He knew from his years working with his uncle not to load more on a horse than you had to.

Jana had packed him dried meats, fruit and berries. She had given him her favorite wine pouch filled with fresh spring water, warning him to be careful about where he refilled it.

Louis stood holding the reins of Alimar's horse. Alimar noticed that in addition to his saddle bags there was a scabbard strapped to the saddle horn for easy access when riding. He recognized the scabbard from all the training his uncle had done with him over the years.

"Uncle, I can't take your sword. It is your most prized possession."

"That is where you are wrong, son. You and your aunt are my most prized possessions. This sword is very dear to me because your father had it made for me. It is a fine sword, use it well. If something better comes along, don't hesitate to sell it.

Here is some coin, too. Remember to always keep it inside your tunic, especially in the cities. You'll get robbed blind and not even know it, if you don't! Now get going boy, before your aunt starts crying again."

Louis thrust a small sack of coin into Alimar's hand, gave him a quick hug, and pushed him towards his saddle. Alimar climbed onto his horse and Fogerden set off immediately. He gave a small wave and tapped his heels so his horse would follow.

He looked back at his aunt and uncle till the horses went around the bend and he could no longer see them through the trees. Part of him longed to stay home and go back to his boring life. There was a part of him, though, that longed for just a little adventure.

They headed west. He wondered where they were going and how long it would take to get there. Alimar knew the kingdom was a vast landmass in the middle of endless ocean.

The ocean was wild and dashed a boat up onto the reef that surrounded the kingdom if it sailed beyond the bay.

The fact that they were heading west told him little. Leaving his home you could only head east or west at first. There were many branches to the trail further down that would lead to different cities and towns Alimar had only ever heard about.

They rode in silence for some time. The trees along the trail were starting to get their spring buds. Wildflowers were beginning to bloom and birds called to each other as they swooped happily across the sky. The trail was well worn and wide enough for a wagon or two horses to ride abreast comfortably.

This was a major trail on the trade route through Asteria, so he expected to see many travelers. So far he had been disappointed. He understood now why he hadn't had much interaction with the travelers who had come to do business with his Uncle Louis. He had been in hiding after all.

Finally, Alimar thought he might get a little information from this stranger. He wondered to himself how Fogerden was involved with all this. He figured he better start out with the easy stuff.

"How long will it take for us to get where we are going?" Alimar started out by asking.

"We've only just been riding for an hour or so; do you need a rest already?" Fogerden asked impatiently.

Alimar realized how his first question must have sounded. He wasn't starting out very well. "No, not at all, I was just trying to make conversation. You don't know me. I don't know you. I just thought we could talk a little to pass the time."

Fogerden grunted at this, but replied respectfully. "If we ride steady and don't run into any trouble, it should take us about three or four weeks to get to Strautin. There will be a couple outposts for supplies along the road, though."

Alimar got the impression that Fogerden wasn't in the mood for small talk. He wasn't quite ready for the hard questions yet, so he retreated into his thoughts and they rode in silence. He would wait until Fogerden was ready to talk.

Many days passed uneventfully. The temperatures were getting a little warmer. The trees also seemed taller to Alimar. He was starting to see some trees and plants he hadn't seen around his home. They spoke little and rode till dark every day. Alimar made it a point not to complain or ask more questions.

At days end over a week into their trip, the shadows stretched far across the trail when Fogerden led them into a small clearing. Fogerden had told Alimar that they would have a day's rest here. There was a creek nearby to wash some clothes and lots of room for the horses to graze. They also needed to get more food as they were running low. Alimar was relieved to dismount from his horse and to have a day off of it to look forward to, but wouldn't have admitted it to Fogerden.

Fogerden went into the woods to set snares for small game. Together, they set up camp in silence and started a fire for warmth. Alimar thought to offer some of his last remaining dried food to Fogerden, but saw him pull out his own. They both settled down by the fire to eat.

"So, I know you have questions, and part of my duty is to answer them. I thought you'd ask when you were ready, but I guess you're waiting on me. Why don't I just give you some of what I know now and then maybe we can both get some sleep."

Alimar nodded in response and Fogerden continued. "I was a young soldier in training when the prince was born. The King, your grandfather I guess, was always worried about the prince.

One day the King was making an inspection on the troops, and there was a new recruit practicing his swordplay right near where I was. He had a strange look in his eye, the new man did. No one seemed to notice but me. He got a fevered look as the King grew near. I realized what he was going to do just in time. As he lunged for the King, I struck him down.

I had never killed a man before. I just reacted. It was my instinct to protect the King. I explained all of this when the King asked me to. He asked the others if they had noticed anything off about the new man. They all said they hadn't. The King asked me to come and see him after training was over for the day and he left.

I was very young, almost as young as you. I thought I was in trouble for killing that man. I thought maybe the King would have me punished or worse for being a murderer.

I knelt in front of the King later that day and asked him to please spare me. I promised not to be so rash in the future. He laughed, the King did. It was amazing to hear the King laugh.

He told me that I was not in trouble. He reminded me that I had saved his life. While all of the seasoned soldiers didn't notice a thing, I saw it and reacted with courage and speed. Then he thanked me.

He asked me if I would be willing to join his personal guard. He asked me if I would help him protect his son. I accepted and was honored. I trained twice as hard and seemed to have a natural ability to sense danger. Eventually, I became the head of his personal guard.

When your father became King, he asked me to continue that role. Eventually, before his death, he asked me if I would take on this duty if he were to be killed. So, young King, I am here at your father's request.

I'm ready to sleep now. We will have other nights for me to tell you more." With that Fogerden started preparing his bedroll.

Alimar did the same. Both of them where crouched down spreading out their blankets. Then a strange chill passed through the air. Fogerden spoke again looking through the flickering fire at Alimar, "Remember the trouble I spoke of that might slow us down? I think some of it has found us already." Fogerden drew his sword as he spoke.

Alimar followed the older man's example and armed himself. They stood and turned toward the cold breeze. Four glowing green orbs appeared in the darkness. Alimar realized they were eyes a split second before the creatures they belonged to sprung out of the black night.

Chapter 7

Leaving Home

Alana laughed happily as she slung her pack onto her horse. She was giddy with relief now that she wasn't at odds with her father. She was eager to get going.

Kilian was obviously ready to go too. He had his horse packed and was strutting around the yard in his new armor. Alana admired the workmanship of the custom made piece longingly.

"Afraid some creature is going to jump out of the woods at you already, little brother? We haven't even left home yet and you're already stinking up your new armor."

"You're just jealous. Don't think I haven't seen you looking at it. I can't help it if I am the man of the family."

At Alana's dark look, Kilian changed his tactics. "Yours is very nice, you know. And just think of the amazing armor makers in the big cities. Eventually when we have made our fortunes, we can both have the best armor ever made."

Alana and Kilian had practiced into the afternoon after their father had given them the new armor and swords the day before. They had all had an early dinner and Alana and Kilian had gone to pack and get a good nights rest. Their mother had wished them a safe journey and left to go pick berries after the early breakfast they had all shared.

They both knew she couldn't abide by long goodbyes, and understood her hasty departure.

Their father had gone into his storage area to retrieve a parcel, he had said. Kilian and Alana watched him walk towards them with a small twine wrapped box. He smiled at them both in turn before speaking.

"Your mother has left me to do this on my own. I am going to be quick about it so you can get on your way. I can see you're all ready to go.

Take this package to my old friend in Waterful. His name is Kamaron. He is part of the guard in the capital. Waterful is a beautiful city. It will be a good place for you to get a start. Kamaron will give you a good bit of coin for this parcel, too. That will help you once you are there.

The coin I gave you yesterday should get you through till you get to Waterful. I know you'll take care of each other. If you hear of anyone coming this way, try to get word to us.

Now get going. Daylight is wasting. Here is a map to get you to Waterful, and a description of how to find Kamaron once you are there."

He fiercely hugged them both. Then he thrust the map and parcel out to them. Kilian took them and tucked them into his pack. It was suddenly difficult for Alana to throw her leg over her horse. They both waved and trotted off.

On the familiar trail, it was easy to joke and pretend that they were just out for a ride. As they turned off the trail to town down a less familiar path, the seriousness of their journey suddenly struck them both. They grew quiet.

As the time passed, the rhythm of her horse lulled Alana into a kind of trance. She didn't even realize how much time had gone by till Kilian spoke up. The shadows had grown long on the trail.

"It will be dark in a couple of hours. We should start looking for a place to camp." He turned in his saddle to make sure she had heard him.

She nodded her agreement and tried to shake off the lethargy of the long ride. The trail was narrow and slightly overgrown. It was almost full dark before they came to an area with a small clearing they could camp in.

Kilian gathered some twigs and brush to start a fire while Alana unloaded the horses and took off their saddles. She gave them each some water, and tied them loosely so they could graze.

As they settled in by the fire, they spoke of what it would be like in the city of Waterful. They each had visions that varied, but both of them imagined riches and fame waiting for them. They did agree that it would be exciting and full of adventure.

They spoke of the journey to come and Alana wondered how many others sat in the dark on their way to places they had never been before. She thought about the places they would see. She wondered about the people they would meet and how their lives would change.

As they settled down to sleep, Alana heard noises in the woods. The horses seemed to shift about as they too heard the noises. She sang a soft lullaby to calm the horses as well as her own nerves. Then it was quiet again, and sleep washed over her.

She dreamed a strange dream. She was walking late at night through an unfamiliar town. The streets seemed deserted, but then three men stepped out of the shadows.

They started walking towards her with purpose. She reached for her weapon, but found that she was unarmed. One of the men laughed a mean laugh and she knew they meant her harm. She turned to flee.

She found herself cornered in a small graveyard. The fence around its perimeter was topped by vicious spikes. As she turned to go back out of the graveyard, the three men blocked her way.

She prepared to fight. As the men approached her, she saw from the dim light of the waxing moon that they were large and strong looking men. She didn't see how she could fight them all without a weapon. Desperation filled her.

Suddenly the ground beneath her feet began to shift. She was thrown aside, and cracked her head sharply on a crumbling tombstone. It took a few moments for her to shake off the blow.

She looked over and found that the three men had been surrounded and were being battered by several corpses. She couldn't believe her eyes. She looked around to see if any were coming for her, but they seemed not to have noticed her so far.

She crawled towards the fence furthest from the fighting. She covered her mouth with her hand as a scream threatened to rip free of her. The men were being torn apart now, and it was just a matter of time before the corpses turned their attention to her.

She began to crawl towards the gate. A few seconds later, it grew silent. She wasn't even half way to the gate yet. She turned her head to find that the three men were dead or unconscious. The corpses turned and looked at her in unison. She screamed as they started shambling toward her.

"Wake up! Alana, wake up." She heard Kilian's voice and opened her eyes. He was shaking her gently. Once her eyes opened, he grinned. "First night away from home and you're having nightmares. I am never going to let you live this one down."

Alana groaned and shrugged him away. She didn't want to admit how frightening her dream had been. It had seemed so real. Then she saw that day was breaking.

"Let's just have some breakfast and get going. You can laugh it up later." Alana said irritably. She didn't know what was wrong with her. Her dream had washed away all the excitement she had felt the day before. It had left her with a feeling of utter dread.

Chapter 8

Shelter

T he next few days went by slowly. They didn't see anyone else on the trail. Alana had been quiet and sullen
since the dream. She had been sleeping fitfully afraid of having it return.

She did have variations of the same dream a few more
times in the days that followed. Each morning after the dream
she was lethargic and irritable. The first week passed and they
found a rhythm and routine to traveling. They were grateful
of the skills their father had taught them. They took turns
catching fresh game, Kilian with his bow and Alana with her
blowgun. It was a rare night they had to dip into their dried
supplies.

If it hadn't been for the dream she would be enjoying
the journey more. Just when she would think it wasn't going
to return, it did. Still she found her excitement for the future
growing as each days riding took them closer to it.

Kilian tried to joke, like he always had done to lighten a
mood she might get in, but the mornings after she had the
dream it didn't work. He finally decided to let her get over it
in her own time. He had thought talking about the troubling
dreams would help, but she refused.

Talking about the dreams seemed to Alana like it would
only make the memory of them stronger. She wanted them to

fade away like most dreams did. So far they had remained as vivid as a real memory.

Alana looked up as a crack of thunder rumbled in the sky. She realized as the day had progressed the clouds that had been building for the last couple of days were full and black with rain. In the distance the rain had started and a thunderstorm was coming their way.

The trail had started to widen and in the distance a fork had come into view. Kilian took out the map to see which way they were to go. Then he spoke.

"We'll take a right at that fork. If we push our horses a little, we might make it to Trail's End, a town that's just a few miles off the main road we're to follow. Maybe we can find somewhere there to wait out the storm."

The wind soon was whipping across the trail. The horses were well trained and tucked their heads down and kept on walking. Kilian kicked his horse up to a trot, but soon felt that visibility for both horse and rider made the faster pace a bad idea. He quickly slowed his horse back down.

Alana and Kilian hunched over in their saddles as the wind picked up the dust from the trail. Alana began looking forward to the rain starting when her eyes and lungs started to burn from the dust. Her eyes were watering and it hurt to take each breath and then, finally the rain came.

It felt wonderful. In just moments the air cleared and her breathing eased. She turned her face up towards the sky and let the rain wash the dust from her eyes and face. Kilian was doing the same.

Then the rain started coming down harder. Soon they were both soaked through. As good as the rain had felt at first, soon it was as miserable as the dust had been. The water came at them sideways. The wind caused each drop to sting as it hit like a needle.

It seemed like an eternity had passed and they still hadn't come to the side trail that led to Trail's End. They did see a short trail that went in the opposite direction. The trail was narrower than the one they were currently on and the trees were tall and thick.

They could see a flicker of light somewhere in that direction and decided to turn off. The trees on the smaller path gave them partial shelter, but the ground below was saturated with water already and ribbons of water were quickly connecting and forming small rivers across the trail. There was no place to stop where they could get warm or dry.

They continued plodding along. Horses and riders were weary. It had been several days of riding already, and this storm was quickly taking its toll on all of them. They were wet to the bone and painfully cold.

"I can't go on much further!" Alana had to shout several times before Kilian heard her. Her horse had started stumbling. She was worried about it getting injured.

As Kilian turned towards her to answer, he spotted something through the rain. As Alana turned to see what he was looking at, a flash of lightning lit up a two story farm house. He waved her towards it.

Alana spied a good size barn as they came around the bend and hoped that there would be room in it for their horses. Then she reminded herself that they were strangers here. Maybe the people inside would turn them away.

The thought made her shudder. She hoped that whoever lived here would offer them shelter. She felt a desperation she had never had in her life. She realized why her parents had not wanted this life for her. She saw now just how hard things could get.

They left their horses tied near the porch and Alana and Kilian both stepped under the protection of the porch roof. Alana could see firelight flickering through the window and she almost cried with hope. She couldn't stand the idea of going back into the rain.

Kilian rapped sharply on the door. A moment later, it opened. A woman looked out at them for only a moment before speaking.

"Louis, come quick! Some folks are here that need some shelter. Come in you two and let me get you something warm to drink."

Alana and Kilian stepped inside gratefully. A man came into the room. Looked them over carefully and smiled.

"Well, you both look like you just about drowned out there. Do you have horses or belongings?" At their nods, he took charge of the situation.

As he grabbed a jacket from a hook by the door, he nudged them towards the fire. "Go get warm. I'll see to your horses and bring in your things. Don't worry about getting the floors wet. They have been wet before, and will be again." With that he went out into the rain.

The woman came back into the room as Alana and Kilian still stood dripping by the door. She had fragrant steaming mugs in her hands and blankets slung over her shoulder. She gave them each a mug and then held out the blankets to them.

"Hurry up you two, you'll catch cold if you don't get by the fire and warm up. Wrap up in these blankets till we can get some of your other things dried off for you. Come, tell me all about yourselves."

Kilian started out telling her about their parents and how they were on their way to Waterful to find their fortunes. Alana cut in explaining that the area they were from didn't offer a lot of opportunities for young people and that they wanted to see what might be available for them in the city. Alana cut a look to Kilian that she clearly thought his explanation had sounded immature.

The woman laughed. "My name is Jana, by the way. The two of you being here makes me feel happy. I am sorry that you got caught in such an awful storm. Our boy left not long ago himself. Seeing you together makes me wish we had had a child for him to grow up with. Being the only one can be so lonely.

Alimar is a little younger than the two of you. His time to go out and find his way in the world came a little early. Listen to me go on. Drink your tea. I'll see about getting some of your things dried for you."

The door opened and in came Louis loaded down with their belongings. Jana rushed to his side to help him. As she left the room with Alana and Kilian's wet bedrolls and clothing packs, Louis set the rest by the door while he got out of his wet jacket and boots.

"We should help, you're both going to too much trouble." Alana said as she shrugged off the blanket to get up.

"You two stay right by that fire. It's a joy to have someone to fuss over, especially for my wife. I dried off your horses and tucked them away in the barn. I also gave them some oats. They'll be fine for the night." He took up their weapons and armor he had brought in.

"I am going to get these dried and oil this leather so it won't stiffen. You both just rest and we'll get your beds made up."

As they sat in the warmth of the fire sipping their tea, the fatigue of the journey so far washed over them both. When Louis and Jana came back into the room it was to find them leaning against each other more than half asleep.

Chapter 9

The Nocturnals

Alimar had hunted with his Uncle Louis many times. They had also had sparring sessions regularly since Alimar had turned four and received his first wooden practice sword for his birthday. He felt unprepared for this attack in the dark, nonetheless.

From the glow of the small fire, he could see that the creatures were as big as large wolves. Their fur was so dark they seemed to blend in with the night. Their green, glowing eyes were all that were truly visible until he saw one open its mouth. Then the fire revealed a double row of wicked, blood stained fangs. As the two creatures paced towards them he could hear their huge, knife-like claws scraping against the rocks.

Alimar felt the fear trying to take hold of him and remembered what his uncle had always said. "Fear only brings hopelessness. There is no place for hopelessness in battle. Hopelessness is death. Push the fear aside and pull your intellect and strength of will into its place. Then you will be victorious."

Alimar straightened his shoulders and bent his knees readying for the first strike. The creatures were coming around both sides of the fire, flanking the man and boy. Alimar saw Fogerden turn towards the one on his side of the fire, so Alimar did the same. As the creature grew closer, Alimar could see it a bit better in the light of the fire. It was lean and strong looking.

At the same moment, both creatures leapt. Alimar saw their haunches bunch only a moment before the creatures were in the air. He knew the sheer weight of the thing would take him to the ground. So he knelt and, at the same moment, thrust the sword into the beast. It let out a cry, but as it came over the top of him, caught him in the shoulder with one set of razor sharp claws.

Alimar let out a hiss of pain and Fogerden turned suddenly from his beast and leapt across the fire. Fogerden thrust his blade into the beast as its jaws snapped at Alimar's throat. The beast Fogerden had left behind him suddenly had his jaws locked on Fogerden's shoulder. He turned back to it with a cry of pain.

Alimar knew he had been wounded, but the pain was not important now. The creature was now wounded twice, but Alimar's sword was still in the beast as it started to fall. He turned with the creature and pulled his sword free as it landed. He felt sure that he or Fogerden must have struck a mortal blow, but the creature turned to him for more.

The only sign it had been wounded was the way it moved. Alimar did not want to give it an opportunity to build its strength for another attack. He stepped in and slashed the sword across the beast quickly. It stood for a moment looking unchanged. Then a gout of blood seemed to rush out of it's now gaping throat as it fell to the ground.

Alimar turned to Fogerden with a victory cry on his lips. What he saw turned the cry into one of dismay. Fogerden's sword stuck out of the beast, but it was still alive. It had managed to pin Fogerden underneath its weight, and was almost at his throat. Fogerden was barely holding the beast back and was losing fast.

Alimar could see the glistening of blood, but couldn't tell in the dim light where it was coming from. It could be from man or beast or both. Alimar leapt over the fire and with a vicious thrust, speared the creature through its ribs. He must have pierced its heart because it immediately fell over dead.

As Alimar knelt over Fogerden, he was disheartened to see that much of the blood spilled belonged to Fogerden. He had large scrapes down one leg and a bad bite on his left shoulder. Alimar knew that the worst of the wounds were from when Fogerden had turned to help him.

"You shouldn't have helped me. You had your own beast to deal with. Why did you risk your life for mine?" Alimar asked quietly.

Fogerden opened his mouth to speak, but took two tries to get any words out. "I have spent my life proudly putting my King's life before my own. You are my King now Alimar. Don't you understand that yet?" He groaned in pain.

"In my pack... Get the healer's bundle." Then Fogerden passed out. Alimar rushed to get the bundle. He was glad he knew what he was looking for.

Alimar had spent much of his time with his uncle. There were times that he spent with his Aunt Jana, though. She knew more about herbs and remedies than most healers. He had heard his uncle say it more than once, and the occasional visitor came for her advice.

She had taught Alimar many things. He had thought during those times that it wasn't something he would ever need, but he was glad he had paid some attention now that he did need it. Fogerden was hurt badly.

He found the bundle and it was as he expected. The bundle would not have been very helpful to someone who didn't know how to use it. Alimar found binding salve and the cloth that was soaked in medicine. Both would help Fogerden's wounds heal faster and fight infection. There wasn't much. He retrieved his as well, knowing he would need them both. He would still have to use it sparingly as Fogerden had grievous wounds. He also found a small quantity of pain remedy his aunt had packed for him.

He applied the salve and treated cloths to Fogerden's wounds and mixed some pain remedy into a small bit of water. He held Fogerden's head up and poured it into his mouth. He hoped that some of it made it down Fogerden's throat, but couldn't tell in the dim light.

He half drug, half carried Fogerden over to his bedroll. Then he tried to drag the smaller of the two beasts away from the campsite, but wasn't strong enough. Its fur was coarse and sharp. It felt greasy and was caked in dirt, but left little residue when he rubbed his hands together after touching it. The creature smelled of woods and dark, dank places.

Alimar's wounds were burning, but he had done his best to ignore the pain. He wasn't nearly in as bad of shape as Fogerden. Finally, he wearily sat on his bedroll to see what the damage to his shoulder was.

He hissed in pain as he pulled open his tunic. There were four deep gashes across his shoulder and down onto his chest. He deliberated over whether or not to use the last of the salve on himself.

He finally decided if he had to he could probably find the ingredients to make more if they needed it. His aunt had taught him how to gather herbs around their home. If he didn't use it and got the fever, then they would both be in trouble.

He carefully applied the last remaining bit of salve to his wounds. He had used all the treated cloths to cover Fogerden's wounds. He got one of his spare shirts from his saddlebag and put it on. The salve stuck to it, but at least it was clean.

Alimar sat for a while. He had hoped Fogerden would wake up, but he didn't. He got up and checked on him. He wasn't fevered, but he looked very pale.

Alimar was very tired and wanted to go to sleep. He was worried that more of the creatures that had attacked them would come. He didn't think he would have the strength to fight anymore, and he was so tired. He built up the fire, moved his bedroll closer to Fogerden, and curled up around his sword.

Chapter 10

Herbology

Alimar woke to a dead fire and early morning sunlight shining through the trees. As he rolled over and shook the sleep from his head, his shoulder burned in protest. The memory of the night's events rushed back to him.

He twisted free of his bedding almost wounding himself on his own sword. He reminded himself to find a safer way to sleep armed. He took one look at Fogerden and groaned. Without having to feel his forehead, Alimar already knew Fogerden had the fever.

In the light of day, Alimar soon discovered a score of smaller wounds he had missed dressing on the older man. Cursing himself for using the last of the salve on his own wounds, he quickly got his water skin and last clean shirt. After cutting the shirt into strips, he cleaned the red jagged cuts the best he could.

He thought back to the times his aunt had taken him into the forest near their home. He wished he had paid closer attention to her lessons. While he played at trapping a rabbit or daydreamed of greater things, she had given him all the tools he needed to fix the mess he and Fogerden were in. Maybe she had known someday he would need that knowledge, but he hadn't.

Using the rest of the strips of his shirt he wrapped Fogerden's remaining wounds as well as his own. The last strip he wet and placed on Fogerden's fevered brow. With the last of the water in his skin, he tried to help the still unconscious Fogerden drink. Most of it ended up running into his beard, but Alimar told himself that some had managed to trickle down his throat.

Alimar tended the horses and ate some dried meat while trying to recall all of the herbs that his aunt used to make the salve he needed. He remembered two of them for sure. He also was pretty sure there were only two others that were in the healing salve. One had little red flowers, or were they pink?

Alimar looked at the beasts lying dead in their campsite. He realized in the light of day that he knew from some books his uncle and aunt had used to teach him with what they were. They were called Nocturnals. He remembered they typically traveled alone or in pairs, but only at night. They also were obviously carnivorous. He knew that they normally wouldn't have come into the light of the campfire. Their eyes and skin were very sensitive to the light. They must have been extremely hungry after winter's end.

He had not felt strong enough the night before to move the creatures, but he didn't want to leave them there while he tended Fogerden. He tried, once again, to drag the smaller one towards the forest. It didn't budge. The smell of it was already getting worse. He had to get it out of the campsite.

He finally tied it up to his horse, though it obviously didn't want to come closer to the creatures. He had the horse drag it off where he could then roll it down a small slope so it was out of sight, and more importantly smell. He repeated the process with the other one.

Fogerden's waterskin was still half full, but he needed to refill his own anyway. He took them both down to the nearby creek and refilled them. He was grateful they had camped so close to water last night.

Alimar placed Fogerden's now full waterskin beside him in case he regained consciousness while he was gone. Then he slung his own waterskin over his unwounded shoulder. He looked around the camp one last time. He knew he had done everything that needed doing before he left. He was just feeling so unsure of himself that he was hesitating needlessly.

Finally, he squared his shoulders, picked up his sword and set out into the woods. He found the first herb almost immediately. His spirits rose a bit. Then he remembered his aunt saying that you could find it almost anywhere in the Kingdom.

Sometime later, just when he was starting to despair, he found his second herb. The second one he found was not the one he had remembered. As soon as he saw it he was reminded of his aunt showing him the small shiny leaves. She had said this was the one with the best healing qualities. He quickly gathered it as she had shown him.

Worried about how Fogerden was doing on his own for so long, Alimar looked at the position of the sun. He had spent so long with his head down as not to miss any herbs, he had lost track of time. Realizing it was already late morning, he started back to check on Fogerden.

In his rush to get back, he almost missed the little red flowers. He had found the third herb. After gathering some of it up, he tried to think of what his aunt had said about the last one he needed.

As he walked towards the campsite, he remembered her saying it was rarer than the others. He also recalled her saying it was the one that disinfected the wound and stopped the spread of infection.

He got back to the campsite to find Fogerden worse off than how he had left him. The fever was definitely higher. When he looked at the untreated wounds, he knew he had to find that last herb. They were beginning to fester and would continue to get worse the longer it took him to tend to them.

Alimar had a little to eat, and tried again to get Fogerden to drink some water. This time he was sure Fogerden didn't swallow any. He knew that he needed to find the last herb fast.

He went off in a new direction this time. He checked in every grove of trees, and in any bush he thought it could hide behind. His neck soon ached from looking at the ground so long. His stomach began to rumble too.

He took a moment to rub the worst of the kinks out of his neck and saw, with dismay, that more time had passed then he would have thought. He only had a couple hours of daylight left. He was sure that Fogerden wouldn't last through the night without the salve.

Suddenly, a horrible thought occurred to Alimar. As soon as he realized that Fogerden needed more salve, he should have gone for help. There had been a small house off the road several hours back. They also had passed the occasional traveler. He had risked the man's life on the slim chance that he could find ingredients he could hardly remember.

He wouldn't have been able to get Fogerden on his horse, even if it had been safe to move him. There might have been a chance to save him if Alimar had left out first thing in the morning. Now here he was at the end of the wasted day without the ingredients he needed. Alimar felt foolish.

Alimar started heading back to camp. He kept trying to remember everything he could about the missing herb. He had already remembered that it disinfected the wound. He was frustrated that he had only found three of the herbs he needed. He wished there was something else he could use to disinfect the wound.

He stopped, his brow knitted in concentration. Was there something else he could use? He thought back to all the times he'd come home injured. His aunt had had a remedy for everything, from a scratch to a bee sting. The salve he was trying to re-create she had used on his more serious cuts, but she always said even a scratch can get infected. She'd used something else for scratches, though. She'd said it worked just as well for something small, without such a sting.

Now that he thought it through, he had seen that other herb. It might not work as well as the one he couldn't find for the salve, but it was better than nothing. He started running through the woods back towards camp. He was out of breath, by the time he caught sight of the horses through the trees.

He turned in the direction he had originally gone in the morning. He soon found a familiar outcropping of rocks, and there he saw the herb his aunt had used on his scrapes and scratches. For the final ingredient he found a wounded tree and scraped some sap onto his knife.

He had helped his aunt mix ingredients many times. He got out his cooking pot, crushed the herbs, added the sap, and set to lighting the fire. Once the fire was going it was just a matter of heating and blending the ingredients. At the last, fearful that his replacement herb wouldn't be strong enough to do the job, he doubled the amount of it.

Once the salve was cooled, Alimar quickly but thoroughly applied it to Fogerden's untreated wounds. Fogerden was very hot and groaned occasionally, but had obviously not regained consciousness all day. Alimar used the remaining water to cook a broth and re-wet the cloth to cool Fogerden's forehead.

Alimar propped Fogerden up and tried spooning some broth into his mouth while massaging his throat like he'd seen his aunt do once with a sick farmer. It was a slow laborious process, but he was pretty sure some of it got down. He stoked the fire and bundled Fogerden up. His aunt had always said those that have a fever catch a chill easier.

As the darkness of night fell, he worried. He worried that more Nocturnals would come, or some other beasts. He worried that Fogerden wouldn't get better and it would be his fault for not getting help. Mostly he just worried that he was not cut out for all of this.

He dozed on and off, each noise of the night making him start. Finally, unable to stay awake any longer, he tucked his sword away while keeping it in reach. Hoping the morning would find him and his traveling companion still alive, he fell fast asleep.

Chapter 11

Uninvited Guests

Kilian and Alana woke the next morning, hardly remembering being ushered into the small bedrooms that they had occupied.   Sun was filtering through the curtains on the windows. The storm had broken. They would need to leave soon.

The smell of breakfast was what woke them almost simultaneously. Famished, they both rushed through dressing and grooming. Kilian beat Alana to the small landing outside the bedroom door, but hearing her movements from the room she had occupied waited there for her.

As the two came down the stairs together Jana caught sight of them from the kitchen. "I knew I could trust the smell of breakfast to roust you two out of bed. It works on our Alimar every time. Now come to the table and eat before it gets cold."

Eagerly rushing to the table, Kilian and Alana's eyes met. They broke into a fit of childish giggling that stopped abruptly at Jana's curious look. As she put plates on the table in front of them, Alana spoke up. "Sorry about our lack of manners. After all these days of traveling and being caught out in that storm, this feels almost as though all of it was a dream, and we never really left home."

"Well, it surely warms my heart for you to say so. It's only been a short time, but I've been lonely without Alimar. Having you both to cook for this morning made me feel almost as though Alimar was going to come to the table himself." Jana sniffled a little bit at the last.

Not knowing what to say to that, Kilian and Alana got down to the business of eating. They finish quickly, and thanking Jana, went up to their rooms to pack. Alana had just set her pack out on the landing and was straightening the small bed, when she heard Louis come into the house and speak in a low voice. She couldn't hear what he said to Jana, but could sense the urgency in his tone.

A moment later he called up to them. As Alana stepped out on the landing, Kilian opened the door to the room he'd slept in. Looking down at Louis's face, made it clear something was wrong. "Please, both of you, grab your things and come out the back. I think some trouble might be coming, and I need your help."

Grabbing up their packs, they rushed down the stairs, Kilian right behind Alana, to follow Louis out the back door. As Alana passed Jana, she saw the fearful look on the older woman's face as she stood in the kitchen, wringing her hands. Back over his shoulder Louis called her. "Quickly now Jana, go upstairs and make it look right. Then check the rest of the house too."

When he reached the backyard Louis wasted no time. He held their armor and the swords hanging in their sheaths. He turned to Alana and Kilian and spoke quickly and with authority. "Okay, listen closely, I know you don't know us well, but I need to ask you to trust me. I just heard word from a neighbor down the way a bit. He says a rough looking bunch might be looking for my boy.

Kilian, I need you to pretend to be our son. You shouldn't be in any danger. They're not looking for anyone like you. It sounds as though they have a description of the one they are looking for and we just need to get them to think that the boy that lives here isn't the right one. I am just hoping to fool them so they get it out of their heads that my Alimar is the one they are after.

Alana, I need you to take these packs and the rest of your things and run into the woods. You can carry all of this, can't you? I don't have time to come up with a story for you being here. There's a small clearing straight back. Hide there till we come for you."

Kilian and Alana only looked at each other for a moment before Alana took the swords and slung them both over her shoulder, took the packs in one hand and the leather armor in the other and ran as quickly as she could towards the woods as Louis had directed.

"In our time of need, you treated us like kin. We're grateful to have the chance to return the favor." Kilian looked straight into Louis's eyes as he spoke.

Louis then quickly explained his plan to Kilian. As he did, he moved into the house and proceeded to make some final preparations. Once Kilian understood what he needed to do, he went upstairs. As he passed the room Alana had been in, he saw that Jana had obviously erased every trace of their female guest.

Entering the room he'd slept in, he began to familiarize himself with the things in it. He hadn't paid much attention upon waking, but it was obviously Alimar's room. He had made the bed and straitened up. Thinking of how his room had always looked at home, he mussed up the bed and went to scatter a few items of clothing on the floor.

Upon opening a drawer in the bureau, he realized the clothes that Alimar had left behind were much too small for his build. If the room was searched anyone could see that he wasn't the one who occupied it. He quickly went to the next room and explained the problem to Jana. Nodding in understanding, she rushed downstairs. While she was gone, Kilian quickly bundled the clothes up and shoved them far under the bed.

Jana soon returned, shoving a stack of folded clothes into Kilian's hands. He placed the new clothing into the bureau realizing that they must belong to Louis. Then he threw a couple things in the corner like they had recently been worn. He would've liked to take more time, but just then Louis called up to him. "Kilian, come on down boy. I can hear horses approaching. I think this must be them."

While Kilian had been upstairs, Jana had reset the table. He had never been one to turn down a second helping, but he knew he couldn't eat a bite. Obviously Louis and Jana wanted their actions to appear to be the normal routine of a household. He could feel his heart beating wildly in his chest. He hoped he didn't give everything away.

Then he heard the voices outside calling to one another. A moment later there was a pounding at the door. Even though he'd been expecting it, he jumped a little in his chair. Louis and Jana looked at each other and then both of them gave Kilian reassuring looks. Louis got up from his chair and calmly walked to the door.

The four men that walked uninvited into the kitchen were unkempt and didn't look as though they had washed in some time. The smell that rolled off of them proved that they hadn't. Kilian was glad he had already eaten. Louis took their invasion in stride. He seemed relaxed and unaware of the malice that poured off of the men. "What can we do for you men today? You need horses or boarding?"

One of the men stepped forward. Kilian was sure that this was the man in charge. The man narrowed his glaring dark eyes. He had long greasy black hair that hung about his face like a hood. He was dressed all in black. He looked from Jana to Louis and back again. Then he looked to Kilian, and his eyes narrowed even more.

"We don't need no boarding, and our horses are right outside. What we need are some answers and you lot will be given 'um to us." Turning to the other men he said,

"Take a look around boys, while I asked these nice folks some questions."

The men scattered into the house as he turned, with a sneer, back to the table. Then putting his hand on the hilt of his weapon meaningfully, he continued. "First off, where's this nice son of yours we been hearing so much 'bout round these parts?"

Alana was out of breath when she reached the small clearing. She wasn't sure running was necessary, but Louis's tone had given wings to her feet. Her arms burned from the load she had carried. The grass and trees were still wet from the storm the day before.

The sun hadn't had a chance yet to dry the branches and the ground was well saturated as well. She had slipped a few times, but been able to keep going without losing her footing completely. She was soon as wet and chilled as she had been out in the storm.

She had then hidden the packs in a small cluster of trees just in case she had to move in a hurry. She strapped her sword on in case she needed it, but had left Kilian's sword as well as their armor with the packs. She had wrapped the leather so it would stay dry. Louis had obviously spent some amount of time oiling and cleaning all of it for them.

She then proceeded to get busy with her least favorite task, waiting. She began to pace after only a few minutes. She wasn't happy to have left her brother behind. Louis had said he should be safe, but she would've felt better if they could have stayed together. She was worried, too, about the couple that had treated them so kindly. The thing she liked the least, though, was that she didn't know what was happening.

None of what Louis had said made any sense to her. Why would men be looking for Louis and Jana's son? Hadn't they said that he was even younger than they were? What could be so important about a young country boy?

Alana realized she had a lot of questions, but no answers. She was too far from the house to see or hear anything.

Maybe if she left their things hidden here she could get a little closer just to see what was going on. That way she could at least see if they needed her help.

As she snuck back through the woods, alarms were going off in the back of her mind. She shook them off and continued on. Alana had always been prone to getting into a bit of trouble in times like this. Her curiosity was always winning out over her common sense.

Chapter 12

Bloodshed

"**W**ell then, let's have it. Where's your boy?" The glaring man ignored Kilian and narrowed his eyes at Louis.

Louis had a feeling that his ruse wasn't going to work on this man, but felt compelled to try anyway. "You don't have to look far. He's right here in front of you, isn't he? Now see here, if he's gotten into some sort of trouble, I'm sure we can..."

"Stop your blatherin'! Do you take me for a fool? This boy's at least three years older than that of the boy I'm referrin' to. I know your son is younger, smaller, and has totally different coloring than this one. The families south of here were very...helpful. So, I have a new question for you to go with my first one. What are you trying to hide?

Forget it, don't even bother answering. Just the fact that you're trying to hide something already answers both of my questions. I don't want to waste any more time listening to you lie to me. I think I know enough to say that your boy is the one we're after. One of you three will tell me where he is." With that he began to pull his sword.

Kilian watched the exchange with growing concern. These four men obviously meant business. Where had the other three gone? He had heard one go up the stairs. He thought one had gone out the back door, but that still left one. Where had he gone? Was he behind them even now?

He felt clumsy and inexperienced. As it became clear that this man was not going to accept that he was Alimar, fear that had already been growing blossomed in his belly like an uncoiling snake. Jana was slightly behind him and he couldn't see her face, but he was sure she was terrified. He wished he had a weapon. He wished too that he knew where all the men were.

As the man in front of them started to draw his sword, Kilian's thoughts grew frantic, but his feet seemed rooted to the kitchen floor. He knew he needed to look for a weapon or find a way to defend himself and protect this kind couple. What happened next was so unexpected that Kilian reacted totally by instinct.

It had seemed as though Louis was leaning casually on the table. Now, he straightened and came up with a small blade in his hand that had been hidden by a napkin. He closed the distance to the man very quickly. Putting his left hand over the man's right, the few inches of steel that had been revealed were thrust back into the leather of the scabbard.

Louis's right-hand, holding a small knife, went to the man's throat. Without any hesitation, he jammed the blade straight up under the man's chin and slit his throat before pulling the knife free. Then he turned and pushed him towards Kilian.

It all happened in just a second, but Kilian would always remember every detail. It was the first man he had ever seen killed. Blood poured from the horrid wound that the knife had left behind. The man's eyes were already losing the look of surprise and glazing over in shock.

Instinctually Kilian caught the now dying man. The weight of him caused Kilian to crouch and turn slightly so as not to drop him. He caught sight of Jana's face. The fear he had expected to see was not there. Instead he saw a quiet determination. Moving just as quickly and decisively as Louis had, she pulled back the long tablecloth and gestured to Kilian. Realizing she wanted him to hide the man's body under the table, he quickly shoved him under.

As he straightened, Kilian caught sight of movement out of the corner of his eye. Seeing it was Louis creeping quietly up the staircase, Kilian marveled that in the time it had taken him to hide the body, Louis had snuck around them and was already halfway up the stairs. Now that the kitchen was quiet he could hear movement in one of the bedrooms.

Just as Louis disappeared upstairs, another man stepped from a storage room off the living room. Jana, dipping her hand into her apron pocket, walked toward him smiling. The man seemed to notice his missing friend and either saw or smelled the blood in the kitchen. Just as Jana took her hand from her pocket, she stepped up to the man and blew a fine dust into his face. Jana stepped aside and carefully dusted her hands off on her apron. The man just stood there blinking for a moment. Then he started to walk carefully towards Kilian and the kitchen, as if drunk or wandering in the dark.

Kilian began to look frantically around the kitchen for a weapon, but then caught sight of Jana who just shook her head softly. Kilian stepped aside bewildered as the man passed him heading towards the door he and the others had entered through. Louis came down the stairs looking slightly bloodier than before. He took in the scene, and with a glance towards Jana seemed to relax.

Jana and Louis followed the man outside. Confused, Kilian followed behind. The man wandered towards five horses. A fifth man was waiting with the horses. At first, upon seeing his friend, he stepped forward. Then glancing toward the house, he realized something was wrong. He quickly helped his friend onto his horse and dove towards his own as Louis began walking towards them.

As the two began to ride away, Louis deftly flipped his small knife into the air and catching it by the blade, threw it with seeming ease and precision into the fifth man's back. He didn't even seem to break his stride as he continued towards the horses.

One of the two riders fell from his horse before Louis got there, but to Kilian's surprise, it wasn't the one with a knife in his back. It was the one that Jana had blown dust at. As Louis reached the slowing horses, the man with the knife in his back finally tipped out of his saddle hitting the ground with a dull thud.

Upon reaching the horses and unceremoniously retrieving his knife, Louis turned back towards the house, "Kilian, will you take these two to the stable for me? Jana, would you mind seeing to the mess in the kitchen? I need to find the last one that came through the house. Only one was upstairs. We need to move quickly; there could be others nearby."

Jana quickly disappeared into the house. Kilian just stood there, dumbfounded. It seemed like hours had passed since the four men knocked at the door. In reality, Kilian knew it'd probably only been a few minutes.

Kilian's father had told him many times that it was a brutal world they lived in. Kilian had thought he knew what that meant. Yet learning swordplay, being aware that strangers on the road may not be your friends, and knowing to tuck away your valuables did not prepare him for this morning's events.

The quick readiness of Louis, and even apparently Jana, to kill may have saved all of their lives, but being witness to it made him realize this is what his father had really meant. These men had come here with the intent to do harm and now had lost their lives. It truly was a brutal world. Finally, shaking off his shock, he went to deal with the two horses and the dead men who had been riding them.

Alana peered at the back of the house through the branches at the edge of the woods. She didn't see anything for a few minutes and was getting frustrated. She continued watching the house for a moment more ready to give up and leave the woods for a better vantage point.

She was glad she had grabbed her sword and the weight of it across her back was reassuring. She wasn't sure what was happening in the house but she had a bad feeling. She was also glad that she left the rest of their things hidden so she could move quickly if she needed to.

Then just when Alana was about to move into the yard, Jana came to the back door with a wooden bucket in her hands. Jana stepped out and dumped the bucket away from the house. It caused Alana some alarm to see the water tinged dark red, obviously with blood. All she could think was that something may have happened to Kilian in her absence.

Then she saw a man. He was watching Jana and pulled his sword at the sight of the bloody water. He waited until Jana turned her back and went into the house. He began creeping towards the house with malice in his eyes.

Alana came out of the woods and snuck up behind the man. She should've never hidden in the woods, while Kilian might've been put in danger. She had come along and planned to do her share. The man must have sensed her presence behind him and turned.

"Lookie here, I got myself a pretty one to play with."

He stepped towards her with his free hand reaching for her. She leapt back out of his reach with ease. He growled and came at her faster; she rolled away through the grass. Once more the man tried to grab her with the same luck. She smirked at him. She hadn't been training every day with Kilian to be bested by this big oaf.

Then he swung his sword suddenly. She had to dive out of the way of the blade not expecting him to get nasty so fast. She pulled her sword as she came up and waited to see if he meant business. It became obvious that he did when he lunged at her.

She wanted him to go away, but she didn't even know who this guy was. She wasn't going to let him hurt her, but she only wanted to make him leave her alone. When he swung at her next, she rolled away like a cat and cut his arm on her way up.

She saw the man inspect the small ribbon of blood with a surprised look and hoped he would see that it was best to leave. Instead he became furious. He was clumsy with his rage and she continued twisting and dancing away from his blade thrusts cutting him almost every time as he recovered. Soon he had small cuts lining both arms and thighs.

She wished he would take the hint. She was getting tired. She could only do this for so long before one of them got seriously hurt. She was determined that it wasn't going to be her.

He was tiring too. He was moving more carefully now. That was bad for her. He had been so angry that he had telegraphed his moves. Now he was taking his time and moving more carefully.

He swung and as she dodged, grabbed his sword with both hands and thrust it in the direction she was twisting. He would surely kill her this time if she didn't act quickly. She had to use her sword to stop his momentum and it slid in between his ribs almost effortlessly.

He fell to the ground dead. She had actually killed him. It had been him or her, but it still made her feel sick to see him lying there. She sat down in the grass stunned and pushing with her heels on the grass scooted away from the body.

Before she could recover Jana was back at the door. Jana came out backwards bent over dragging something that was obviously causing her some strain. Jana noticed Alana about the same time Alana was able to see it was a man she was dragging.

"While Louis might be unhappy you left the woods before he came for you, I'm glad to see you, as I could use your help. Grab his legs and help me carry him to the woods, will you?" Jana wiped her brow and stretched her back looking expectantly at Alana. Then she saw the body sprawled out in the grass. Looking at Alana carefully she obviously saw the blood on her sword and the stunned look on her face.

"What in Asteria happened? Are you alright? You should never have come out of the woods before Louis came for you." Jana came over and took a closer look. She could see that Alana was unharmed. Then she looked at the man that Alana had killed.

"You sure did manage to take care of yourself. Don't worry, Kilian is fine too. We'll have to talk about the rest after we take care of the bodies. We could still be in danger. Now please grab his legs and let's get both of them into the woods for now." Alana followed her instructions. By the time they reached the woods with the second body Alana understood what they meant when they said "dead weight".

Both women were breathing hard by the time they tucked the second of the bodies behind some trees out of sight from the house. Wordlessly Jana marched back towards the house with Alana, following close behind. Jana headed straight upstairs, while Alana peeked through the living room into the kitchen. She could see the still drying wetness on the floor, and it looked as though the tablecloth had been replaced on the table. Shaking her head she began to follow Jana up the stairs.

Just then, the kitchen door opened and Louis came in, followed by Kilian. They both had blood on their clothes and hands. Kilian's eyes were wide with shock, and his skin was pale. Alana practically fell down the stairs in her rush to reach Kilian and confirm that he had not been hurt.

"Alana, what are you doing back from the woods? Didn't I make it clear that we'd be back for you? You're lucky you didn't walk into the middle of this whole mess." Noticing the shock on Alana's face, Louis stopped and shook his head for a moment. He didn't realize yet that she had dealt with her own trouble. "He's fine Alana. We all are. I hoped we'd be able to deal with this without bloodshed. Once I knew it couldn't be avoided, I made sure the blood shed was theirs."

"So did I." She told them what had happened in the back yard. Kilian's eyes grew big and he looked her over twice to confirm she was not wounded. She repeated one phrase a few times throughout the explanation. "It was self defense, he wouldn't stop."

Kilian spoke for the first time since this whole thing had started. "You didn't have a choice then, Alana. You did what you had to do. I understand that.

What happened in the front was a different story. Louis, those last two were on the run. My father taught us you don't stab a man in the back. That's just what you did. Why, why did they have to die if they were running?"

"You both best be sitting down. You're looking more than a little shaky to me. Jana, come on down here. We've got some talking to do." Alana and Kilian both sat down in the living room, reluctantly. Louis pulled up a chair from the kitchen. Jana came quietly down the stairs and sat on a bench next to Louis.

"First of all, let's clear up your concern about these men. We'd all be dead now, if we hadn't done what had to be done. Those last two, they were just going for help. Not the kind we'd like either. They would come back with more like them. Let me assure you, there are more like them somewhere close by. All I did was delay them by hours or maybe a day if we're real lucky.

We told you about our boy, Alimar. What we didn't tell you is that he's special. I had hoped he'd be long gone, before anyone even knew he had been here. Unfortunately, the other men that worked with this group are going to know for sure they're on the right track as soon as they realize that their friends have gone missing.

Alana, I put you in those woods to try to make it seem like Kilian was our boy. I'd hoped to mislead them. So they'd think they were on the wrong path and go follow some other lead. And Kilian, I'm sorry you had to see all of this. I don't like to kill, but I need you both to understand; it was necessary and my only choice.

Now I gotta put a whole lot of faith in both of you. I'm going to tell you some things about our Alimar. I'm going to tell you things we've never told anyone. I'm going to gamble that you're as good and noble as I believe you to be. I pray I'm right about you two, because I think you are our only hope.

Chapter 13

Dorn Deepaxe

Dorn Deepaxe had developed a routine. He got up in the morning. He went to work and swung his axe all day. It wasn't the life he wanted, but it was the one he had anyhow.

Strautin was just the city for a lumberjack or wood-worker. It was surrounded by dense forest on all sides. Strautin was known all over the Kingdom for its amazing hardwood called Strautin Oak. The trading route came in, circled the city and went back out, but other than that the forest was so thick it was almost as good as any wall.

While most cities in the Kingdom boasted of their lakes, rivers or ocean, Strautin was all about wood. In fact, the water source was in the center of the city and came up from underground. It had been a natural spring, but as the years passed and the small settlement turned into a town and then a city, they had improved it so that it fed most of the city in an ingenious underground water system that utilized hollowed out saplings and magic both.

Strautin was the name of the man that first settled in these woods. He had discovered the amazing qualities of the oaks only found here. He soon had a thriving business and so much trade was coming through the settlement just grew up around him. When the settlement grew into a town the folks named it after him.

The city of Strautin had some hired men to keep peace and lock up anyone that got too rowdy. There was a mayor, not that he seemed to be too worried about law enforcement except when it came to his own gain. They got some riff-raff coming in to the city from time to time, but mostly the riff-raff was everywhere these days anyway. Who needed a wall to keep them out when they were living in the city already?

By the end of the day swinging his axe, Dorn was hot, hungry and very thirsty. He liked to have a meal and more than a few pints of ale before heading home. There were only two taverns in Strautin worth mentioning. One of them, the Gem, just happened to be on his way home. He really wasn't much for the other one anyway.

The Gem was just his sort of place. Back when he'd been a fighter, it was the type of place he'd always looked for when he came into a town. The three things he would try to find were good ale, greasy food, and a slightly rowdy clientele. The Gem had all those things, and a bonus.

Ruby was the owner of The Gem. Dorn often wondered if she was referring to herself or the establishment when she named the place. There may have been a time that Ruby was pretty, Dorn wasn't sure.

As long as he had been in Strautin, she had been a barrel-chested, ruddy cheeked loudmouth. She had bright red hair that stuck out in all directions. Her lip rouge was always smeared, and since it was bright red, it didn't do her coloring any favors. She was rude, and sometimes her service was slow.

Dorn got into a heated argument with Ruby almost every evening. They traded insults every time she came around to fill his mug. He would never have admitted it to Ruby, but he enjoyed her company. Secretly, it was the highlight of his miserable days.

Dorn had grown up in a town not unlike Strautin. His father had been a lumberjack. His father's father had been a lumberjack. He had known from an early age that everyone around him expected him to be a lumberjack too. Swinging an axe had always been as natural as eating for Dorn.

Lumberjacking may have been in Dorn's blood, but he had always despised it. He could take down at least two trees to another man's one. He could also keep up that pace all day long. By the end of the day he was taking down three times as many trees as anyone else. He made sure he was compensated for it too.

He was determined to get out of Strautin someday soon. He had saved all of his wages to that end. The only thing he spent money on was ale, food, and a place to sleep, in that order. Occasionally he had to have the tailor make him a couple new breeches when he wore the old ones out, but that was pretty much the only exception.

When he had told his father all those years ago that he was leaving home to become a fighter, his father had not argued. He had looked at Dorn with the knowledge of experience. He didn't try to talk him out of it. He just matter-of-factly said, "Mark my words son. You will be a lumberjack."

Dorn had even tried to give up the axe. His large size ruled out many smaller weapons, but he had tried training with the few that fit his frame. No matter how hard he tried he had been a total klutz with the broadsword. He gotten pretty good with the great hammer, but as soon as he picked up any sort of axe he was unbeatable. His tool of choice, in the end, was the same whether fighting or lumberjacking, the great axe.

His great axe had double blades of the finest quality dwarven steel. It had a stout wooden handle that was Strautin oak with a solid metal core to make it ridged. He had commissioned it to be made for him in the glory days of his fighting and kept it in perfect condition.

Once he had admitted to himself that the axe was the weapon for him, he had settled into the fighter's life with ease. Everything about being a fighter had suited Dorn. He had loved the traveling, the adventure, and the variety of companions. Most of all, though, he had loved fighting the good fight.

Dorn had always picked his jobs carefully. He made it a point not to accept any work for scoundrels or thieves. Unfortunately, once the King was dead, good work dried up fast for a fighter. Scoundrels and thieves soon became the only employers he seemed to be able to find. Finally, he turned to the only other job he knew; lumberjacking.

As Dorn approached The Gem he passed a mother holding the hand of a small child. Upon catching sight of Dorn, the little girl gasped and cowered behind her mother's skirts. Dorn attempted to shift his scowl into a friendly smile. At that, the mother looked frightened, picked up her child, and moved to the other side of the street. Dorn let his scowl settle back onto his face. It was his natural expression these days, anyway.

The Gem sat between a traders shop and a tailor. Since the trader and the tailor did most of their business during the day and The Gem did most of her business at night, everyone seemed to get along alright. The Gem was larger than her neighbors, but all three buildings had standard size doors and ceiling height. Unfortunately, this caused Dorn some issues.

Dorn was a large man. His arms and legs rippled with muscle. Even in a loose shirt, it was obvious that his chest and stomach were just as sculpted. His shoulders were too wide for a doorway, and his feet were too big for almost all boots. His width, however, caused him less difficulty than his height.

There were a few different races living in Strautin. Humans made up the vast majority as in most of Asteria. There were some Dwarves and Elves that had settled in Strautin for the same reasons the humans had, the Strautin Oak.

Dwarves loved the wood because it paired well with the metalworking they were renowned for. Elves used it for the intricate carving of weapons like bows and staffs as well as for various arts that they had perfected. Most of the residents got along, and the ones that didn't learned to avoid each other.

Humans were tall by most civilized race's standards. Many races had bred with humans and so there were some of mixed blood. Dwarves and Elves had fewer offspring than humans and because of their longer lifespan didn't grow in population very much.

He had dark brown hair that was almost black. Working outside, Dorn kept his hair as short as it was practical. His eyes were brown and he had been told his gaze was fierce. He was rugged and his facial hair started coming in as soon as he finished taking a razor to it. He didn't consider grooming a necessity other than to keep himself clean and comfortable. He wasn't ugly, but no one was going to give him a prize for his looks either.

Dorn was mostly human. He had human features and looked human in all ways but one. He stood at least 2 heads higher than the tallest man in town. Getting through a standard size door was no easy trick.

Dorn started by taking his ax and gear off his back. He opened the door to The Gem and, carefully reaching in, placed his things inside. He then turned sideways, squatted down, and shuffled carefully into the tavern. Once he was through the door he could stand fully upright, but his difficulties weren't over.

While the ceiling was barely high enough to accommodate his height, the periodic rafters and chandeliers were not. So, upon retrieving his gear, he carefully wove and ducked his way towards the bar.

The Gem was eclectic to say the least. On one hand it was rustic with its great length of polished wooden bar, carved stools and sawdust floor. This was a lumber rich city after all.

On the other hand Ruby had strange taste in her décor. She had paintings on the walls of all kinds of places she wanted to go one day. Some were well done. Some looked like they had been painted by children.

Then there were the chandeliers. She had about a dozen of them hanging from the ceiling. Not one matched another. They went from plain to downright gaudy. Some were simple brass. A few of the others had fake jewels and gems set into them in intricate patterns. One almost matched the bar being plain polished wood.

A couple years after Dorn had settled in Strautin, and became a regular customer with Ruby, he had been presented with an unexpected kindness from her. It had been this act that made him look deeper than her rough exterior and find the true gem of The Gem. Upon reaching the bar, it sat waiting for Dorn, as it had since that night years ago.

It was a hand carved stool much like the others at the bar, but it was much wider, slightly taller, and definitely sturdier than the others. The first night it had been there waiting for him Ruby had simply said, "I'm getting tired of you wearing out my stools, you big oaf. You sit in this one from now on. It wasn't cheap either, so you better keep coming long enough to make it worth my while."

Placing his things in the corner, he sat on the stool Ruby had had made for him all those years ago. Scratching absently at his beard, he tried to recall how many years it had been. Was it eight? That seemed about right.

"Dorn, you look lost in thought. I have to know, what is that pea size brain of yours trying to reason out?" Ruby liked to start right in as she served his first ale.

"I was trying to decide how long I've been coming to this dump. I'm kind of sick of this place. How much longer do I need to keep coming in to pay off this stool?" Picking up the mug Ruby had set before him, Dorn took a long satisfying pull.

"Well, you've been coming here for more than 12 years. I only got the stool about 10 years ago. I'm pretty tired of seeing your big head come through my door pretty near every night. Unfortunately, we're going to have to put up with each other a while longer. Apparently, it wasn't easy to find a tree big enough for that ars. Now I got other customers."

Dorn hid his chuckle behind his mug. Ruby like to bring you your ale, give you a good tongue lashing, and leave while she still had the last word. It was just part of her natural charm. On nights like these, he drank a little faster than usual just so he could get to the next round quicker, not for the ale, but for the insults.

Looking around the tavern, he noticed that many of the other regulars were already settled around the bar. There were a handful of tables and chairs. A regular or two might nod a careful greeting in Dorn's direction from time to time. There were almost always a few empty stools next to him, though. He was used to being feared, avoided, or even challenged. These people had at least gotten used to him, even if they didn't want to make friends.

The door opened a few times letting in other faces Dorn recognized as regulars or at least residents of Strautin. Dorn's stool sat in the corner of the bar. He liked his back to the wall. Old habits from his days as a fighter still stuck with him. Even though he swung his ax all day as a lumberjack, he still practiced with it as a weapon as well. He was also still a careful observer of his surroundings. So when the strangers walked in, he noticed them right away.

Strautin got a fair amount of trade and other travelers passing through. Strangers weren't unusual, but these were. Dorn took in their sharp eyes and the fact they were all well armed and knew these were not typical strangers. They took a corner table and leaning in towards each other spoke in a secretive manner. Dorn's interest was piqued. That hadn't happened in a very long time.

Sitting by himself in the quiet corner, only a couple tables away from the strangers, he was able to make out bits and pieces of their conversation. There were four of them. One spoke louder than the rest. Another occasionally raised his voice enough to be heard. He couldn't make out anything the other two said.

The little he heard didn't give him much, but it was enough to make something stir within him. At first, he couldn't identify it. When Ruby returned with a refill and was obviously ready for another round of insults he just shook his head softly. He had never turned down either before and she was obviously surprised as she retreated to the other end of the bar. Then he realized that what he was feeling, for the first time in years, was purpose.

Chapter 14

Eavesdropping

"So how do they know he's heading here then?" The man that said this was talking louder than the others. Dorn wished the rest of them would speak up a little louder too. Trying to piece together the small snippets he overheard was giving him a headache.

Dorn sat on his stool not drinking or even moving for fear he might miss a word. He was also leaning at a funny angle to try to get his ear a little closer to the conversation. He was starting to get a stiff back.

Some of the conversation he heard so far had gone something like this. "Once we've taken care of him, mumble, mumble, mumble. Whisper, whisper, whisper, he'll be in charge and we'll all be rich."

They kept referring to a boy. The loud one had asked why he was so important. That was the question Dorn kept asking himself. He just about tipped over his stool trying to lean even closer to hear the answer. He wished whoever had the answers would speak more clearly, but Dorn hadn't heard any of the response to that question or most others. What was clear to him is that the boy was indeed important.

Dorn was starting to think that he was getting the basic idea. The whole conversation seemed to be about this boy. If taking care of him meant killing the boy, and killing him meant someone would be in charge of something that would make this lot rich, then he just might have to do something about that.

He would have to come up with a way to get more information. He needed to learn who this boy was and who was after him if he was going to do something about it. Then he heard something that gave him an idea of how.

"We're going to have to find some local help. We'll find a guy or two that can help us get a better idea of how things work around here. Some cheap muscle that knows this town and won't ask too many questions is what we need."

Dorn was out of his stool and didn't even know it until his head grazed the beam above. He moved away from the bar with his plan still forming. He hoped this worked or he would have a hard time coming up with any other ideas. This approach would alert them to his interest.

As he carefully approached the table of strangers all four sets of eyes turned towards him with suspicion. Suspicion turned to disbelief as they took in his size. The loud ones mouth even dropped open.

When he got to the table, Dorn tried to appear even more oafish than he already did. He didn't want to seem too dumb, but he didn't want to come across as smart either. "Did I just hear one a you say sumthin' bout needing some help? I could sure use some work. I didn't catch what kind o work you needed done, but I can do a lot."

At first, Dorn was sure he'd made a mistake. All four men just stared dumbly at him. Finally, they looked at each other and broke into laughter. Dorn couldn't figure out what was so funny, so he went ahead and joined in the laughing. That just seemed to make them laugh harder.

As the laughter died away, one man looked at Dorn again. The suspicion was back in his eyes. "So, you heard us talking about needing help, did you? Tell me, my large friend, what else did you hear?"

Dorn should've known this question would be asked. His decision to approach the strangers this way had been impulsive. Maybe, he should have bided his time and found another opportunity. Now he had no choice but to try to make it work.

"My mug was dry. Just when I was gonna holler for refill, I heard somebody say they needed to find some local help. I'm local, and I'm help, didn't need to hear no more."

That got a couple of the strangers chuckling again. The man who'd asked the question just looked at him searchingly for a moment. Then he seemed to relax and said, "My name is Vorgen, this is Niel, Liam, and Remik. What's your name, friend?"

Dorn knew then that he might just pull off his ruse. He felt truly alive at the thought. He hadn't felt this good in years. He had waited so long for the opportunity to fight the good fight again, that he had given up.

He had thought that part of him was dead. He realized now that this was the opportunity he'd given up waiting for. That long dormant part of him came to life with a vengeance.

"Dorn sir, my name is Dorn Deepaxe."

"Well then Dorn, if you're local then our boss should be able to tell us if you're okay. If you check out with him, then I'm sure we can find a way to use a big strong guy like you. In fact, how bout we go check with him right now."

Dorn had little choice in the matter. He had committed himself and had to follow through. He hadn't done anything like this in so long. He hoped this was the change he was looking for. He hoped this was a good fight to fight.

Vorgen and Liam got up and headed for the door. The other two waited as Dorn turned to begin navigating his way, first to the bar to pay his bill and then, after picking up his things, out of The Gem. They got impatient with his slow lumbering pace through the maze of chandeliers. Their prodding did them no good.

He caught Ruby watching him curiously. He offered her a small nod so she'd know everything was okay. She shrugged back and turned to wipe down the bar. When she didn't think he was still paying attention she looked back at him with concern on her face. He wished he could go back and tell her everything was going to be alright.

When Dorn finally reached the street, all four men were shaking their heads and commenting rudely on his size. He ignored them and followed along agreeably. He'd been teased plenty and by better men than these. He didn't let it get to him.

He was lost in thoughts about how his life might be about to change. He wondered at the adventures still to be had in his lifetime. He wondered about the future. Most of all he hoped to never swing his axe as a lumberjack again.

His step was lighter with these thoughts. He hadn't felt anticipation for anything in so long it was like warm ale in his belly, rich and filling. The weight of his axe was a comfort instead of a burden for the first time in a long time.

Chapter 15

Griff Borrowmore

Waterful was the most beautiful city in Asteria and the most fortified. Sheer cliff faces filled the back third of the city. Waterfalls ran in beautiful crystal clear cascades down the cliffs. The different levels of Waterful were clearly delineated by the natural and manmade irrigation system that flowed throughout the city.

The top level included the castle and its acres of lush green landscaping. The castle had its own moat and drawbridge. Even though the city was well fortified, the castle was even more so. If an enemy made it into the city, they still would have equal difficulty getting into the castle itself.

This had been designed and built some centuries past. There had not been a need for it since, but it was carefully maintained anyway. Whether this was in case of a future threat or just for appearances, no one seemed to know.

The next level below that of the castle was filled with grand homes of nobility and upper class. There were three more levels down to the main streets and a mote around Waterful. While each level was not as rich as the one above it, the whole city sparkled in its splendor. Not even the lowest level could be considered poor or ill kept.

Griff Borrowmore was in his element. As he wandered the streets in the day's fading light, he looked at each passerby.

He didn't speak to anyone, although there was an occasional nod his way.

Under his breath, from time to time, he would say, "Mine." Each time he said this he would smile happily to himself and continue down the street with a bounce in his step. His eyes never stopped moving over the people in the street.

The streets were lined in cobblestone that the residents had always kept proudly swept clean. Tidy sidewalks lined both sides of even the narrowest lanes. Flowers boxes and hanging baskets added color and fragrance. Oil lamps dotted the streets and were lit at night.

The buildings were kept up as well. Many had stained glass windows and charming awnings. The windows were clean and the signs kept freshly painted. Wooden buildings were whitewashed regularly and stone ones were polished and freshly grouted.

Griff was just what his name implied. He was a borrower. He didn't think of it as stealing. He only took things from people who would hardly notice anyway. Then he would change the item in some way.

He would turn a necklace into a bracelet and pair of earrings for the ladies. He would change the face on a men's pocket watch. A fancy dress would get a new sash and be dyed a new color. It didn't take much and the item was unrecognizable.

Then the people down here on the lower levels of the city had nice things to borrow from him from time to time. He thought of them as his people. No one wanted to admit a dress or pocket watch was borrowed, so everyone liked to pretend they didn't know him.

They sure did know him when they needed something nice for an event or a night out on the town and couldn't afford to buy it, though. They would come knocking on his door acting like he was their oldest friend then. His fees were reasonable and he was very discreet.

He always knew who had each item and when to expect it to be returned. He very rarely had to go after it. Everyone knew that if you tried to cheat Griff Borrowmore, he'd come by and borrow *more*. He'd take back his item along with a few extra things. He had to cover his expenses after all.

His favorite pastime was to go out during the busy time of night and see all his things. Each time he saw a person that was borrowing an item he would quietly say, "Mine."

On a good night as he roamed the streets he would be saying to himself, "Mine, mine...mine. Oh, and that too. Mine." Those were his favorite times.

Griff stood at least a full head shorter than most men. He rarely stood even with women unless they were quite petite. He always held his head up high with his chin slightly raised. He believed he didn't have to be tall to stand tall. He was a self made man after all.

Griff had intelligent brown eyes and wavy brown hair. He was slightly portly which he felt was something to be proud of. Only the poor are thin, was what he always said. He wore quality breeches with a matching vest and jacket. His tunic was made of the finest silk. His shoes were always shined and his nails were always clean and trimmed. He never left the house looking less than his best.

He was proud of his accomplishments and loved his place in Waterful. His cousin worked for him and aspired to be just like him one day. Griff wasn't going to give him too much responsibility just yet. He had to earn his way up was what Griff kept telling him.

Griff was nearing the end of his twenty forth year. His cousin Tabot was barely twenty. When Griff had been twenty he hadn't even been sure where his next meal would come from. He had worked hard for everything he had. Tabot needed to be grateful for any opportunity Griff gave him.

Just then Tabot came dashing around the corner. His brown eyes searched the crowd, obviously looking for Griff. His hair was much curlier than Griff's, and he wore it longer and it was quite unbecoming, in Griff's opinion. Griff made sure he had a decent suit of clothes, but he didn't keep them as clean and pressed as Griff would have liked.

Spotting Griff he stopped in his tracks. Griff had given him strict instructions that when he was out for his evening stroll he was not to be interrupted unless it was an emergency. Tabot motioned to Griff. Griff sighed in frustration. The evening had been going so well.

With one more, "Mine", Griff made his way to Tabot. Tabot was a bit taller than Griff, but slumped so badly that it didn't seem like it. He had a worried look that Griff didn't like.

"Griff, we've got some trouble and I knew I had to come and get you as soon as I heard. Here is the ..."

"Shhh, you idiot, we don't talk about unpleasant business in the street." No one seemed to be paying them any attention, but Griff was upset that Tabot hadn't figured out the first rule of the Borrow More business. The public should only see the clean polished side of things. That way his customers keep coming back.

Griff marched off down the street with Tabot rushing to keep up. They didn't speak again until they got back to Griff's house. Not even a single "mine" was uttered. That was proof that Griff was bothered by the trouble Tabot had mentioned.

Griff lived in a very small home behind a little bakery. He woke to the smell of fresh bread and pastry every morning.

Sometimes he would slip over and get something warm and sticky before they were even open to anyone else. The owner liked to borrow from him now and then.

He enjoyed living off the beaten path. The house didn't feel nearly as small to him as it was. The ceilings were very low, but just made him feel taller. He kept it clean, but it was extremely cluttered. There were trinkets and gadgets in every nook and cranny.

His favorite room in the house was the kitchen. It only had four cupboards, but he had all sorts of gadgets hung from the ceiling and practically spilling off of shelves. He loved to cook and tried some new recipe almost every night before his walk.

Tabot had asked him why he had so much junk when he had first moved to the city and seen where Griff lived. Griff had replied that he didn't like to throw things away. He had told him it wasn't junk and that Tabot wouldn't last in the business unless he figured that out. Tabot had nodded solemnly but looked around in disbelief.

The second rule of the Borrow More Business, Tabot learned later, is you never know when you might find a need for something. Griff didn't even know what some of the stuff was, but if his customers ever needed whatever it was, he would have it. He figured that would show Tabot a thing or two.

As soon as they were both through the door Griff slammed it and turned to Tabot. "Well, let's have it then. What was so urgent you took me away from a very pleasant evening stroll?"

Tabot sighed to himself before speaking. "I heard it from Mara that one of the militia was asking questions about you and the business. She overheard him saying there were some complaints and it looked like you were finally going to get what was coming to you. I figured you'd want to know as soon as I heard. I wouldn't have bothered you otherwise."

Tabot and Mara had been courting for a few months now. Mara worked in a city office, and was full of information. One of her favorite pastimes was gossiping. Unfortunately, for Griff, her gossip usually turned out to be true.

Griff didn't answer. He was trying to figure out who would have complained to the militia about him. What could he have possibly done? He admitted to himself that not everything he did was exactly lawful, but he was very careful. What was he to do?

"What are you going to do, Cousin?" Tabot asked quietly.

"What am I going to do? Well, nothing. They can't prove a thing. I am a good citizen of this city and provide a great service to my community. They will realize their error and drop the whole thing." Griff said this with more confidence than he felt.

"Griff, I don't think I made the situation clear. They already are looking for you to take you in. They are going to lock you up in the jail, or maybe even the dungeon.

Mara doesn't think they are even going to give you a trial. You know how things have gotten. The Militia is not run by good honest people anymore. If someone up high enough in power wants you to disappear, you will."

Griff was beside himself. He wrung his hands in frustration. Tabot may be young, but he was loyal and had obviously come to him with a real problem. Griff would be a fool not to heed his warning.

Chapter 16

Incarcerated

Griff started throwing some essentials in a small bag. Looking around in dismay, he realized that until he figured out how to fix this, he would have to leave Tabot in charge. He felt sick at the idea. How would Tabot possibly keep track of all of his things? How would he make sound business decisions without Griff there?

He looked at Tabot, and with a great inhale, began explaining how he had to get out of the city for a while and Tabot would have to be in charge so he needed to listen well to his instructions. Griff didn't like the look that came into Tabot's eyes. He thought it might be excitement.

Tabot had been asking for more responsibility. He was also hinting around for more pay. He had been talking about wanting to be able to afford his own place so he could propose to Mara soon. Right now he was staying in a bunk house with other single men like him.

Just then they heard voices followed by a loud knock. Griff looked around in alarm. There was nowhere to go. His house backed up to a sheer wall of earth. The front door was the only way in or out. He realized he needed to move if he got through this ordeal.

The door crashed open. Suddenly the small room was filled with militia. They were grabbing Griff and Tabot both.

One said, "Which one of you is Griff Borrowmore?", as they dragged them both out the front door.

"I'm Griff. Leave him be. I am the one you came for." Griff hollered as he was trying to keep his feet. He couldn't have both of them taken away. Tabot had to keep things in order. The thought had crossed his mind to try to trick them into taking Tabot instead of him, but once they realized their mistake they might both be locked up, or worse.

As they hauled Griff out to the main road, his thoughts were in such turmoil that he didn't even think about what was coming next. Then they threw him into the back of the paddy wagon. He realized with a groan that the joy he had been feeling at everyone being out this evening was about to become horror.

Sure enough, as they began the trip up to the next level of the city, he saw many people he knew. He tried to hide his face, but he could tell he didn't fool anyone. He heard his name and peeking out saw the sneers and smirks of some of his very own clients. In fact, there were some of his things right now.

It seemed to take forever, but they finally reached the alleyway behind the jail on the third level. At least back here in the alley there was no one to watch his disgrace. He should have been happy they hadn't gone straight to the dungeon, but he was so humiliated he found it hard to care one way or the other.

They hustled him out, grabbing at him like a common criminal. Dragging him through the back door his feet didn't even reach the floor. Then just when he thought it couldn't get any worse, they threw him into a rat infested cell. He was in his finest clothes too.

The cell was the most awful place he had ever been. He hadn't always led the comfortable life he had now. When he had first been on his own, he had not had it easy, but this was far worse then anything he had endured back then.

There was a bucket in the corner. It had been used and was still half full of waste. The straw on the dirt floor was damp and moldy. The straw bed was not much better than the floor and it was where the rats had run when he had been shoved in. He wasn't going to be sleeping on that if he could help it.

There were three other cells. Only one held a prisoner and it looked to be a drunk sleeping it off. A short hallway led to the front of the jail.

One guard was on duty at the back door. He looked less than enthusiastic and scowled at Griff when he caught him looking at him. Griff quickly looked away. He didn't want to make friends in here, but he surely didn't need any enemies either.

That got him thinking about why he was here in the first place. He didn't understand how he had gotten into this mess. Just then the door to the front opened. He expected a guard to come through. Instead it was the Constable himself.

The Constable was not a nice man. No one would dare say it to his face, but he wasn't liked. He was tall and wiry with close cropped hair and colorless eyes that seemed to look right through you. While the position had always been one of some power, this man acted, and was treated, like he ran the city.

Waterful, being the capital city, had always been beautiful. It still was beautiful from the observer's vantage point. He was proud that the streets were still swept and the cobbles replaced often. The water was clean and sparkled like always. Everything looked the same.

Unfortunately, some of that was due to it being required now. You had to pay an extra fee if your street was found below standards. There were also fees for running a business, fees for living in the city, and fees for just about everything. It just got worse and worse every year.

Everyone that lived in the city knew it was corrupt. It was like a piece of fruit that was rotting from the inside. It looks okay on the surface, but then you take a bite and it's bad. This guy was part of that rottenness. He was handpicked by the mayor, and ran the militia like his personal bully club.

They walked the street handing out slips to everyone that owed a fee. People were starting to have financial difficulties that had never had before. People were moving out of the city or being forced to close their business due to the new fees that they couldn't afford to pay.

The constable walked up to Griff's cell and looking in gave a mean chuckle. "Griff Borrowmore, look at you. I expected a taller man. It's hard to take such a little one seriously. In any case, Griff, you are in deep, deep trouble. Are you aware of that?"

Griff had to clear his throat before he could form a reply. "No sir, I mean yes, sir. What I mean to say is that no, sir I don't know why I am here. I think there has been some sort of mix up. And yes, sir I am obviously in some sort of trouble since I am locked in your jail."

Suddenly the constable's eyes went cold and he dropped the faked nonchalance. "You know exactly why you are here. It really doesn't matter, though. You are never getting out of here. Not alive, anyway.

I don't really know who you stole from, but it must have been someone up close and personal with the mayor. All I know is the mayor says you're to go out of business, permanently. I guess you could say you are in some sort of trouble all right. You sleep well tonight. Tomorrow, well, we will see if there even is a tomorrow for you."

The constable left through the same door he had come in by. Griff was stunned. Tabot had been right about the new way things were being done. He was in a serious situation. He started looking around more carefully. He was small, that was true. Small and nimble had gotten him out of a lot of scrapes in the past.

The bars were wood. They were in good repair, but had a little give to them. The guard eyed him suspiciously as he checked them. That was his biggest problem. How could he even attempt to break out of here with a guard watching his every move?

He could hear talking coming through the bars in the door leading to the front. He realized, after a moment, that it was the constable talking to someone. His ears perked up at the subject matter.

"Now that we know where it is supposed to be, I don't want you taking any chances. You take the best men we've got, the best horses too, and get it. The mayor won't understand any excuses. He must have it. Get it and we will all be set for life.

Come back empty handed and you will not see the next day. Understand what I am saying? Now go through it again so I know you've got it. Where is it and what are you going to do when you find it?"

Griff heard everything. He knew exactly what he had to do. He even knew the place they were talking about going to. He had to get out of here and get to it first.

Then he could come back to his city and back to his things and he would be set for life instead of the constable and his men. This was right up his alley. He just had to get out of this jail and the rest was just borrowing.

Chapter 17

Chance Encounter

Alimar stood on the hill. The breeze blew the tall grass making it seem like some great serpent was moving through it. He felt as though he was rooted to the ground, like he was heavy and encumbered. He looked down and saw the gleam of his armor; felt the weight of his sword. He flexed his arm that was holding the sword. It was larger and well muscled. He felt taller and stronger too.

Then he saw a man standing slightly behind him. He somehow knew he was a friend. As he stood there others appeared one by one on the hill. Soon the hill was filled with soldiers all around them. They were all wearing armor and were also armed, and seemed ready for battle. They all stood there waiting. He realized he was waiting with them. He just wasn't sure for what.

Then he heard it. The thrum of power was vibrating through the ground throughout the hillside. He also heard the sound of many feet marching towards them. The trees below began to move as the approaching army came closer.

The man behind him said something calming to the soldiers around them. Alimar looked at him, trying to figure out how he knew him. The man smiled and said, "We're here Alimar. We're all here for you, our King. Are you ready? Are you ready, Alimar?"

Alimar woke. As he shook off the dream, he noticed he was his scrawny self again. He was so used to having one dream that having a new one was disorienting. What did this one mean? He suddenly felt time rushing by. That moment in his dream was coming. He had to make sure he was ready for it. Would he be ready?

Alimar thought about that while he fed the horses and checked on Fogerden. Fogerden was still pale, but the fever had broken sometime in the night. His salve had worked, at least for now. Alimar still wasn't sure if it was a good idea to move him, but did he really have a choice?

They were also out of food. He remembered the snares that Fogerden had set the day before and went out to check them. He found two rabbits and took them and the snares back to camp. He cleaned the rabbits and set them to cooking on a spit over the fire.

He had used all of his new salve he had made. Most of all, he was pretty sure the dream meant he was running out of time. He had to make a decision. It was time to move.

He used some heavy sticks, his blanket, and twine to build a litter for Fogerden. It would drag behind his horse. They wouldn't go very fast, but it was the only way for Fogerden to travel at all.

He made some broth and packed up the rabbit meat for a later meal before dousing the fire. He spoon fed some of the broth to Fogerden and drank the rest himself. He made quick work of packing up camp. Now that he had made the decision to get moving he was ready to move.

It was midday by the time they got started. As he had thought, the going was slow, but after stopping to make a couple adjustments to the litter, he was able to go some distance. By the time the sun was setting, and he knew he had to stop for the night, they had made about a quarter the distance they might have in the half a day. It had been tiresome to get that far. He and the horses needed to stop, and Fogerden was surely getting parched pulling up the rear.

The next few days were slower. He stopped often to check on Fogerden and adjust the litter. Twice he had to make repairs to it. They were out of food again and he was frustrated by the slow progress he was making. He could see no improvement in Fogerden's condition either.

He found a spot not far off of the trail. He didn't want to delay getting out the next morning by scouting around for a place more sheltered. He knew they were a little too exposed here, but he was too tired to care. Dragging Fogerden around was making him so tired. Watering the horses, forcing Fogerden to drink, and starting a fire so Fogerden wouldn't get a chill was all he could do before he slumped over exhausted.

. . . .

Kilian and Alana were barely staying in their saddles. They had ridden harder than they ever had before. They had only seen a few groups since they left Louis and Jana's. One was a family with children they had passed. The others had all been headed in the wrong direction and definitely didn't include a boy of fourteen.

They didn't dare ask if any of them had seen the boy either. They didn't know who was looking for Alimar and couldn't take any risks. After the experience they had with the strangers looking for Alimar, they weren't taking any chances they might talk to the wrong people.

They were only afraid that if they did manage to catch up to Alimar and Fogerden in time that they might pass them up. Surely they would be staying out of sight as much as possible even without knowing men were out looking for them. What if they had made less progress then Kilian and Alana were estimating and they passed right by them?

Evening had fallen and this part of the trail was not safe for the horses at night. A broken leg would not make the journey any faster. They were all too tired for another all night ride anyway. Kilian slowed his horse and started looking for a place to get off the trail and rest. The change of her horse's pace jostled Alana out of her half doze.

"What's happening?" She asked, slurping slightly.

"We need a break. The horses need to get off the trail in this dark. It's too rough through here for nighttime riding. Look for a spot we can rest for a few hours." Kilian replied warily.

They were quiet for several minutes while they both peered around in what little light the stars were offering. They both saw the faint light at the same time.

"What's that?" Alana asked quietly.

"I think it's a fire." Kilian whispered back.

"Oh, a fire sounds lovely."

"We can't risk it. What if they're bandits or something?"

"Come on, Kilian. We can't just pass it up, either. What if it's the two we're looking for?"

"Not a chance, they wouldn't be right out by the road like that. Besides, there is no way we caught up to them this fast. You know they must be at least two maybe even more days ahead of us as fast as we've been going. We need to just get past and find a different spot."

They had determined they were riding twice as fast as they normally would. So if Alimar and Fogerden were traveling at a normal pace, they might be two to five days behind them. As they closed that gap more they would have to slow down and keep a closer watch for them.

As they quietly started to pass the glow of the fire, Kilian could just make out a slumped figure. It seemed small. Suddenly he knew that Alana was right. They had to be sure. What if this was them and Kilian and Alana went right by?

He got off of his horse and motioned for Alana to wait for him. Even in the dark he could tell she made a face at him. She had made it clear to him that she didn't want to separate in times of danger anymore after what had happened at Louis and Jana's.

He crept quietly through the narrow band of trees between the trail and the clearing the camp was in. The camp was only partially set up with one bedroll. The slumped figure just sat in the dirt.

As he snuck around to see the figures face, the boy turned and looked at him. He was obviously tired and Kilian was worried that he might pull a weapon at the sight of a stranger. It was dark and Kilian had come up behind him suddenly.

"It's you," was all Alimar said.

Chapter 18

Introductions

All three of them sat around the fire tired and weary. The only thing keeping them awake was curiosity. As soon as Alimar had seen Kilian's face, he knew he was in no danger. While he had never laid eyes on him before, he was the man in his new dream. He was younger then he had been it the dream, and even a little smaller, but it was definitely him.

It made sense that once they had introductions out of the way the first thing that Kilian would ask is, "How did you know me? What did you mean when you said, it's you?"

Alimar thought about how to answer. He wished he hadn't blurted that out. He'd been so tired that he had almost thought he was dreaming again when he had seen Kilian's face.

Now he was stuck and had to come up with some sort of explanation. "Well I saw you, not really, but sort of. You were in a dream I had." Seeing the looks on Kilian and Alana's faces he stopped.

Kilian and Alana exchanged their look that translated into "This guy is a horse or two shy of a full barn." Then Alana remembered her own dreams and looked into the fire thoughtfully. Her dreams sure did seem real while she was having them. Maybe Alimar had those kinds too.

Seeing Alana retreat into her thoughts, Kilian looked back at Alimar. "Well, I don't really understand what's going on, but let me explain why we're here." He went on to tell Alimar what had happened at his home.

Alimar was upset to realize his aunt and uncle had been in danger. Then he was relieved to hear how easily they dealt with the five strangers. He was grateful that these two had been there to get the word to him so that his uncle wasn't forced to make some other decision, like leaving his aunt to come find him. More strangers would surely come to their home; Louis needed to be there to keep Jana safe.

"I want to thank both of you. As you can see, Fogerden is in pretty bad shape." He explained the encounter with the Nocturnals and everything that had happened afterwards. Kilian and Alana both listened with rapt attention.

"I should get to a town in the next few days with Fogerden. He said we would pass through a couple trading posts on our way to Strautin. Once I see he's safe, I will make sure to avoid whoever is looking for me. You must already have gone out of your way. I wish there was something I could do for you in return, but I can't think of a way to repay you. I will find some way in the future. You can trust me on that."

Kilian and Alana exchanged another look. This one said, "We can't abandon this kid just yet." Alana spoke up this time. "Let us help you get Fogerden to town. After all you've gone through, it is the least we can do. We're here now, and a couple more days won't make a difference for us. For now, lets all get a little sleep."

Both Kilian and Alimar let out a yawn at that. They all smiled and went about setting up bedrolls. Since Alimar had used his blanket on the litter for Fogerden, Kilian shared his. The next thing any of them knew, the sun was peeking through the trees.

Alimar woke to find Fogerden awake. He was very weak, but was able to stay awake long enough to drink some broth. As Alimar tended Fogerden, Kilian and Alana got the horses situated and food for the rest of them cooked. Alimar had been grateful of Kilian and Alana's offer to go hunting and they were back in no time with breakfast. Alana turned it into a quick stew and they all enjoyed the simple meal.

Alimar was secretly very relieved to have help. He had been trying so hard to be self sufficient, but he felt as though he was failing miserably. Between causing Fogerden to almost be killed, and then camping in plain sight where anyone could have found him, he wasn't doing a very good job.

Kilian was thinking just the opposite. He was amazed at Alimar's accomplishments so far. Alimar was almost two years younger than Kilian and here he was out here on his own since Fogerden had been hurt. Not just on his own either; he was caring for this man, having to even find herbs to heal him with.

Kilian knew if he had been in the same situation that Fogerden would have died. It was a sobering thought. He was coming to respect this kid a lot in a short period of time. Kilian was glad they were here to help him, but obviously Alimar had been getting along without them. He could tell Alana felt the same way.

With all three of them working at it, they got on the road right away. They made a lot more progress than Alimar could have alone, and by the end of the fourth day of being together made it to the town of Woodman's Ville. No one was more relieved than Alimar to find an old healer that immediately got to work on Fogerden.

Alimar stayed with Fogerden while Kilian and Alana went to restock supplies for all three of them. They hadn't mentioned where they were going from here, but they wanted to make sure he wasn't seen in town more than he had to be. They hoped to at least help keep whoever was looking for him off his trail.

Alimar couldn't even guess how old the old healer was, but she was as thin and bent as the stick she used as a cane. Her name was Hester and she was skeptical about Alimar's self made remedy at first. Then she looked at Fogerden's wounds and double checked his lack of fever and wanted to know all about how Alimar had made his version of the salve.

"I just thought about what worked for different remedies and made a substitution. Isn't that what anyone would do if they couldn't find the right herbs?" Alimar didn't understand why Hester was making a big deal out of it.

"No, that is not how things are done. Why, you could have made a worse mess of things. As it is you made a powerful new salve that I have never seen the likes of. You say your aunt taught you about herbology. Who is she anyway?" The old crone asked curiously.

Alimar was trying to make something up as not to give Hester too much information. Fortunately, Fogerden chose that moment to wake up. He asked Hester to give them a minute alone. After some convincing that he wouldn't up and die on her, she finally left with a final shake of her cane.

"Alimar, you did real well. I heard you telling the healer about how you kept me going. You saved my life. You are going to make an amazing King. Now come close so I can tell you who you need to see in Strautin since I can't come with you." Fogerden told him what he knew.

"Fogerden, I hate to leave you here. I get the feeling I have got to keep moving, but I really wish I could wait for you. You saved my life back there in the woods." Alimar didn't want to go and wanted Fogerden to understand.

"Alimar, I was never going to be able to keep up with you once you got things figured out anyway. Those two you have with you are young, but they might be handy to travel with. Ask them to stay with you.

As for me saving your life, I think we must be even in that regard. You did something back in those woods. I was slipping away. I felt it. Then you were bringing me back.

You've got something special in you. If I hadn't already known that, then I sure would know it now. You go find your new friends and get gone. Be safe, you hear?" Then Fogerden drifted back off and there was nothing for Alimar to do but find Kilian and Alana. He just hoped he could think of a way to talk them into staying with him.

Then he thought of his dream. Remembering Kilian standing there on the hilltop at his back, he knew that they would stay with him. When Fogerden had called them his new friends, he had realized that he had really never had any friends.

He got a good feeling about the brother and sister. He thought they would get along great once they got to know each other better. In fact, he was pretty sure they were going to be good friends. With that thought making him feel more confident, he set out to meet them in the woods at the edge of town as they had agreed.

Alimar didn't see the man in the shadows. As he went by the man watched him intently. After Alimar was out of sight, the man nodded to himself and quickly walked to his horse and left town at a gallop.

Chapter 19

Big Little

orn wasn't worried about where they were taking him. He worked hard as a lumberjack, but hadn't made friends or really gotten to know anyone in Strautin at all. He pretty much kept to himself.

Ruby was the only one he really talked to and she couldn't tell anyone where Dorn was from or much else about him, and wouldn't even if she knew. Whoever they were going to meet might know of Dorn the lumberjack, but really couldn't possibly know anything else about him. No one in Strautin knew he had ever been a fighter.

All he had to do was keep up the act of someone looking for a little excitement and extra income. If he kept his head down and listened, he would learn more about the boy these rouges were after and hopefully why. Dorn's interest was really peaked when they arrived at the mayor's offices. This whole thing must be bigger than he had thought.

All five of them walked into the foyer with Dorn going in third. Remik had to squeeze into a narrow space behind the door the area was so full. He glared at Dorn who shrugged an apology. He really did take up most of the space by himself.

The man at the desk only gave a cursory look towards the four men with Dorn. He obviously recognized them. His eyes got big at the sight of Dorn who only looked bigger indoors. Dorn sometimes just wanted to yell out, "What are you looking at?" or something like that to make people stop staring.

The city offices were pretty much the same as you would see anywhere. In this front area there was the foyer they stood in as well as desks that sat outside the larger offices. Some doors were open, but only one office had light coming from within. Dorn could see the office with the mayor's name on it was closed and dark.

The man got up from his desk and poked his head through the open doorway that was lit. He obviously told someone inside the office who was here because Dorn heard someone say. "Well, send them in. What are you waiting for?"

The man must have said something about Dorn then because soon another man came to the door to look out. He waddled really. Dorn was a big man, but this man, while average in height, had him beat in girth. There was no polite way to describe him; the man was fat, really fat.

He was balding and his beady eyes seemed to regard Dorn with familiarity. Dorn had never met him, but though they were surely different, they were very alike in one way. He and Dorn regarded each other like men that were used to getting looked at.

He was dressed in fine clothing that had to have been tailor made. He had a double chin that disappeared into his lacy shirt collar. His feet seemed too small to carry such a load, but somehow he didn't topple over as it seemed he should.

"I see what you mean. I guess I better come out here. This big boy is not fitting in my small office." Waddling out of his office was obviously not an easy task for the fat man. Dorn sympathized.

"I'm Deputy Mayor Little. Who are you?" It was all Dorn could do to keep a straight face. This man was Deputy Mayor Little? Dorn had heard of him, but he hadn't heard how big Little was. He almost wished his own name was Tiny, just to see the look on Little's face when he introduced himself.

"My name's Dorn sir, Dorn Deepaxe."

"What do you do Dorn Deepaxe?"

"I'm a lumberjack sir."

"Well, I guess that's obvious. Come to think of it, I have heard of a really big, very productive, lumberjack. I bet that's you. What are you doing with this lot, then?" Little was ignoring the four men with Dorn completely. They just listened and waited. This must be the way the Deputy Mayor did things.

"They said they needed local muscle. I'm local, and I guess I fit the bill in the muscle department too. I thought I might help em' out. For a change of pace, you know?"

Little chuckled, then his chuckle turned into a very large belly laugh. The other men started laughing too, even the man behind the desk. Dorn smiled even though the joke was obviously on him.

Little started turning red in an alarming way. Dorn thought he might keel over. Everyone watched him with concern and the laughter died away. Then with a mighty coughing fit, and a few deep breaths after that, he seemed to recover.

"Dorn, I like you. I think we can get you a few days off at the lumber mill. They may not like having to go without such a productive hand, but I think you're just the type this bunch needs. I just have two questions for you first." At this he leaned forward and his eyes narrowed on Dorn.

"Will you kill if you have too? If so, can you keep your mouth shut?"

Everyone seemed to wait for Dorn's response. The answers to both questions were simple. He just didn't quite think that what he had in mind matched the Deputy Mayor's ideas.

"No problem, Deputy Mayor Little. I am very good with my axe." Dorn replied meeting Little's look squarely.

After another few seconds, Little nodded. "OK, boys, you know what needs to be done. We're pretty sure that the boy is headed here. We know he's coming here for some sort of message. He isn't going to get it.

I want a man posted at the main South road at all times. I want men posted at the inn and both taverns in case he gets past the man at the road. Stay sober and alert. Bring the boy to me. If you can't get him alive, kill him. Is that understood?"

The men nodded their heads and left the building. Dorn wasn't happy with the idea that they were to split up. What if one of the others caught the boy first? "I'll be happy to take the south road, I know what most locals look like and I will most likely spot a boy that doesn't belong here."

Vorgen looked at him suspiciously. Dorn may have not played the idiot well enough with that forward thinking. Finally, he relented, but sent Remik with Dorn. Obviously he wasn't taking any chances on Dorn's loyalty.

As the two men walked towards the main road, Dorn had time to think. If the Deputy Mayor was bold enough to meet thugs in the office even at night, then Dorn had to assume that the Mayor was in on this too. The offices and businesses on the street may have been closed, but there were still people out. Someone was bound to notice activity at the mayor's office.

They arrived at the south road. It was getting very late now and less people were out. It was an uneventful night, very few people came along, and not one of them could have been confused for the boy they were watching for.

Dorn had gotten a basic description out of his companion. The boy was traveling with an older man, Dorn learned as well. Then Remik had promptly fallen asleep under a tree leaving Dorn to keep watch.

The next morning Vorgen came to check on them and seeing Remik sleeping went over and kicked him. "You are supposed to be keeping an eye out. Get up and take over so the big guy can go get some sleep. What good are you anyway?"

He went back into town while Remik got up rubbing his side where he had been kicked. "Go home and get some sleep, I guess." was all he said to Dorn.

Dorn couldn't risk the boy coming in to town with him at home sleeping. He had to stay put. He was really tired, but just had to get over it.

"I'm okay. I don't need much sleep anyhow."

"Suit yourself. I'm going to get something to eat then. I'll bring you something back."

Dorn was pretty sure he could stay up through another night, but after that he was going to need to rest. He had no idea when the boy would arrive. If he was honest with himself, he knew the boy might never come to Strautin at all. He despaired at the thought.

If the boy didn't come, could Dorn just go back to his miserable life as a lumberjack? He shook his head. No, if the boy didn't come through Strautin, Dorn would go find him. He was sure it was what he was supposed to do. All of his instincts screamed at him to protect this boy.

He took a short nap after Remik brought him breakfast. He didn't really sleep, worried that he would miss something important, but he felt a little better for the downtime. He took up his post and got through the day thinking about how great it would be to get out of Strautin. He made a promise to himself right then and there. No more lumberjacking for him. Whatever happened he was done cutting down trees for a living.

That afternoon Liam replaced Remik. Dorn was again offered a break to go home. Again he declined. Someone was sent with dinner. The second night seemed very long. Dorn's eyes were gritty from lack of sleep.

The following morning, just when he thought he was going to have to risk another nap, a rider came up. Both man and beast looked exhausted. The man dismounted and came over to them. His name was Dal. It turned out Dal was one of several scouts that had been sent out to the smaller towns along the trade route to watch for the boy.

After making sure with Liam that it was okay to talk in front of Dorn, he explained that he was confident he had seen the boy they were looking for in Woodman's Ville about a week away. He had ridden at breakneck speed and believed he was at least two maybe even three days ahead of the boy and his new companions.

One thing was for sure, Dal told them, they were headed this way. He explained that the man the boy had been with was wounded and he had been left behind. The boy had two new companions, but they were both young and "wet behind the ears". Then he told them he had learned the boy's name. It was Alimar. Dorn was so happy to finally have a name he barely heard the rest of what the man had to say.

Both men headed into town to report to Vorgen. Remik told Dorn he may as well take the rest of the day off and report back in the morning. "I don't want to hear how you don't need the rest. If nothing else, you need to wash. You really smell."

Dorn happily walked home ready for a meal, a wash and sleep, lots and lots of sleep. He wanted to be ready when Alimar did arrive. He was so elated as he washed and ate that he had confirmation that the boy, Alimar, was coming. He had to wonder as he lay down to sleep, was he saving Alimar, or was Alimar really saving him?

Chapter 20

Trouble in Strautin

The next morning Dorn was rested, clean and already posted by the road into the city when all four men approached. They had a determined look about them. Dorn had woken up with an idea. It had bounced around in his head as he had prepared for what could be another long wait till Alimar arrived. He just needed the right opening to present it.

Vorgen saw him standing there and shook his head with a grin. "Dorn, last to leave and first to be back, you're showing these boys up. You might come in handy after this job's done. You certainly have the scare factor. What do you say about that?"

Not in this lifetime was what Dorn thought, but what he said was, "That might be alright."

"Good. Now I know that Dal said we had a couple, three days before this Alimar and his new friends arrive, but I want to be ready. Little really wants the kid alive, but the other two will just get in the way. We need to kill them quick and knock out the kid. That way we can all get a big bonus and get out of this city. What do you boys think about that?"

The other three men nodded and smiled. It didn't look like Dorn was going to get the opportunity he'd been waiting for, so he better just jump in and hope for the best. He put on his best imitation of a thoughtful but not too smart expression.

"I just got one question about your plan. Where are we doing it?"

Vorgen gave him a mildly annoyed look. "What do you mean? We'll do it as soon as they ride in. Get them while they are still outside of town. Why, what do you care?"

"I just was noticing how many people are around this area. Being that this is the main road in, there's the main trading post right there in plain sight, and that's the hiring office for the mill. Look at all the people this time of morning.

It's not so busy at night, but we don't know when they might ride in. If we just up and start killing these young people out in the open in front of everyone, don't you think there might be trouble with Little?" The four men looked around and seeing that Dorn was right, three heads swiveled back to Vorgen for a reply.

"Dorn, you're a might smarter than you seem aren't you? Okay, I see what you mean, but what are our options? You got any brilliant ideas you want to share?"

Dorn did. As he explained his plan to get Alimar without raising any alarms, the others look skeptical at first, and then seemed impressed with his idea.

"That just might work. We have to be careful he doesn't get away is all. It's got some risks, but if we do it right, we won't have to knock the kid out like we'd planned. I like it Dorn. If it works as smooth as you say, you will have earned part of that bonus I was talking about.

Everybody knows what to do then? Okay, let's get ready." Vorgen had taken to Dorn's plan like it was his own.

Dorn let out a breath he hadn't even known he was holding. All he had to do now was get to Alimar and his friends first and he could make sure everything went smoothly. He ran one errand to get everything set. After that he came right back and got settled in, keeping a constant eye on the road. No more naps for him till this was done.

The rest of the day and night went by his attention only wavering slightly by meals and the occasional traveler that came down the road. The next day came and went too. He was starting to worry that his exhaustion would get the best of him as night started to fall again.

. . . .

Alimar and Kilian were getting along great. Alimar had been right about him. Alana was another story. She hadn't planned to stay with Alimar this long. She and Kilian had already gotten so far off course that it would be weeks before they got back on the right road to Waterful.

She had told Kilian that she didn't see where it was their problem. They had helped get Fogerden to a healer hadn't they? When Kilian had explained that he just couldn't leave Alimar alone, Alana was a little hurt. When had this kid become so important to her brother, and why?

"I am sure when we get to Strautin and Alimar is able to get the directions he needs there will be someone that can help him out. For now, he can't go on alone. It just isn't safe. You see what I am saying don't you?"

"What about the package we told Da we would deliver to his friend in Waterful? We made a commitment to him to get it there."

"I'm sure he would agree this is more important. A few weeks won't make a difference one way or the other. We'll get there soon enough, Alana."

Alana couldn't really argue without sounding like a cold hearted cretin. She went along with it, but she clearly wasn't happy. They had a plan, and they were not sticking to it.

As the days went by they camped well off of the roadway. Alana or Kilian would go out and hunt every other night or so. Alimar didn't mind tending the horses and usually took care of them. They took turns cooking and washing. Everyone took a turn on watch too.

Alimar and Kilian became fast friends while Alana grew more sullen. Kilian would try to get her to join in the friendly discussions, but she would make excuses about being tired or having a lot on her mind. She wasn't used to Kilian having a friendship that affected her this way. She felt left out.

Finally, they were rounding a bend and there was the city of Strautin. The trees had been cut all around the growing city. As it grew, more trees were cut to allow for the addition of buildings and the expansion of the trade road.

Stumps lined the edge of the trail and circled the city. Some of the stumps had been there for some time. Nature had started to reclaim them and they were covered in moss making them seem like forgotten tombstones.

The entry in to the city was crowned by an impressive guard tower. It was a wooden structure that spanned the entryway like a bridge. It was as wide as it was tall. The view from it stretched across Strautin and the roadway.

Alana immediately felt better. Soon they would be on their way again, just her and Kilian. "Thank goodness. We finally can get off these horses and sleep in a bed. I can't wait." She said happily.

. . . .

Dorn saw the three before they seemed to spot him. He acted quickly before Remik could do anything that might foul his chance. He stepped away from the trees and left his great axe leaning against one of them. He scared people enough even when he wasn't carrying it. He had better make this good.

"Hello there. Might one of you be Alimar?" He said as they rode closer. The three looked from him to each other obviously trying to decide how to act. He kept a friendly smile on his face and tried to seem as non-threatening as possible. This was the riskiest part of his whole plan. If they tried to run now, he wasn't sure he could protect them.

He had a chance to take a closer look at the three and it was obvious which one was Alimar. He was too young to be such a threat to whatever was going on. Dorn felt protective of him already and they hadn't met yet.

"My name is Dorn, and everything has been arranged for your arrival. I can take you to your rooms so you can get the dust of the trail off of you and rest up a bit. I'll see to your horses while you're here too."

Just then the one he had identified as Alimar slid out of his saddle. The other young man with him hissed, "What are you doing? You don't know who this guy is."

Alimar approached Dorn looking into his eyes. Dorn felt an indescribable urge to look away. He met Alimar's eyes instead and tried to project his need to be trusted.

"I am Alimar. Do you mean me harm?" The boy said quietly. He seemed calm and unaffected by the idea that Dorn might want to hurt him. Dorn towered over Alimar and yet he didn't seem to fear him.

"I mean you no harm. In fact, I wish to keep you safe. Please come with me so I can do so." Dorn replied back very quietly, hoping his companion would not be able to hear the earnestness in his voice.

Alimar looked at him a moment longer searching his face. Finally, he nodded once as though understanding all that was unspoken between them. "This is Kilian and Alana. They were kind enough to have traveled with me for a little while. Can you speak to their safety as well?"

Dorn had hoped that he could focus his efforts on protecting Alimar. He had intended to try to keep all three of them from harm while making Alimar his priority. If he gave his assurance to him, he would have to keep all three safe for certain. He would just have to find a way.

"I can. I will make sure you all leave Strautin safely." Dorn finally replied.

With that Alimar turned to the other two, trying to project his confidence in the situation to them. "Kilian, Alana this is Dorn. He's here to help. He has some rooms ready for us and will get the horses taken care of as well."

Both of them warily dismounted and started leading their horses into town. As they passed Remik, who it seemed obvious was with Dorn, Alimar looked at him suspiciously. Remik was not doing anything to make Dorn's job easier. He had a menacing scowl on his face aimed right at Alimar.

Alimar looked to Dorn with an inquiring expression. Dorn shook his head meaning two things. One, the man wasn't to be trusted. Two, Alimar didn't need to worry about him. Alimar seemed satisfied with whatever he read from Dorn.

Dorn could see from the expression on Alimar's face that this was his first time in a city. Alana and Kilian wore matching expressions as well. He tried to see it through their eyes.

Walking under the guard tower the three looked up in amazement. It had giant wooden supports that were fortified with iron brackets. It towered above them and was the tallest wooden structure in the kingdom as far as Dorn knew. It was quite impressive. He had just gotten used to seeing it every day.

The streets were simply dirt; no cobblestones paved the way in this city. Along the side of the buildings there were occasional spots of sawdust. It was cheap here, and it worked great on mud puddles. The buildings were almost all wood construction; some were made of log, and others of milled timber.

Some of the buildings had covered front porches with wooden gangplanks leading up to them. Others had wooden walkways leading to the door. The storefronts had painted wooden signs. Some were fancy and some were simple. There was an occasional awning, although they were mostly wood like everything else.

The streets were very wide and it was obvious why as they passed mammoth size wagons pulled by six Yegoxen. The three newcomers obviously had never seen the creatures before as they stared in awe.

The Yegox was a four legged creature with three tremendously muscled trunks. It looked like a cross between an elephant and its cousin, the ox. It had short, dense fur that kept it dry even in the pouring rain. It was twice the size of a regular ox and at least three times as strong. As they passed, the earth shook from the concussion of the six creatures walking.

The wagons were filled with Strautin Oak logs and towered above the smaller wagons and riders they passed on the street. They were the biggest wagons made and used only for logs. When the wood was milled it could be handled by smaller wagons as well as draft horses or regular oxen.

They got to The Gem where Dorn had arranged with Ruby to have rooms ready. He dismissed the other man to take the horses to the stable down the street and he did it, but didn't look too happy. Dorn took them up the back staircase to the little veranda that all the rooms shared.

There were four rooms over the tavern. They were small, but clean. He handed them each a small key. As they turned to go, Dorn left them with one whispered sentence. "Don't trust anybody but me, not anybody!"

The three went into their rooms where Dorn knew that Ruby would have heard them on the stairs and send up water basins with warm water and soap as well as a hot meal. This was the errand he had run. He had come to The Gem and asked Ruby to get three of her rooms ready and be prepared when he came up the back stairs.

She seemed curious, but could tell that he wasn't prepared to answer any questions. So she had just agreed without any of her usual banter. If Dorn didn't know better he would think she was worried about him.

Dorn took up position outside the rooms. So far he had managed to keep things on track. He just hoped his luck held out. By morning he would know for sure.

Chapter 21

Deception

𝔄limar hadn't known what to think when he first spotted Dorn coming towards them. When he called out to them he was surprised to hear his name. He knew then that the trouble had caught up to him.

He hadn't been sure at first what Dorn was about. He had looked up at the hulking man thinking he would see menace behind the smile. He hadn't, instead he had seen a look his uncle had given him before he had left. He thought it was protectiveness.

He decided if he was really to be the King, he had to see if he could read people properly. He hadn't had much practice and yet he was confident that he was reading Dorn right. Something was going to happen, but whatever it was, Dorn was on their side. He was betting all of their lives on it.

He hadn't liked the looks of Dorn's companion. He got the feeling that Dorn didn't either. Once the man had taken their horses, and they'd gone up the back stairs of the tavern, Dorn still didn't seem comfortable saying much. What he did say spoke volumes to Alimar. It was also clear that this was not the time to ask any questions of Dorn.

So, Alimar sat quietly in his room. He would've liked to sleep, but thoughts filled his head. Every time he thought he was adjusting to all the new things happening to him, something else came along and made him realize how over his head he felt. He knew Kilian and Alana didn't understand why he trusted Dorn. He wasn't sure he even understood it.

One thing was certain. Alimar had to find the woman Fogerden had told him about. Her name was Shari and she lived on the north side of the city in a big house. She had a message about the next part of his quest. Fogerden had said that she might even offer him another story about his past.

He thought about Kilian and Alana and how they would probably go their own way from here. He knew it was selfish, but he wished they would stay with him. Alana was against that for sure. He wasn't sure why she didn't seem to like him. She scared him a little. She was so beautiful and self assured.

There was a knock on Alimar's door. He walked to it and opened it a crack. Then he saw the prettiest girl he'd ever seen besides Alana. She had long golden ringlets and pale glowing skin. She was about his age and looked at him with curious interest.

He opened the door wider and saw that she had steaming hot food. She must've already made a couple of trips up the stairs, because sitting outside his door were two other trays of food and three basins with warm water, washcloths and soap.

The girl spoke. "My name is Pearl. I'm Ruby's daughter. She owns the place, if you don't know. She doesn't really like me to come around the tavern much. Tonight she sent someone to fetch me to give her a hand with all of you. I brought up some food and water to wash with."

Alimar was having trouble remembering how to form the words his brain was firing to his mouth. Finally, after taking a careful breath, He was able to reply. "Hi Pearl. Thanks for all of this. Sorry your mother had to have you come and help out on our account. I hope it wasn't too much of a bother."

"Oh, no bother, it's a relief to get out. She doesn't want me around any of those bar flies. She acts like I am too delicate to take care of myself. Usually when she has guests there is a boy that will come and help her out. Tonight I was the only help she could get. I'm glad."

Alimar had never heard someone talk so fast. Pearl could really talk. He wasn't quite sure what to say and he was really tired and hungry. In fact now that he saw the soap and water, he realized he really needed to wash as well. Pearl saw him eyeing the food and water.

"Listen to me ramble on. Here's your food. I'll just get your friends fed too. You go on now. I hope I see you again. You're quite the looker, even dirty." He set the food on a small table by the door and was stooping to retrieve the basin of water.

"Will I see you again, then, maybe tomorrow?" Pearl asked.

"I don't think so. We have to leave, maybe even tonight." Alimar replied as he reached for the basin.

Suddenly Pearl bent forward and kissed him right on the mouth. She looked as surprised as he was. "I've never done that before. You're the first boy I thought I might like to try kissing. Since I wasn't going to see you again I just, well, did it."

She stepped back, giggling, and knocked on Alana's door before Alimar could quite recover. Alana opened her door, took in the scene and scowled at Alimar. He took his basin and closed his door.

He was not sure how things worked in the city, but being kissed by strange girls he just met wouldn't have been on his list of things to expect. He hadn't hated it, but it was not what he had expected at all.

He washed, ate, and fell fast asleep. It was still dark when he heard the quiet knock on the door. He pulled on his pants and opened the door a crack. It was Dorn. He opened the door wider and Dorn ducked his way in. Then Dorn closed the door behind him.

"Alimar, we don't have much time. I couldn't speak to you sooner because I have that other man watching every move I make. I sent him to prepare for our arrival. We have to hurry.

These men have been waiting and watching for you. I joined them to keep you safe. Don't ask why. I am still trying to figure it out myself. Now we have to trick them into thinking I tricked you. I warn you, there will be some blood shed this night. We just have to make sure it's theirs.

This place is being watched. The roads are being watched. None of you will survive if you run for it. Even if I came up with a way to get you out of town, they would give chase with the full force of this city, I have no doubt. Our only chance is to strike first and strike hard when they least expect it. If we take care of them the way they planned to take care of you, we'll have some time to get out before it's discovered.

Now get your friends and tell them to be prepared for a fight. You all must act like everything is fine until I give the word. They will trust you more than me, so go tell them. Then get ready. I will be waiting in case one of the men comes to check on us."

Alimar got Kilian and they both went and woke Alana. Alana shooed them out while she got dressed then let them back in. Standing in Alana's room, all three of them still bleary eyed from lack of sleep, Alimar told them what they must do.

"I'm so sorry that I got the two of you involved in this. I'm sure that when my uncle sent you he did not intend for you to end up in harm's way either. It sounds as though if you try to leave you will be killed."

Kilian replied, "I can't speak for Alana on this, but I have come to value our friendship Alimar. I knew when I left home to become a soldier that I would be in harms way eventually. Just the trip there could have been dangerous. Instead of meeting the Nocturnals, like you did, we met you.

My father gave me a sword and told me to only use it when I was forced to. These men mean us harm. I say we are being forced. I for one am with you, Alimar.

Alana, I know you wanted to get on with our adventure. I have to say that this feels like adventure to me. For some reason people want Alimar dead. I couldn't leave him alone to face that even if I wanted to. What about you?"

Alana looked from Kilian to Alimar. Her expression was unreadable. She closed her eyes and gave a great sigh before answering.

"I have been so desperate to get on with our plans that I wasn't even really thinking about why we left home in the first place. The real reason, I mean. Yes, we were going to Waterful, but that was just a destination.

I realize now I have been jealous. Here you are making great friends with Alimar and instead of trying to do the same I have been sulking like a little girl. You're right Kilian. This is a great adventure.

I do wonder why you are of such concern to these people, Alimar. I think when this is done we all need to have a long talk and try to reason it out. For now, I am with you both. No more sulking for me."

Alimar and Kilian smiled in relief. They went back to their rooms to prepare. A few minutes later a brisk knock on the door brought Alimar to it again.

Dorn stood there looking grim. "It's time to go. Remik is waiting at the bottom of the stairs. Ignore anything I say until we're there and I give the word. You just act as though nothing alarming is happening."

He knocked on the other doors and soon all four of them where tromping down the stairs in the light of the moon. "I guess I forgot to tell you that this is Ruby's place. The Gem is a good place to tip some back. This is where we all met, eh Remik?"

They walked through town with Dorn acting like he was giving a tour. Alimar suspected that he was trying to keep everyone calm and distracted. Soon they slowed. Alimar saw they were at the mill.

"This is where I've worked for many years now. No one works here at night, but I thought this was the best place to get together and give you that message you were coming for."

Four more men were waiting for them inside the expansive yard. One, Alimar noticed was extremely fat. The rest looked ready to fight. All of them were armed but that wasn't so unusual. Some of them had their hands on their hilts already, though. They weren't pretending this was a friendly meeting very well, he thought.

Dorn was standing between Alimar's group and the others. Remik had moved up to join his group. Alimar had definitely been aware of the Dorn's large size. Suddenly though, he realized just how big he really was.

The axe on his back was what really drove the truth home. The blades were bigger then Alimar's whole torso; the handle as big around as one of his thighs. Alimar was pretty sure that if it was balanced on its blades on the ground, it would be taller than he was. This was the weapon Dorn would use this night. Alimar was very glad he was on their side.

The fat man spoke. "So this is Alimar. A lot of people are curious about you, my boy. I think I might see a resemblance to someone I once saw. Dorn, step out of the way so I can get a closer look.

I think I finally understand why everyone is looking for him. I would have never thought it was this! Move out of the way, you big oaf!" The fat man was getting pretty excited. His face was turning red in an alarming way. The men with him drew their swords. One stepped towards Dorn with bloodlust in his eyes.

Then Dorn spoke, "I don't think so, Deputy Mayor. In fact, now is the time to end this charade." With that he drew his axe just as the man facing him swung his sword. Dorn's axe was just a blur he swung it so fast. Alimar realized that it was time to fight or die.

Chapter 22

Mercy

Dorn swung his axe and it was like he had been reborn. The steel of his axe met the steel of Liam's sword. His muscles sang with the vibration of steel on steel. The sword broke in two and Liam's wrist twisted with the force of Dorn's blow. He yelled in pain, but was reaching for the knife in his belt as Dorn cut him cleanly in two. He had been cutting down trees bigger than these men for many years.

He saw Alimar and his two friend step boldly next to him with weapons drawn. Dorn was pretty sure the most deadly of this lot was Vorgen, so he stepped towards him with his axe ready. He saw Alimar step up to Remik and was torn. He wasn't sure what the boy's abilities were and he wasn't quite paying attention when out of the corner of his eye he saw Vorgen swinging his blade towards him.

Dorn may have been a big man, but he could move as fast as the most nimble fighter. Even so he barely dogged and had to parry just as fast. He realized that Alimar was holding his own. Adjusting himself as he fought Vorgen he saw that Kilian was fighting Niel and doing fine there.

Then he noticed something that surprised him. Alana had already disarmed Little and was holding him at sword point. She looked pretty pleased with herself too.

Vorgen was tiring and Dorn was just getting warm. He ended it quickly beheading the man. He turned to Alimar to give him a hand. He had already finished the job. He looked a little green around the gills, but he pulled his sword free of Remik and stood ready for more. Glancing toward Kilian proved that he had dispatched Niel as well.

As quickly as it had started it ended. Dorn stepped forward to finish Little so that Alana wouldn't have to. Little saw the look in Dorn's eyes and shrunk back in fear.

"I'm disarmed, aren't I? What harm can I do now? Please spare me. I beg of you."

Dorn shook his head. Then he looked at the others. Alimar, Kilian and Alana all shared looks of pity. Dorn swore under his breath. These three had done okay in the heat of battle, but this was the hard stuff. They had a lot to learn. He wasn't happy to be the one to teach them this lesson.

"Deputy Mayor Little, let me ask you some questions. If we let you live, what will you do when we are gone? Will you forget you ever saw Alimar? Will you call off the search for him?

Alimar, come over here. Remember when we met? You seemed to be able to look right into my heart. You knew I meant you no harm. Look at this man. You tell me what you see. "

Little looked confused. Dorn could tell he put on his best innocent face and answered with all the sincerity he could muster. "Alimar, I swear, I'll forget you were ever here. I mean you no harm any longer. I am done with the whole business. Please tell this man to spare me."

Alimar looked at him for a long time. Little couldn't meet his eyes for more than a moment. Finally, Alimar stepped back sadness filling his face.

"He lies. As soon as we're gone he will have us hunted down. I don't know how I know, but I am sure of it." He said this with a voice full of wisdom that aged him. He was drawn and even his face looked older.

Little gasped, "It is you. I thought it might be when I saw first saw you. Now I see it for certain. You are the one. Now I know why they want you dead so badly."

Dorn didn't want to cause these young people any more heartache than he already had. They had all done well. He could spare them from this.

"Wait for me outside the fence. I will just be a minute. Go on now. I don't want to talk about it or have you argue with me, just go." Then he marched over and took Little by the collar. Alana lowered her blade and stepped back.

"Dorn, wait. You wanted me to get the truth from him. You asked what you wanted to ask, but I have one more question for him before you do this." Dorn nodded, a bit frustrated by the delay. Once he decided killing was the right thing to do, he liked to get it over with.

Alimar turned to the Deputy Mayor again. "Do others know I'm here?"

Dorn could see that Little was at first trying to decide how to answer. Then realizing his chance he croaked out, "Yes! Two others know you are here. I think one of them even knows who you are. Killing me will do no good. They know everything that I do." He looked at Alimar in triumph.

Alimar searched his eyes. Then he turned to Dorn. "He tells the truth this time. Killing him won't do us any good. I wouldn't feel right about it."

"Your uncle did. He killed one of those men outside your home with a knife in the back. He said he had no choice. What's the difference here?" Kilian asked.

"I know my uncle did what he thought was right. Maybe in that situation it was the right choice. I can't say. I am not ready to let a man die in cold blood if it will do us no good anyway."

Turning back to Dorn he continued. "Can't we just knock him out and tie him up somewhere? By the time he is discovered the others will already know something went wrong."

Dorn saw the wisdom in that this time. What about next time, though? Would the boy still hesitate when it was not a choice? Not all kills were simple self-defense.

"Okay, I will only tie him up and knock him out. You all go outside and wait for me. I may be a few minutes hiding him and the bodies."

"One more thing, and then we'll go as you ask. Little, hear me well. You seem to know who I am. If that's true than think this over very carefully. You might want to reconsider your choices from here on out. I had mercy on you this time. I am young and foolish. Next time you may not fare so well. Understand?"

With that he turned and walked out of the yard. Alana and Kilian shared a confused look as they followed. Dorn was also trying to figure out what was going on. He wanted to get to the bottom of this.

After they were outside of the mill yard fence he asked the questions he had that the deputy mayor seemed to have the answers for. "What did you mean? Who is he? Tell me or I may kill you still."

Little looked at him curiously and then he shook his head bewildered. "You didn't know? Why did you do all of this if you didn't know? What would you care for a strange boy unless you had already- I won't tell you. Do what you like, but you won't get another word out of me."

Dorn stood there. Suddenly it dawned on him. No, it couldn't be. He quickly knocked Little over the head. He processed the idea while he hid Little in a supply shed. He would certainly be discovered by morning.

Then he rolled the rest of the bodies behind the building. There wasn't much point in going to too much trouble since Little would be discovered so quickly anyway. Last, he covered the blood soaked ground with fresh saw dust.

He took one look around while his thoughts continued marinating. There was a massive main building that housed the offices and the shop where tools were repaired and maintained. Then there were the many out buildings like the storage shed where he had hidden Little.

There were also the stables where they housed the Yegoxen. The Yegoxen didn't just pull the giant wagons to deliver Strautin Oak. They also used their three thick trunks to move the logs from the time they got cut to the time they were loaded into the wagons as logs or run through the mill to make lumber.

In addition to all of that there were the millworks themselves. The giant trench brought up water from the underground spring. The millwheel was turned by massive cogs. The blades were also very large and kept especially sharp for cutting the dense lumber.

Dorn would likely never see any of this again. He turned to leave. He wasn't going to miss this place at all. He was glad to be going.

As he walked away he was still arguing with himself over the answer that he had finally come to about Alimar. It really was the only thing that made sense. Little may as well have given him the answer he was so sure what it was. Alimar was his King.

Chapter 23

The First Link

Alimar thought he might be sick. He knew Dorn wouldn't kill the fat man. He had almost let it happen though. Was the heart of a King that hard? If it was, he wasn't sure he would ever be ready.

He had heard Dorn call the man Deputy Mayor Little. He was in too much shock to see the irony of the Little part. What had his thoughts all in a jumble was the deputy mayor part. What had happened to the Kingdom in the last fourteen years? Why would a leader in a major city like Strautin be after him? Obviously Little hadn't even known who he was until the end.

He saw Dorn coming out of the gate to the mill. It was too late to ask Little any of the questions Alimar was finally realizing he should have asked. Dorn seemed strange. He wasn't meeting Alimar's eyes for the first time since they had met. He wasn't sure what that meant, but it worried him. Was Dorn wishing he hadn't helped them? Well, whatever the problem, soon they would be out of Dorn's hair.

"I cleaned things up the best I could so no one will realize what's happened here right away. Saw dust works wonders on blood stains. The bodies won't be found for a while either. Even so, it won't take long till someone will be looking for those men, especially the Deputy Mayor.

We need to get you all out of town right away. I hope you grabbed all of your things from your rooms. We don't have time to go back there. I had your horses moved to a stable near the south road after Remik dropped them at the one closer to The Gem. That way we can head straight there and then..." Dorn was looking squarely at the ground while he spoke.

Alimar saw where this was going and had to interrupt. "Dorn, I am here for a reason. I have to find a woman who has something I need. Without her I won't know where to go from here. Whatever dangers remain in Strautin have to be risked long enough for me to see her. You can go. You all can go, in fact. I have to do this; none of you do."

Dorn shook his head fiercely. Finally, after a battle with himself he looked at Alimar. Seeing something new in Dorn's eyes, Alimar suddenly suspected he knew what was different. Dorn had found out what Little had known.

"I will not be leaving you. I will stay by you and protect you even if it means my death. Where you go, I go. Nothing could convince me to do otherwise. If we need to find this woman, then let's find her. The sooner you have what you need and we can get out of town the better."

Alimar saw Kilian and Alana exchange bewildered looks. Alimar was a little bewildered too by the sincerity in Dorn's oath to him, but unlike Kilian and Alana he knew what had made Dorn act this way. He was sure now that Dorn knew who he was.

Without further ado, Alimar quickly explained all he knew of Shari. Dorn wasn't totally sure, but he thought he might know the house that Fogerden had spoke of. They quickly headed that way. Kilian and Alana seemed on the verge of asking questions, but knew they didn't have time for that now.

Soon the four stood in front of a grand home. It was backed by the forest and at the end of a small road, so it was at least not on a main thoroughfare of the city. It wouldn't be long before first light and then the city would wake around them. Already they had passed a man delivering fresh milk. Fortunately, in the dark he couldn't have made out much of their group.

"Are you sure this is it?" Alimar asked.

"No, I'm not sure. This is just the only house I know in this part of town that fits the description you were given. Want me to knock?" Dorn replied.

Alimar considered that, but then looking at Dorn's hulking figure and thinking of the hour, decided he would be a little less intimidating. "No, I'll do it. This is my task to complete. I think it best that I go up to the door alone."

Alimar walked up the carefully tended path. He tried to be mindful of the flowers that encroached on the cobblestone walkway. The house was as picturesque as the yard. It would have been more fitting for it to be in the country.

He knocked lightly on the door. After a few minutes he realized he would have to knock harder for anyone asleep inside to hear him. He knocked louder.

Just when he thought he still hadn't been heard an oil lamp flickered to life through an upstairs window. Soon he heard movement and could see the light moving down the stairs and towards the door.

The door opened and an old woman peered out. Her grey hair was swept up in a nightcap. She clamped one hand in the fold of her robes while the other griped the handle of a lantern. Her face and hands were lined with age. Her eyes were bright with intelligence and clarity. She held the lamp out to cast light across Alimar's face. She gasped and almost lost her grip on the lamp as her hand started shaking.

Alimar thought she might be afraid of her late night visitor, but that turned out to be a false assumption. She spoke before he could say something to try to calm her. Her words made it clear that not only did she know who he was; she had been expecting to see him at her door.

"Oh it's you! After all of these years it's you. Come in quickly. I am sure your time here is short."

"My friends..."

"No, no, what I have to tell you is for you alone. Your friends will have to wait. I am sorry. I usually am very hospitable, but this is not time to worry about that."

She ushered him inside. He looked back at his three friends and saw that Kilian and Alana looked more confused than ever. Dorn just looked alert. He was surveying the street around him with no concern about being left outside.

Alimar realized he probably would have stayed outside anyway to keep watch. He had to admit to himself that Dorn knowing the truth about him and promising to stay with him was a huge relief. He felt unworthy of such a commitment, but grateful nonetheless.

As soon as he got inside the door, the woman he assumed was Shari got the fire going and lit a couple more lamps. Turning back to him she let out a small cry. Looking down at himself he realized why. He had been sprayed in blood. She must think he had committed murder. Again he was wrong in his assumption.

"Oh my, they already found you then. I guess you made it here so you must have been raised to be a competent fighter. I have wondered all of these years who had charge of you. Can you relieve me of my curiosity?"

When Alimar hesitated she went on. "How about if I go first? Then maybe you will feel you can share a little with me, hum?

Let me get you a cloth to wash a little of that stickiness from your face and hands. Then while you clean up a little I will tell you my story. Here, sit down by the fire."

She stripped a pretty throw off of a sturdy wooden bench so he could sit down without ruining the throw. He removed his sword and jacket and hung them on a hook by the door. He sat down carefully waiting only a moment till she returned with a basin and several cloths. It reminded him of Pearl. He wondered if he would ever see the strange girl again.

She settled down and began speaking in a slow even voice. "I guess you know my name is Shari. I was brought to the castle to be the nanny to your father. Once he was grown he made me an independent woman with enough gold to be very comfortable doing whatever I wanted to do.

Of course, I told him "thank you very much", but I was not an old useless woman to send off. I wanted to be nanny for his offspring too. Hadn't I done a good job with him I wanted to know? Oh, how your father laughed! I loved him like my own. I would have done him proud with you, too.

He said he had just wanted me to be free to do whatever I chose. The fact that I wanted to stay on only proved what an amazing nanny I would be to his children. He was a kind and generous King, your father. I still think of him often.

Anyway, I was just as excited as the King and queen to realize a baby was on the way. They were worried, though. The trouble had already started and there were rumors of spies in the castle. They wanted to keep it a secret that the Queen was with child.

These things never stay secret for long. The Queen's handmaidens would be whispering about it when they left her dressing room. People close to the King and Queen eventually figured it out. Word gets around a castle. No one was trying to hurt them with this gossip. It was just a joyous event everyone wanted to share.

Soon the queen was on constant guard because of an attack on one of her handmaidens that might have been an attempt on the queen and her unborn child. Your father was so worried he began having meetings with all of his key staff. These were secret meetings that no one talked about; then the day came that he called for me.

I wasn't sure what to expect. Then your father explained that he needed to prepare things for you. He was organizing his troops to go out and meet the Dark Lord in battle. If he didn't make it back he had to be sure you would be safe.

I wanted to argue. I wanted to reassure him. I knew that he had to do this to go into that battle knowing he had done all he could for you. So I bit my lip and listened.

Then he told me that if he were to die, his child would have to disappear. He told me that though he wished he could send the child away with me, that that would be the first place his enemies would look for you. He asked me to settle in a city where everyone could see I had no hidden child. That would keep me safe, he said. Then I was to communicate with only one person about my whereabouts and my involvement in the chain.

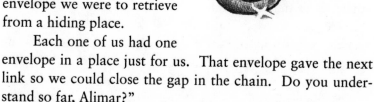

That is what he called what he was doing. He was building a chain. Each link had to be strong on its own, but lead you to the next link. If a link was broken, in other words killed or compromised in some way, there was an envelope we were to retrieve from a hiding place.

Each one of us had one envelope in a place just for us. That envelope gave the next link so we could close the gap in the chain. Do you understand so far, Alimar?"

After thinking about what Shari had said so far, Alimar answered honestly. "I guess I understand what he was doing and even why he was doing it. What I don't understand is why would all of you agree? You have put yourselves in danger for over fourteen years now, for what? In case I came along asking questions? Why would you risk everything for that?"

Shari looked puzzled for a moment and then seemed to come to a realization. "Alimar, you have lived in a Kingdom without a King. I assume that up until a short while ago you had no idea who you really were. So the best way for me to explain is to say, we are your humble subjects.

If I try to imagine myself in your position, I can see how daunting that would be. By the way, do you realize that today is your fifteenth birthday? What a strange coincidence that I was there the day you were born and when finally I see you again it is on your birthday. Fifteen and you have to go through all of this.

As for our willingness to do as the King asked, we agreed to do his bidding without hesitation. Of course we did! Our lives belonged to him. Now, Alimar, they belong to you. Many people will fight to hang on to the image of freedom they have grown accustomed to over these long years, but in the end I have every faith that you will be embraced as our King.

I hope you understand a little better now. Let me get on with my story. Where was I? Oh, that's right, I had explained the chain.

So if one link was broken we had a way to mend the chain. Your father said he didn't dare give us access to more than one additional link. If we were compromised, the most we could tell is who our link was and the hiding place of one other. More than that your father felt was too big of a risk.

He was worried that if more links than those were lost over the years that your journey would be impossible. So he asked us all to be extra cautious. I hope the chain remains complete for your sake.

Several weeks ago a man I had known all those years ago came to see me in the dead of night like you have. His name is Fogerden. He said he was on his way to meet you and that I was his link in the chain.

He just wanted to make sure before he set out to meet you that I was still here and uncompromised. That is the first time I realized that your father had made me the first link other than Fogerden. I prepared for your arrival.

Here is what I have for you, Alimar, a scroll written to you by your father. I also have the location of an item your father wants you to find and I can finally give you my link in the chain. Would you like a moment alone to read the scroll?

He nodded, trying not to show his emotions at the idea of reading words his father had written to him. What a birthday present. To read a message from his father was the best present he could have received.

He took it carefully noticing the seal still intact after all these years. He was afraid his glistening eyes gave him away by the look of sympathy he got from Shari as she left the room.

He began opening the scroll reverently. It was made of very sturdy parchment, the best quality he had ever seen. The seal had the King's emblem in wax. He was careful not to break it as he pulled the scroll open. He unrolled the scroll and saw that it had hardly aged. Shari must have kept it in a very safe place.

When he first saw the fine penmanship he choked back a sob. He finally felt the full gravity of his situation seeing his father's message that had waited all these years for his eyes, and only his, to see.

It read:

Dearest Alimar,

If you are reading this, then I am long past. For that I am sorry. I wish nothing more than to see you grow into the fine man I know you will become. I also do not wish this curse on your future.

By the same token, if you are reading this then you live on. For that I can be grateful. I held you for the first time only moments ago. I leave for battle in just days. My time with you will be precious even if it is short. Every minute I am not preparing for the worst, I will be with you and your mother.

As you read this, know that I am with you in spirit. You must be strong and get even stronger. This is just the beginning of a very long journey which will end at your rightful place, the throne.

The people you will see have been my most trusted advisors and friends. The items you will retrieve are my most precious besides you and your mother. Take great care, my son! There are those that will do you harm in our own Kingdom.

This parchment runs short as I ramble on. Know that my love for you can never die. I have one thing left to say, dear Alimar.

Be King. Be a great King!

Yours truly,
Devlin Aster
King of Asteria, and Your Father

Alimar read the letter twice. He was totally unaware of the tears streaming down his face until Shari came back into the room and handed him a handkerchief.

"Keep that in a very safe place, my young King. It is just one of many items you may need to prove your birthright at the end of your journey. Now, let me tell you where you need to go next and who you will want to see after that for your next set of instruction.

The sun will soon be up. By the looks of you you've already gotten through a bit of trouble. I don't want to delay you anymore than I must. More trouble is bound to come for you if you linger here to long."

Shari gave Alimar the description of the place he would find an item left for him. She also gave him the identity of the person he needed to find next as well as the hiding place of the identity of the next person up the chain in case the first one was dead or compromised.

Then she ushered him to the door and gave him a small hug and excused her familiarity by saying, "I was to be your nanny after all. Now be safe young King, and happy birth-day."

At the last minute as he walked through the door Alimar turned back and said, "To answer your question from earlier, it was Louis my father had take me away. I was raised by Louis and Jana."

As he walked down the path, towards his waiting friends, he heard her reply almost to herself, "Of course it was Louis and Jana. I should have guessed. They did a fine job of it too, if I do say so myself."

Chapter 24

The Plan

The four got out of town as quickly as they could. By the time they collected their horses and got down the road out of sight of the city the sun was coming up over the great forest. Dorn's horse was of mammoth size. It was a draft horse that normally would have been used to pull large wagons.

Alimar finally had to ask, "Dorn, why are you so big, anyway?"

Kilian and Alana both choked back a laugh at the bold question, but then listened curiously for the answer. Dorn shrugged and replied. "I'm part giant. My father's father was a giant. I guess that makes me a quarter giant. Honestly, my father wasn't really any bigger than me though. It might have helped that my mother was big for a human woman.

Honestly I wish more people would just ask me that question. People stare and whisper, but I think it has been years since someone just came out and asked me why I am so big. It's not like it's a secret. I guess people just like to gawk."

Alana and Kilian looked embarrassed. Dorn didn't seem to notice. Obviously neither one had even thought to just ask. They had wondered and even talked to each other about it in a whisper a couple of times.

After that they fell into the rhythm of riding. They were all tired and lost in their own thoughts about the events that had transpired. It was early evening when Dorn suggested that they find a suitable campsite far from the road to rest and plan. Everyone gladly agreed.

Once they were settled around a fire in a small clearing far off of the road, Dorn asked the question that was most on his mind. "Where are we going?"

Alimar thought about the answer for a moment before reminding himself that that was not the question that needed to be answered first. "Dorn, can we get to that in a moment? First we need to establish the who and then we can get to the where."

He turned to Kilian and Alana. He knew that this could be the place where they would go on separately. Yet the vision from his dream kept reminding him that Kilian was supposed to be with him. He decided he should start there.

"Kilian, do you remember when we first met and you asked me how I knew you? I had a dream. This was no ordinary dream. I can't really explain why just yet. Anyway, in this dream we were older. If I had to guess I would say you looked three, maybe as much as five years older. The point is that we were together. I think that is how it's meant to be. I know it sounds crazy, but I believe that.

Alana, I don't know what to say to you. I wish I had seen you in my dream too. There were so many other people in it maybe you just weren't in sight. I didn't see Dorn, but somehow I know he will be there.

I guess all I can say is that I know that you and Kilian had a plan. I wish I could tell you everything about what is happening to me, but I need to be very careful, especially if we end up going our separate ways. What I can say is that this is really important.

I will understand if you decide not to stay with me. I do have Dorn now, so I am not alone. That really makes me feel better about everything, to be totally honest." Alimar looked at Dorn as he said this with a nod of acknowledgment. Then he looked back towards Kilian and Alana. "I may be totally selfish to say this, but I really want you both to stay with us, too."

Kilian and Alana looked at each other. Kilian was the first to look back at Alimar. When he spoke he seemed subdued like he might have bad news.

"Alimar, you know I like you. I respect you too. For being so young and in so much danger, you really keep your wits about you.

To be totally honest in return, I want to go with you. I made a promise to my parents and to Alana that I can't break. Alana and I have to stay together.

I don't really understand the dream you had. I don't think I understand most of what is happening with you. We'd probably be safer if we didn't stay with you. To be fair, though, I didn't leave home for safe.

I guess the answer from me is this. If it were just me I would stay with you, but it's up to Alana. We are staying together no matter what. So, if she is willing to stay with you for a while, then I am too. Otherwise we both go."

Alana looked at Kilian like she wanted to hit him. Then she did. "Kilian Kenny, how could you put this on me? I can't win with the two of you ganging up! If I say we will stay with Alimar, I am a total push over who is willing to give up her dreams. If I say we go, I am just a bad, hateful girl."

With that she got up and ran to the trees. There was audible sobbing so it was pretty clear that she was crying. Kilian sighed, "Oh Dark Lord's Realm! I hate it when she cries. I better go figure out how to fix this."

He got up and went to her. Soon they were talking to low to hear. Alimar looked at Dorn. "Dorn, do you understand women?"

Dorn started laughing, "Alimar, no man really understands women. I am definitely out of my league with them, though!"

His laughter was catching and soon Alimar was laughing too. He felt as though he hadn't laughed in years. Tears started rolling down his face and he was getting a side ache. He couldn't seem to stop. Then he remembered the scroll that was buried safely in his pack. The laughter stopped but the tears kept coming for a little while. Dorn pretended not to notice, adding another log to the fire.

It was a while before Kilian and Alana came back. Alimar had gotten himself under control by then. They just sat quietly for a while. Alimar could tell something had been decided but he wasn't sure what. It was making him nervous.

Then Alana finally spoke, "I really don't see any harm in us all traveling together for a bit. We're still young, after all. We'll have plenty of time to go get cooped up in some city. I decided this is what I want. It has nothing to do with anybody else. I just figure, why not see the Kingdom a bit first, right?"

Kilian and Alimar grinned at each other. Alimar realized he needed to include Alana more. He turned his grin on her. She smiled back and he was reminded how beautiful she was. Dressed in nondescript traveling clothes with trail dust for face paint, she was still a sight. He broke eye contact before he embarrassed himself.

"Okay! Let's talk about where we are going." He started. Then he gave them the description of the place that Shari had given him.

"That's it?" Alana asked skeptically.

When Alimar looked confused Kilian added, "That does sound hard to find, Alimar."

Dorn spoke up then. "What we need is a cartographer."

"A cart-what?" Alana looked like she already doubted her decision.

"Yes, a map maker. They would surly know the region well enough to get us there. Um, where do we find one?" Alimar was first excited, then unsure.

Dorn had the answer. "I know of one. He is famous for his maps. I'm sure he can help us. I think we can find him easily enough. He puts his location on all of the maps he makes so customers can find him. He lives off of the beaten path, though, so only serious buyers will bother him.

By the sounds of the place we need to find, it may not be on any map, but maybe we can hire him to guide us. I just happen to have a map done by him. I think it will take us a couple of weeks, maybe three, but it sounds like it's in the right direction, anyway. We can head there tomorrow."

They all agreed they had a plan. Everyone was very tired. It would be the first full night of sleep any of them had had in too many days. Dorn insisted they set up a watch schedule, but when the others groaned, he offered to go first. It was fortunate that they weren't attacked. They were all too tired to fight.

They traveled rather slowly. When they heard other travelers approaching them they would either get off of the trail or hide their faces from view and hurry by. The problem with staying on the road was Dorn.

Between him and his horse he towered above everyone. He tried walking beside his horse and ducking out of sight when others came along. He tried riding in the ditch to look smaller. They soon realized that they stood out no matter what Dorn did.

The spring had come into full bloom and summer was right around the corner. Time was marching on without Alimar even realizing it. The nights were warmer and some of the days got downright hot. After a long day on the trail with

Dorn trying to stay out of sight, they finally agreed to travel at night and stop during the day. It was hard to get used to, but after a long night of riding they all managed to get some sleep anyway.

They camped well off the road and Alana and Kilian continued taking turns hunting. They grumbled a bit at how they had to hunt almost every day with Dorn eating half the food, but it was all in jest. It may have been hard to hide with Dorn with them, and it may have meant more food, but they were all glad to have him and his axe along.

The group never had to go without firewood with Dorn around. It was too hot to need a fire for heat, but they still used it for cooking. They usually would extinguish it as soon as the cooking was done. Alimar was used to caring for horses and didn't mind seeing to them. So they all pitched in and got along okay.

By the beginning of the third week they were traveling on a side trail that no one seemed to be on. That was a relief to all of them. They had agreed to continue traveling at night for a while, just to be safe. It was cooler anyway.

It took them four more days to get to the cartographer's vicinity. It took almost another full day to find the hut he lived in. Dorn's map did have it marked, but the scale of the map was so that it left plenty of margin for error in finding one small hut.

The area was marshy and wet. There were few places they could find that were high enough to offer a dry place to camp. Alimar worried about the horses hooves being wet all day.

There were much fewer trees and the trees were nowhere near as big as they had been closer to Strautin. They hadn't seen a Strautin Oak in at least two days by the time they reached the hut. The hut was built between three trees on one of the few small hills in the area.

It looked like it had been built by weaving small saplings together and tying the corners with some sort of twine. The roof was thatched and the whole thing seemed to only be able to stay standing due to the fact it was tied in the corners to the three trees. Even with that support it listed to one side and leaned on one tree hard enough to be causing it to bow.

The door was so crooked on its frame that they wondered aloud if it would even open. After knocking on the rickety door they heard someone say, "Oh, bother. Who is that, now?" Then it took a long time for the door to open. It only did so with much scraping and obvious effort on the other side.

"What is it? I am busy, can't you see?" The cartographer was a strange looking old man. He wore glasses so thick his eyes seemed huge in his little round face. He had very little hair left and what hair he did have seemed to grow from his slightly pointed ears. His back was so curved it looked as thought he may be beginning to reach down to touch his toes. He used a cane; it seemed, to keep himself from tipping over forwards.

"We heard you are a map maker. We were hoping that we might be able to hire you to take us to a place that sounds hard to find." Alimar explained.

"Oh, I couldn't do that, now could I? I can't get around anymore. Perhaps we can find a map that will help. Do you want to come in?" The man opened his door wider with some effort.

As they all stepped inside, they looked around in amazement. His hut was one large room. Fortunately for Dorn it was taller in the middle. Dorn carefully moved there and was able to stand up straight.

There was a post holding up the beams at that point. Dorn eyed it suspiciously. It didn't look very stable. He made a point not to bump it. If he did, the whole place would surely come down around them.

Every inch of wall, table, and ceiling were covered in maps. Alimar had to wonder how this man was able to get the maps on the high ceiling. Then he saw a strange ladder in the corner with a pole on the backside. It looked as rickety and unstable as the rest of the hut. Alimar wondered if this man actually climbed it.

"Wow, you have a lot of maps." Kilian observed.

"My family has been map makers for generations. No one knows this Kingdom like I do, do they?" The mapmaker responded.

"What about your children, can one of them guide us to this place?" Alana asked sensibly.

"That's the problem. See, I got so involved in making the maps, I forgot to have any, didn't I?" It seemed to be his custom to ask a question every time he completed a thought.

"Well then, might we be able to buy a map from you that will tell us how to get there?" Dorn asked.

The crooked, old man craned his neck around at an uncomfortable looking angle to look at Dorn. "I'll need to know where it is you're trying to find before I can tell you if I have a map to get you there, now won't I."

Alimar sighed. This was some kind of crazy adventure his father had sent him on. He wasn't sure, but he thought maybe along with everything else, his father might have wanted him to develop a sense of humor. In any case, he was developing one whether that had been intended or not. Then he began to tell the map maker all he knew about where they needed to go.

Chapter 25

Alana's Nightmare

Alana was in the graveyard. She was standing on the far side of it and could hear the waves crashing against the rocks below. She was excited; waiting for something. She looked over and saw Alimar standing in the hole Dorn had dug.

The tombstone behind Alimar's head gave her the creeps. It was like a bad omen or something. Alimar came up with something in his hand. Everyone bent over to examine whatever he had found. She was too far away to see. Kilian helped Alimar out of the hole.

A small man that Alana had never seen rubbed his hands together in anticipation. "What is it? What is it?" He kept saying.

"Can you keep it down, little man? There are people in their homes not far from here. Do you want them to come find us digging up their cemetery?" Dorn whispered harshly.

"Little man, he says. Big brute, I say." The small man replied though he was quieter. He crossed his arms with a huff. He still watched Alimar with the gleam of anticipation in his eyes.

Suddenly, men stepped out from the shadows. One was right behind her before she knew what was happening. She didn't have time to pull her sword before she was wrapped in his steely grip. She looked back over her shoulder all she could see was a dark hooded face with dark eyes.

She was frightened for herself as well as her brother and friends. She turned back to see what was happening. She watched helplessly as her brother, Alimar, Dorn and the new man were quickly engulfed in fighting. They were outnumbered.

Even though she struggled she couldn't get away from the man's strong hold on her. He had her arms trapped by her sides and her feet barely touched the ground. She was in a panic and her heart felt like it would burst free of her chest it was pounding so hard.

The ground began to rumble and shake. Was it an earthquake? She had time to wonder this before the first body broke free of its grave. She screamed. She couldn't see her brother and friends through the wall of corpses now joining in the fight.

Then the man holding her began dragging her away. She screamed for help. She screamed as loud as she could but no one came. Some of the corpses turned towards her. She couldn't stop screaming.

"Alana, wake up! Come on, you're having a nightmare. Stop screaming! You're going to wake the dead." Kilian shook her awake. She was shaking and her throat felt raw. She could still smell the upturned earth and the decay of the corpses.

She struggled from her bedding and crawled towards the woods. She didn't quite make the tree line when she vomited. Kilian was there with water when she finished.

"That must have been a bad one. Want to talk about it?"

She gained her feet and looked around. Dorn and Alimar stared at her with concerned looks that matched Kilian's. She wondered how they would feel if she shared her dream with them. They would no doubt think she was crazy or just had an active imagination and tell her it was only a dream.

"Just a nightmare, like you said. I just want to try to forget about it. I'm going to get cleaned up. Excuse me." She practically ran to her gear and then moved into the woods for some privacy so she could get her bearings.

This time it had been bad, Kilian was right about that. She had been there. If she had picked up a handful of that dirt while in the dream, she was sure she would still be holding it. Maybe she was crazy.

She took a few shuddering breaths and washed out her mouth and cleaned her face. She wanted to get her composure back before returning to the group. She was already "the girl". They had seen her cry. They treated her differently, especially Alimar. She didn't need to give them any more reasons to tiptoe around her.

They had been traveling for weeks now. Summer made travelling more of a challenge since the horses needed much more water then they had when it had been cooler. Some days they didn't get very far. If they came to a spring or creek, even if it was only midday, they would stop and camp to give the horses a break, a thorough watering and get themselves and their clothes washed up. She knew they were getting close to the place the map maker had marked on the map for them. He had also drawn a smaller more detailed map of the area surrounding their final destination. He did that after she had mentioned that it had been pretty hard to find his place with the map they already had.

He had replied, obviously insulted, "It's all a matter of scale, isn't it?"

When she finally went back to the campsite, she saw that Alimar and Dorn were studying the map very intently. As if she hadn't seen that one before. It was the old pretend you don't see her routine. Kilian had stoked the fire and was making porridge. At least he looked up when she came into sight.

"Better?"

"I'm fine."

"Sorry, sis, but you look like you've just been to the Dark Lord's realm and back. I know you aren't fine. Was it like the other ones?"

Alimar's head popped up at that. "Other ones, have you been having a recurring dream Alana?"

She glared at her brother for bringing it up. All he did was shrug in that way he did that meant, "Gosh, I sure am sorry about that. What's done is done."

She couldn't talk about this now. As it was the contents of her stomach was still rolling around. She felt her heart still beating too fast. No, now was not the time for this.

Who was Alimar to ask anyway? He obviously had lots of secrets himself. She was not going to start yammering on about her dream that they would just think was silly.

"I'll share when you do Alimar." Leaving him with a look of surprise on his face, she turned on her heel and marched back to the woods.

She stayed there for a while leaning on a tree. Her stomach was finally settling and she was thinking she should get some porridge before Dorn ate it all or it got cold. Then Kilian came through the trees holding out a bowl like a peace offering.

Seeing the look on her face he handed it over and went back the way he came. She ate while the sounds of the campsite being packed up finished calming her nerves. At least as calm as they might get until she had a few dreamless nights.

She finished her lumpy breakfast and returned to the campsite. She wordlessly started helping pack up. The horses had had enough room to graze so they didn't have to give them much of the precious grain they were quickly running out of. Dorn's gargantuan horse ate most of it. To be fair, though, he carried most of it too.

As they set out for the day no one said much. When they did talk it was about random unimportant things just to fill some silence. She usually would participate. She enjoyed getting a rub in once in a while when Dorn got a round of insults going. That seemed to be something he liked to do.

She also liked to see the looks of respect when she actually knew something about whatever was being talked about.

She was a girl and Dorn and Alimar sometimes treated her like she couldn't even start the campfire without help. Even though she helped with the hunting and did her share, she still felt she had to earn everyone's respect.

She didn't participate in the conversations today. She wasn't mad or even still upset that much over her dream. She was just enjoying listening and riding. Maybe it was the normalcy of it all, but it made her feel better.

Riding for days on end gave her plenty of time to think. She could let her mind wonder and was able to figure a lot of things out. She had been thinking a lot about how she and Kilian didn't seem as close as they had been at home. She told herself that it was natural for them to get around others and make new friends and not be as reliant on each other for companionship.

She admitted to herself that it bothered her that Kilian and Alimar had grown so close while she felt like a third wheel most of the time. That got her thinking about Alimar and all the weird things that seemed to be going on with him. All the people that were looking for him and all the people that seemed to know him, made her wonder what they still had to learn about him. Of course, no matter how much she pondered Alimar's situation, she couldn't make sense of it.

When Louis and Jana had asked them to come after Alimar and tell him he was in danger, they had given her and Kilian an explanation of sorts. They had said that Alimar was special.

They said that he was on a quest of great importance to the kingdom. Other than that, she still knew very little. It drove her crazy.

After they made camp that night, she listened while Dorn and Alimar looked over the detailed map. They were getting close to some sort of landmark that would indicate they needed to start up a rise. From there it seemed like even with the map it would be difficult to find what they were looking for.

Basically at the crest of a small peak was a cave. It wasn't visible from the ground so they would have to follow some pretty cryptic directions to end up at the right part of the peak. She was glad she wasn't the one having to try to figure that out.

She realized that Kilian had been keeping himself pretty busy. He was always offering to do the hunting or cleaning up around camp. She realized he didn't want the responsibility of trying to figure out where they were going either. She tucked that fact away for future teasing.

Alimar and Dorn had stopped talking and were looking at both her and Kilian. Alimar had a hopeful but slightly bewildered look on his face. Obviously they had figured something out without her or Kilian needing to examine the map.

"We're almost there, we should come to the pillar shaped rock sometime tomorrow. That's where we'll turn. After that it shouldn't take us more than a day to get there, if we don't have trouble finding it. I wonder what will be waiting for us. I wonder what we will find."

They all pondered that thought. No one had any idea, of course. They set up the guard rotation and took their turns sleeping. Those same questions were on all four minds when they each drifted off to sleep. What was waiting for them? What would they find?

Chapter 26

The Great Escape

G riff had made the mistake of kicking the bars in his cell just to test them out when the guard had started to doze. The bars might have some flexibility to them, but his throbbing toes were only a testament to their strength. He thought something might even be broken.

Add that to the fact that he was not going to sit anywhere in this cell due to the filth and he was pretty uncomfortable. He had to get out of here. He examined the bars closer in the corner where the guard couldn't see him as well.

The wood was very hard and smooth. It hardly had any grain to it. Then it hit him, this was Strautin Oak. He wouldn't be able to break it no matter how hard he tried. Strautin Oak was four times denser than any other wood in the Kingdom.

The only reason wood was used so much in Waterful was because iron rusted terribly with all the dampness in the city. Between the waterfalls cascading down behind the city, the irrigation ditches running throughout, and regular precipitation it kept everything a little dewy.

He started to pace, trying to remember everything he had ever heard about this wood. The pacing aggravated his hurt foot and the rats living under the bed, but it helped him think. Four times denser, yes. Wait, in contradiction to that, it was also the most flexible wood in the Kingdom.

He wondered who had sold these bars to the city. Someone who wanted a way out if they ever were put in the jail themselves? He liked the idea. It was something he would do himself.

In reality it was probably someone that sold it to a buyer that needed strong wood by only describing that virtue, while selling it to someone who had a more flexible application the same way. It was genius. He took a moment to admire the sales skills of such an individual. Now that was someone he could use in his business.

He started testing the bars every time the guard dozed. The problem was that while he could bend one bar pretty far it took both hands to do it. He needed to bend the bar next to it the other way if he had any hope of fitting through the gap.

He understood now why the flexibility of the bars wouldn't have been a concern to those building the cells. A normal sized man could have never stood a chance of fitting through. Even he wasn't sure it would work, but desperation is the mother of invention after all. Finally, he realized he would need something to help him.

He waited until the guard seemed to be napping pretty well. He braved the walk over to the disgusting rat infested bed, and shooing the rats into the corner, he padded the bed so it would appear he was sleeping under the filthy blanket.

He walked back over to the bars and with one more look at the guard he began. First, he pulled off one of his shoes and stripped his foot of one of his favorite woolen socks. After slipping his shoe back on he wrapped the sock around two bars and started twisting it.

The bars started bending and the sock held. He was elated. Then he let go and the sock quickly unwound. No matter how he stretched it, it wasn't long enough for him to tie in place. Since he needed both hands to bend the other bar he was stumped over what to do.

He finally got a new idea. He twisted the sock around the bars again. Then he pressed his foot against the ends to hold them in place. He started pushing the adjacent bar with his hands and his shoe slipped off the sock. After trying it a few more times, with the same results, he shook his head in frustration. The bottom of his shoe was too slippery.

He rolled his eyes at his own daftness. He took off his shoe once again. This time after he had his sock twisted around the bars he used his bare foot to hold it in place while he pushed the other bar in the opposite direction with both hands. It was working. He had a gap. Then he tried to figure out how to ease through the gap and realized he was not at the right angle to hang on and get through.

Stepping back from the bars he thought about how he would have to be aligned to be able to hold the sock, hold the adjacent bar, and keep holding both while slipping through. Somehow he had to be sideways to the bars, not facing them. With one foot on the sock he couldn't step through either. He switched feet and after stripping the other was ready to try anew.

He turned to the side after getting the sock twisted this time. He bent the leg furthest from the bars back behind him and up to hold the sock. Then he pushed the bar in front of him with both hands. He had the gap, now how did he get through?

Then he had it. After a careful review of the guard's level of sleep one more time, he just tipped his body through the gap. As soon as he let go, the bars would snap back into place and he would fall over. He tried to make sure all of his torso and backside were through before being forced to let go.

He started to fall over as he had known he would. Unfortunately, he hadn't quite cleared the bars with his rump. He was left hanging with one leg and his upper body out of the cell, but one hip and leg still stuck inside. Since he had expected to fall and was trying to do it quietly, his head and hands were already almost touching the dirt floor.

It was very uncomfortable. Not only was he still desperate to escape the jail, he was now in a very embarrassing and painful position he really wanted to get out of. He got his head raised a little, but couldn't straighten all the way due to the angle the bars held him.

He grabbed the bar with the hand he could reach it with, but that wasn't going to do him much good. He was unable to get to the bar with his other hand no matter how hard he tried. He wiggled his hips a bit and while the bars gave a little he couldn't budge.

Finally, he tried the only thing left to try. Leaning back towards the floor, he was able to touch the ground with his outside hand. Bracing himself that way, he lifted up his outside leg. His hand was now the only thing holding him up except for the vise grip of the bars across his hip and buttock.

Raising his foot as much as he could he began pushing the bar. Then he began twisting his hips as much as he could to help the pressure of his foot open the gap. It was working, but he had to be careful and take it slow. His arm was shaking from the effort of holding him up. His leg was cramping at the impossible angle it was bent in to exert any pressure on the bar.

He inched his hand forward little by little, adjusting his foot and hips ever so slightly as he went. Suddenly, his cheek slid free and he tumbled into a heap outside the cell. Everything seemed to ache; he was filthy from the bars and the floor. To top it all off, he was missing his shoes and socks.

He carefully climbed to his feet and hearing a small sound, turned. To be caught after all of that would be the most unfair thing ever. It was the drunk in the other cell. He had wild hair and bloodshot eyes. His hand was over his mouth and he was holding back his laughter the best he could.

"Nobody gonna believe this story. That was the funniest thing I ever see. You a flexible little man, you are!" He whispered. Then he put his finger to his lips to say he would be quiet.

Griff was horrified to realize he had had an audience through that miserable experience. Here he was half way free and all he could do was brood. At least the old drunk wasn't raising the alarm. So far the guard at the end of the hall wasn't waking up either.

He quickly collected his socks and shoes. Putting them on he realized the sock he had used to bend the bars was stretched out beyond repair. What had been his favorite pair of socks now had one hanging down over his shoe.

Tiptoeing to the guard and taking the keys from his pocket was so easy compared to his ordeal of getting out of the cell he didn't even break a sweat. The key made a scraping noise in the lock though. The guard's head came up and started to swivel his way.

The drunk back down the hall in his cell was still watching. Seeing Griff about to be caught he called to the guard. "Hey you, got a little sumpin' to drink? I'm awful thirsty over hea."

"Shut up you old fool. Too much drink is what got you here in the first place."

Griff used the conversation to cover the sound of his departure. Getting out of town was a simple matter of staying on the back streets and alleyways till he got to the front gate. There were hardly any people out this time of night and he was very good at sneaking around.

He wished he had time to go home and get cleaned up. He wished he had some supplies too. Most of all he wished he could give Tabot more instructions so he was sure his things would be okay. It would have helped to let Tabot know he had escaped and was coming back, too.

All the entrances to the city were locked and guarded at night. Griff brushed himself off the best he could and strolled right up to the front gate. This was risky but he knew his only chance was to act like nothing was wrong.

If the guards got suspicious and he got held up, he would end up right back where he started. He hoped in the dim light of the oil lamps the guards wouldn't notice his filthy condition. That might make them suspicious based on the excuse he was going to use to get out of the city.

"Open the gate or I'm going to be late!" He sang out.

"Awfully late to have business outside of the city isn't it? I'd worry about bandits if I were you." One of the two guards spoke. He sounded a little curious, but not suspicious.

Griff knew soon the word would be sent that he had escaped. Obviously, that hadn't happened yet. The description of him would be all they would need and he would be trapped in the city. He had to get the guards to open up quick.

"No business tonight boys. I have a pretty little farm girl waiting for me to meet her. If I'm late she'll not wait. Help a guy out and open up quick."

They snickered and made a few lewd comments about the make believe farm girl. They opened the gate and out he went. The guards weren't worried about people that were leaving only the ones coming in. He started whistling, then. He had made it out. The rest he could deal with. He was a Borrowmore, after all.

Chapter 27

The Amulet

Griff cursed as the pony stopped in the middle of the road again. He would have to borrow the most stubborn mount ever born. He carefully avoided mules for that very reason. This pony had been so pretty with her spots and beautifully brushed mane. He had thought she would be as nice as she looked. Instead, he was sure from her temperament that when the owners found her missing they would rejoice.

He had walked along the road until he had come to a farmhouse. It wasn't very rich and he hated to borrow from those that could ill afford it. His choices were limited with him being on foot and daybreak fast approaching.

There had been a clothesline in view. He had seen some clothes that he thought might fit him. Once he got closer he saw that the clothes close to his size obviously belonged to a boy who must have had a propensity for skinning his knees. Both pairs of smaller pants on the line had patches. He looked poor but as much as it made him unhappy it would do him well on the road. At least he was a little bit cleaner.

He had also made off with some vegetables from the garden, some fish from the curing shed and a small spade and horse blanket from the barn. It wasn't much, but he could get by and use the spade as a weapon if he was forced to.

He had been fighting with the pony most of the day now. It was not very dignified and every time someone passed him the pony acted up. The road to Waterful was well traveled so it had been a very long day indeed.

It was fortunate that he knew the place that the constable had been talking about. He used to live just outside a town a week or so from Waterful. His family had a little trading post. His father got into trouble now and again with his borrowing, but they did okay.

He used to go wondering. He was smaller than the other kids and treated poorly in town partly due to his size and partly due to the trouble his father had been in. So he would head out into the hills and play.

One day he had spent all day out roaming and realized it was getting late and he was far from home. In fact, he had gone all the way to the far road where he was not allowed. Then he saw something that he was mighty glad now that he had seen all those years ago.

He almost didn't see it in his rush to get back. Then the light of the sun, low on the horizon, shone on it making it almost glow. As he got closer he saw it was a really big rock. It was shaped like a pillar reaching into the sky. He had never seen a rock like it before or since.

He went over to it and realized it was red. Not the orange red of clay, but a darker, truer red like dried blood. He touched it and it was hot from absorbing the heat of the sun. He remembered how late it was getting and ran home. He never went back to that rock, but he had thought about it.

He knew right where it was. That was the place the man talked about having to turn off towards the hiding place of the item. He was sure he could find it based on the description from there.

He camped in spots that the pony could graze since he had no oats. He slept on the smelly horse blanket. He was glad the nights were warm so he wasn't forced to wrap up in it. If this had happened a few weeks ago it would have been too cold to sleep without a blanket to cover up with.

He ate the dried fish and vegetables he had borrowed. He wasn't able to cook or do much of anything. He had no essentials at all. It was pretty awful, really. He even had to drink directly out of the river he passed. The pony drank from puddles along the way, but he could never be thirsty enough for that.

He didn't have time to stop and borrow anything else. He wished he had just a few essentials, and thought of stopping each time he passed a house along the trail. He might have been tempted, but he had to hurry. He had to get to the item before the constable's men.

Days passed and he and the pony were getting along a little better. He was coming up on a fork in the road. The left side led to town the right eventually became the road to Strautin. He needed to take the right fork. As he approached he saw some men arguing and he slowed to listen before he was spotted.

"No, that isn't it. We've got to go this way." One man said, his voice slightly familiar to Griff.

"I thought he said it was near Creekside. That's this way."

"I'm sure he just meant generally towards Creekside. Now we have to turn off here. We're looking for a big pillar shaped rock."

Now Griff knew where he had heard that voice. It was the voice of the man who had been in the constable's office. They had beaten him here. What should he do now?

The worst part was that they were turning towards the right fork. They would definitely get there before him. He had to do something quickly.

"Hello, up ahead." He started in his most nonchalant voice. When the men turned to eye him menacingly he had to swallow before continuing.

"Did I hear you correctly? Are you looking for the pillar shaped stone?"

"What's it to you?" The man who's voice Griff recognized answered suspiciously.

"I'm from Creekside, just down the way, and I know of it is all. If you want to find it you need to go the other way."

"Are you sure about that?"

"Well of course. I don't see why I would say so otherwise."

"Alright, I guess we do need to go the other way boys."

As the men started turning around and heading down the left fork, Griff squeezed by and headed down the right one. He was pleased with his trickery, but knew it wouldn't be long before they figured out he had been lying. He hustled the little pony.

"Hey, I thought you lived in town." The man pointed out.

"Yes, well I am not going home right now. I have to run an errand for a sick friend first." Griff made his answer up on the fly, calling it out over his shoulder. He hoped the man didn't suspect something.

He looked back a couple moments later to see the men had disappeared down the left fork. His superior intellect triumphed again. He smiled to himself.

A couple hours later he came to the pillar. It was not as red as he remembered it, maybe because the sun was still high, maybe because he wasn't a boy anymore and his imagination was more tempered. In any case, it was still just as big and pillar shaped.

He turned down the overgrown trail that must lead him to the hills and rocks above. He had only been here once and had been paying little attention to his surrounding except for the rock. He was going to have to figure out the rest of the way as he went.

Another hour passed and he was starting to worry that he had missed something. Then he came to a small clearing and there it was the tall jagged peak. It was definitely the highest point in the entire hillside around this area.

As he started up, the pony started fighting him again. She was just as lazy as any mule. He fought her for a little while and finally realized he would do better on foot. He couldn't have gone very far up on horseback anyway.

He tied her to a dead tree, broke off a branch to help him with the climb and started up. All he had to do now was find the cave. He was so close he could almost feel it in his pocket, whatever it was.

That was the interesting part. Obviously it must be of great value, but the constable and the other man had not seemed to know what it was. There was something said about knowing it when the man saw it. He thought it was funny that all of them were searching for an item and they didn't even know what it was.

He climbed over two-thirds of the way up to the peak. It was becoming difficult and he hadn't seen any hint of a cave peering up towards the top. It was hot and he was tired and extremely thirsty. The sun was getting lower and then, just like that day so long ago, he might have missed it but for the setting sun.

A red reflection came from one side of the peak. He worked his way towards it as carefully but quickly as he could. Once he was closer he could see it was, indeed coming from a cave. You couldn't see it from below since it was facing away from the trail and the easiest way up to it.

Huffing and puffing he finally made it to the lip of the cave. Looking in he saw a piece of rock that looked as though it had been broken right off the top of the pillar shaped one at the road. It gleamed in the last light of the sun.

Hoisting himself up over the lip was no easy feat. His legs dangled as he kicked and wriggled his way up and over. He lay there for a moment trying to catch his breath not really caring about the dirt for once.

Then his curiosity got the best of him and he rose to his feet ready to find the mysterious item. All he saw as he looked around the small cave was the large piece of rock. Finally, he walked over to it.

Everything in the cave was covered in dust and so was the rock. He reached out to wipe it off and felt the same heat coming off of it as he had the other one years ago. As he wiped it he saw something he couldn't before.

It had a seam. It was almost invisible, but it was there. His nimble, exploring fingers went to work. It only took a moment for him to find a slight indentation in one side of the seam. He lifted and just like that he found it.

The rock opened up like a hinged box. It had indeed been carved carefully into a box and hidden here for who knows how long. He looked inside and gasped at what he saw.

"Oh my, it's so beautiful. It's mine, mine, mine!" Griff muttered excitedly to himself. It was nestled in a bed of silk in the colors of the Kingdom, and rightfully so, too. It was easily recognizable. It was the amulet of the King. In every portrait of every King he had ever seen it was around the King's neck.

His hand shook as he reached for it. It was gold and had a huge gem in the middle. He had never seen anything like it up close. He couldn't even imagine its worth.

He reverently slid his hand around it. "Ouch!" Snatching his hand back he saw a pinprick of blood.

"What is it? Is it booby trapped or something? Well of course it is. No lock, no key, I should have known it would be booby trapped!" Griff admonished himself as he held the wound.

What if it were poison? There was no way he would make it down the rock face and get to help in time. He sucked frantically on the wound spitting out the little blood he was able to extract. He waited to feel the effects of the poison. His short life flashed before his eyes. He had just gotten started.

He realized after a little while that nothing was happening. Surely if he was poisoned he would feel it by now. He was still thirsty and tired, but not poisoned. In that case it was time to get the amulet and get out of here. He looked back into the stone box trying to see any hint of a trigger. He couldn't see anything that might deactivate the trap.

Well it wasn't much of a bobby trap if it only pricked him. It wouldn't be too hard to deal with that. He took a handkerchief out of his pocket and wrapped it around his hand. Then he slipped his hand back under the amulet and lifted it free. It fell to the floor of the cave.

Griff cried out not believing his clumsiness. He had thought he had a good enough grip. He looked down at it. It didn't look damaged, that was a plus. He reached for it again and couldn't seem to get a grip on it.

Then he noticed the chain. It had been wound up tight and had been under the amulet in the box. He hadn't noticed it till now. He gingerly used his fingers and tried to loosen it up. It was in horrible knots. He couldn't get even a single bit of it free.

He tried to pick it up again. Again he failed. He tried using his stick and nudged it towards his hand. It would move towards his hand and then seem to change direction of its own accord.

He lay down beside it and tried to push it into his pocket, no luck there either. This was the most frustrating item to borrow of all his life. He stood back up shaking his fist at the thing. Finally, he grabbed it with both hands thinking that the booby trap must be in the box anyway.

"Ouch!" Dropping it again he decided that it had bit him. He didn't know how, he didn't know why, but the thing had bit him. What was he to do?

Chapter 28

Identity Revealed

Alimar watched in fascination from the lip of the cave. Once they had found the peak it had been no trouble finding it. All they had to do was follow the noises coming from the cave. Dorn, Kilian and Alana pulled themselves over the lip and joined him. They all watched silently as the little man fought with something.

"You will get in my pocket, do you hear?" He threw himself to the ground and slithered towards the small dust covered item. He held his pocket open as wide as he could and it seemed like the item would go in, but it didn't.

He jumped to his feet. "What do I have to do?" He poked at it with a stick and reached hesitantly towards it. "Don't bite me again. I will take care of you."

Dorn stepped forward. "How about you let me have a try with that little man? I don't think it belongs to you any-way."

Realizing he wasn't alone the little man turned to face them. "Well I- What do you mean it doesn't belong to me? I found it. I'm just having a little trouble-I am sick of the little man comments anyway! You are- Oh my, you are really big."

The wind seemed to burst out of the little man's puffed up chest in a great huff of air. He hung his head in defeat. Dorn stepped into the cave. The little man stepped back.

Dorn reached down and scooped up the item then jumped and hit his head on the low ceiling of the cave as the item drew his blood too. It fell to the ground and he rubbed his head eyeing the amulet warily.

"Tall or small it seems we are both in the same boat. Isn't that right big man?" The little man muttered.

Dorn looked back at Alimar and shrugged. Alimar stepped closer and crouched down to look at the item. He gently wiped away the dust that now covered it from it being rolled around on the cave floor. It was an amazing amulet.

"Careful!" Both Dorn and the smaller man said in unison. They glared at each other. Alimar ignored them. It was meant for him after all. He scooped it up. He felt the prick and almost dropped it too. It seemed to warm in his hand. His small pain was forgotten as the amulet suddenly illuminated bright red.

The chain came undone at that. Hanging from his hand tangle free it seemed only natural to put it around his neck and so he did. It glowed brighter still for a moment and then dimmed.

"Oh, it's the bloodstone. Of course it is! That can mean only one thing, though. You must be the King." The little man had watched and realized what the stone in the amulet was. He had stepped slightly forward as he spoke. Then he threw himself to his knees. Mutterings of, "I didn't know. I didn't know," coming from him like hiccups.

Alimar looked at Kilian and Alana. They were looking at the man still on his knees with sudden comprehension coming into their eyes at the same time. Kilian's eyes snapped to Alimar. Alana took longer, but eventually they were both looking at Alimar as though he had suddenly grown horns or something.

"Why didn't you tell us?" Kilian croaked out at last.

"I didn't know how. It was never the right time. I didn't want you to stay with me because of that. I don't know really. Pick one I guess."

Alimar tucked the Amulet under his shirt before continuing. "It changes nothing. Get up you. What is your name if you don't want to be called Little Man?"

The man climbed quickly to his feet. "I'm Griff, sir. Griff Borrowmore is my name, at your service sir."

"Griff, all of you, I am just Alimar. I don't want this to change anything. It's an amulet that's all."

"The King's Amulet-" Griff muttered.

"Not helping at all Griff. Thanks anyway." Alimar interrupted.

"I think we deserve to know what is happening, don't you Alimar. I mean this is a lot bigger than Kilian or I ever would have guessed. We have been with you all this time. Dorn obviously knew. I see that now. Deputy Mayor Little knew.

I think Kilian would agree with me that even with all the clues we never would have figured this out. So, now that we know can you fill us in please?" Alana couldn't seem to look right at Alimar as she gave her plea. She spoke in a hushed reverent tone as though she was in a church or something.

Alimar looked at every one of them in turn. Dorn seemed to be able to see that he was making a decision and asked, "Do you want me to get rid of this guy?" He pointed over his shoulder at Griff.

Alimar looked at Griff. He was a contradiction. He wore shabby patched pants, but very nice shoes. His shirt and jacket, while very dusty, were of quality too. He was small of stature, but held his shoulders square and straight.

"He knows. There's no point in sending him away just yet. I want to hear his story as well."

Then unceremoniously Alimar plopped down on the dirty floor. Out of respect or fatigue everyone else did too. He started with his dream and went from there.

When he was done the cave had grown dark. There was a stunned silence. No one spoke. Alimar finally turned to Griff and asked him to explain why he was here. Looking thoughtful for a moment, he nodded.

"I live in Waterful and have a respectable business there. The city has grown corrupt and someone decided they didn't want me around. I was picked up by the militia and dragged through the streets. Then I was thrown in a filthy cell and told I was going to be killed without a trial.

I managed to escape after overhearing a conversation about this place and an item being hidden here. It sounded important and I didn't want it falling into the wrong hands. I came to get it first."

Alimar could tell he wasn't getting the full story. Dorn seemed to feel the same judging by his frequent eye rolls and even a couple of snorts. It did have some ring of truth to it, so he accepted it for now.

He was more interested in what Griff had overheard. He needed to try to figure out who knew about this item, what exactly they knew, and most importantly how. Somewhere there was a leak. He asked Griff to tell him everything he remembered about the conversation.

It was full dark by the time they finished talking. Griff had asked to travel with them saying, "I can't go home, and I think I could help you."

Alimar didn't get the impression Griff was the most trustworthy man he had ever met, but he seemed earnest enough. He didn't see any harm in it for now. He told him it would be okay as long as he did his part and kept up.

"Dorn, I already know where you stand. Kilian and Alana now you know everything about me. I know you still have your own plans to get on with. I think now is the time to go on separately if that's what you want to do. We came towards Waterful to be here. The next place we're going is not going to get you any closer.

Alana spoke without feeling she needed to glance in Kilian's direction. "Alimar we had no idea you were King. Now we also have learned from Griff that Waterful is not the city we thought it was. Our father taught us that we needed to do right by our Kingdom. I didn't really understand what he meant till now. It's obvious to me that we need to stay with you."

Kilian agreed but thought of one problem. "Our father gave us a package to deliver to a man in Waterful. That's the only thing I'm concerned about. If this man is waiting for the package and we don't deliver it, I feel we'll let our father down. He would also be very worried if he got word back that we haven't made it to Waterful."

Griff replied, "Who was the package to go to? I know pretty much everyone in Waterful."

"The man's name is Kamaron. Our father said he worked for the guard." Alana remembered before Kilian could think of it.

"Your father must have known Kamaron years ago. Kamaron didn't just work for the guard by the time I moved to the city. He was the head of the guard in Waterful.

There's no point in worrying about delivering a package to him in Waterful anymore, though. He and some of his most loyal guard left the city a few years back. He didn't like the way the city was being run and wouldn't have any more to do with it."

"That makes me feel even better about not going there at all then. I guess we'll just have to hold on to the package till we can return it to our father or happen to find Kamaron. We are running short of coin, but we can find a way to get more when we need it." Kilian seemed relieved to have that figured out.

Dorn spoke with a sharp glance at Griff as though wishing he wasn't sharing information with him. "I worked for years in Strautin. I saved up almost everything I made over the years. We won't have to worry about coin for some time. I have more than enough to get us by for some time."

"We can't expect you to pay our way!" Alana argued.

"We are in the service of our King, are we not? Once the throne is his, I am sure we will be fairly compensated. Until that time, my purse is for all of us."

Alimar thought about that and realized that he hadn't even considered all of the financial burden his quest was placing on his friends. He also hadn't considered that he would be in a position to pay them back if he did take the throne. There was still so much for him to learn.

"I hadn't really thought about the fact that we are going along spending all our coin and not making any to replace it. I still have a bit, but eventually I'll run out too. I don't like the idea of dipping into your life savings Dorn. I do appreciate the offer and if we do have to use your coin, I will find a way to pay you back as soon as I'm able.

Dorn's right about that. You are here helping me. It is only fare that the kingdom compensates you for your service. I'm not very knowledgeable about such things, but once I have the opportunity, I will do right by all of you.

In the meantime, you all need to treat me the same way you have. I am just Alimar. I'm not comfortable with you groveling or calling me King. It isn't safe anyway. Let's all agree here and now that until I am actually on the throne we're just friends traveling together, okay?"

Everyone nodded their agreement. They all stood and brushed themselves off and started a careful decent down the steep rock line. It was a dark night with only a quarter moon and starlight to guide them.

There were many loose rocks they sent tumbling down towards the bottom, and it wasn't easy to keep from tumbling down after them. They had to use hands and feet to make the climb safely and it was very slow going.

They had finally reached the point where the grade leveled off a bit and they could walk normally. They all brushed off their hands and continued down. They had left their horses with Griff's and were happy to be heading towards them when they heard a voice in the darkness.

"Who do we have here?" Then a lamp flared to life and six men with weapons ready stood there. They had obviously heard them coming down and waited for them.

As the light illuminated the faces of both parties, Griff made a funny little sound like, "Eep."

The man who had spoken focused on him and smiled, "Well, look here boys; it's the helpful little man that sent us the wrong way. Is one of these nice folks your sick friend then?"

His eyes turned hard and the smile faded away. "You can just hand over the item. We might have been fooled back on the road, but we will leave with what we came for."

Alimar couldn't help but realize that there were a lot of hard men in the Kingdom. This bunch must be the ones sent from Waterful, but they would have fit right in with the group they had fought and killed back in Strautin. Was this his life now? Kill or be killed seemed to be the way of it.

Dorn stepped forward to the front of their group as was his way. He slowly pulled his axe off of his back as all eyes turned to the great hulking figure. He looked even more menacing in the glow of the oil lamp.

"I think a better idea is for you all to turn around and high tail it out of here. We don't want to add your deaths to our consciences, but we will if we have to. I know what you're thinking. You can't go back empty handed. So, don't go back. At least you'll live."

The six men looked at one another, some of them obviously considering the idea. Then the man who seemed to do all the talking spoke again making the decision for them, "We can take 'em."

Alimar appreciated Dorn's effort to end this without more bloodshed. Then he drew his sword as he heard Dorn say, "At least I tried."

Chapter 29

Griff's Surprises

Alimar soon realized how lucky they had been with the last bunch they had fought. This group was much more skilled. Add to that the fact that they had Griff with them. Alimar still wasn't so sure about him. In fact, Griff had disappeared as soon as the fighting started.

There were only four of them. That meant they were outnumbered by two. Three had surrounded Dorn. That left one for each himself, Kilian and Alana.

Alana was a skilled fighter. She had obviously trained hard. Unfortunately, the man she was fighting was just a lot stronger than her. She was dancing about and tumbling away from his skilled thrusts. As fast as she was he was almost as fast. She held her own for a while, but then Alimar could see she was struggling.

He wasn't sure how to help, he was pretty busy himself. The man he was fighting had a flail. Louis had not trained Alimar with a flail and he felt quite out of depth. It might turn out he was the one that needed help. The spiked ball barely missed the side of his head as he ducked.

He saw movement coming from near the horses. He realized it was Griff just as he ran up behind the man fighting Alana. He had a small shovel in his hand. He swung it up at the man's head, and just like that, down he went.

Alimar wasn't sure Alana even saw what had happened Griff disappeared again so fast. She only hesitated long enough to assess who needed her and she quickly joined Alimar. He had been distracted seeing Griff and took the flail to his shoulder. Fortunately the blow wasn't enough to break anything, but the spikes pierced his shirt and arm.

Alana stabbed the man through. Alimar gave her a nod of thanks and they moved to help Dorn. He was still managing, although Alimar didn't understand how. All three men were fiercely swinging their swords.

Dorn was a wonder to behold with his axe. Between the length of his arm and the length of the axe, the men just couldn't get in close enough. One had started working his way around Dorn to get behind him. He had gotten in a couple good slashes and Dorn was bleeding from his side and arm.

Suddenly there was Griff again with his spade. A swing to the head from behind once again, and that one fell too. Griff was like a ghost in the dark. Alimar thought his methods were pretty effective if not very sportsmanlike. Kill or be killed Alimar reminded himself.

Dorn quickly took out the other two with one turn of his Axe. Blood soaked him from arterial spray. Turning to Kilian he saw him breathing hard over his kill with just a small cut over one eye to show for it.

Griff and Alana were the only ones that hadn't been wounded. They were all pretty lucky really. Alimar noticed the two men that Griff used his spade on weren't going to get back up. He had dealt them crushing blows. Griff had taken out two of the men and never really been in harms way. Alimar had to give him credit. His way got the job done.

Griff was suddenly beside him like he had been there all along. "What a rush. I guess we took care of these scoundrels, didn't we?"

When no one answered he went on. "Well, I don't know about you four, but I really could use some essentials. I had to leave the city with nothing. I guess they don't need all of their stuff anymore. I think I'll see what they have."

Griff started heading towards one of the bodies and Dorn blocked his path with a hand on his chest. "We aren't going to rob the dead. We can buy what we need. We won't be resorting to thievery."

"Speak for yourself Mr. Self-righteous. I worked hard for everything I had too. I had to leave it all behind. Maybe if you didn't have such a heavy purse, you'd be checking for loose coin too.

They don't need it anyway. On top of that, any money they have came from Waterful. The people in that city have been getting robbed blind with all the new fees. I was one of them. As far as I'm concerned, that is my money in their pockets. They are the thieves, not me!"

Alimar stepped up next to Dorn. He felt that a compromise was needed so they could all leave on friendly terms. He didn't like the idea of robbing the dead. At the same time, if Griff didn't take coin, it would just go to waste or be taken by whoever found the bodies later.

"Griff, you go ahead and take any coin you find. That's all, though! I don't want you to take any personal items. If these men have families and are somehow returned to them, I don't want some family treasure taken and traded away by anyone traveling with us." Alimar thought that was fair.

"Fine, okay just coin and a better horse," Griff agreed reluctantly.

"No, no horse either. If you're spotted, by someone that knew this bunch, riding one of their horses you'll give us all away. Take only the coin. We'll set the horses free."

Dorn seemed to understand that Alimar was keeping the peace. He took his hand off of Griff's chest and the little man went and searched the men and their things with Dorn watching him closely. Alimar, Kilian and Alana stripped everything off of the dead men's horses and set them free. They stacked the saddlebags next to the men and used the bedrolls to cover the bodies. It wasn't a proper burial but someone would be looking for these men soon. Hopefully whoever that was would see to them properly.

Griff didn't look very happy with the small stack of coin he found, but he shrugged and moved on. "Fortunately I used to live nearby and know the townsfolk just a little ways away. We can go buy what we need there and I can trade this stubborn pony!

The big guy really needs to clean up before we go. A morning arrival will be better anyway. There's a stream I know of towards town a bit. Why don't we camp there and get cleaned up the best we can. Then we can head to Creekside first thing in the morning."

Dorn looked like he wanted to argue, but when everyone else agreed it seemed like a sound plan, he kept quiet. They made their way back to the horses. Then they bound Dorn and Alimar's wounds and Alana dabbed at Kilian's eye till he made her stop.

They rode just an hour or two before the sound told them they had found the stream. They all gratefully got themselves cleaned up in the clean running water. Griff was back to the campsite first and offered to cook. Everyone, even Dorn agreed happily. It had been the least favorite chore as they had traveled together.

At Griff's request, everyone showed him what they had which included half a rabbit Alana had caught and herbs Alimar had collected. He also used the last of the vegetables he had borrowed. Everyone watched him skeptically as he put everything together and added a pinch of this and a dash of that. Soon the smell hit them and everyone's mouths started to water. All of the rabbit stew a la Griff was gobbled down as soon as it was ready.

They all pitched in getting things cleaned up. Then they laid out their bedrolls preparing for sleep. Dorn said he would take first watch and as they had grown accustomed to, the other three chimed in to establish the order for the night.

"I can take a shift too." Griff piped in.

"No offense little man, I mean Griff. I went along with your plan since everyone else did, but I know your kind. You aren't to be trusted on guard until you have proven yourself, if ever."

"What do you mean my kind? I am an upstanding citizen. I took care of two of those men back there. I deserve..."

"You deserve only what you earn, thief. I said I know your kind. I'm a very good judge of character. I am only willing to go on this side trip into town in your company because of the fact you assisted in ending the fight back there. That meal didn't hurt either. Now shut it and go to sleep."

Griff made a noise and looked at the others. Seeing no support coming from them, he muttered to himself about needing his sleep anyway and settled down for the night. The others followed suit.

Kilian spoke up a moment later, "Alana, how about a song? I could use a little tune to send me off to sleep."

Everyone rolled over to look her way. She gave Kilian a look but started singing anyway. She didn't seem to be shy about it at all. Alimar was pleasantly surprised to hear a very well done folksong. It was very restful and melodious. Her singing voice was soft and feminine.

Everyone thanked her and Griff told her they would want a lullaby every night now that they knew she could sing. They all agreed and she just said, "When I feel like it. I don't really mind singing. Our mother always sang to us when we were small. Sometimes I enjoy singing a little tune. It reminds me of her."

The next morning dawned with overcast skies. Moods seemed to match. All but Griff's that is. He whistled while they cleaned up camp and went off towards the creek coming back wearing his trousers he had washed the night before. He was obviously happy to be out of the patched up pants.

They rode to town in silence. Then as the town came into view, Griff sat up straighter in his saddle and ran nervous hands over hair and clothes. Then he plastered a smile on his face that looked forced to Alimar.

Kilian noticed too. "Hey Griff, I thought you used to live here. Why do you seem so nervous?"

"Nervous, I'm not nervous. I did live here. I just was- Hello there, so good to see you after all this time."

As soon as he was in hearing range of the residents he began this chatter. He didn't stop either. Some didn't seem to know him. Others obviously did. The ones that did didn't return his greetings though. They either eyed him warily or nodded lamely.

Glancing back at those they had passed, Alimar saw looks of distaste and distressful whispering. He heard a couple of comments.

"Borrowmore, his father was in our jail more than once."

"What's he doing here? He better not cause any trouble."

Alimar saw Dorn looking at Griff with knowing eyes. He obviously was hearing some of the comments too. He had pegged Griff a thief, and the residents of this town seemed to agree with him. Alimar felt bad for the guy. Griff acted like he didn't hear, but Alimar knew he must have. Some of the comments were spoken like the speakers wanted Griff to hear them.

Griff led them to an inn. "You all can go inside and get cleaned up. I need to trade this pony and pick us some essentials."

Alimar made a decision then. He had to know if he could trust the man or not. "Essentials you say? Well, I know you left Waterful with nothing. Did you get enough coin from those men to pay with?"

Griff looked at his feet. "No, I was going to trade the pony and see what I could figure out. I wasn't going to be able to get much."

Dorn was eyeing Alimar warily. Waiting to see where this was going. "I want you to take a few gold pieces. I know you'll find a way to give it back or work it off. I am not worried about it."

"Alimar..." Dorn began, but was stopped with a look.

"We all have to be able to trust one another. If we can't then we have to go our separate ways." He tried to telegraph the unspoken message to Dorn that a few gold pieces was a cheap way to find out. Dorn seemed to understand because he nodded.

"Thank you, Alimar. I won't forget it. I won't be long and we can get the rest of what we need after you all have had a rest."

True to his word, Griff wasn't long. It was still early afternoon when he returned. Alimar had only just begun to think he had taken the three gold pieces and run. The remaining four had washed and had a hot meal, and napped in a real bed. They were refreshed, visiting in the parlor and ready when Griff returned.

"I got the essentials out of the way. I also found out what everyone has available this season. Let's make a list and get our shopping done today. Then we can get a good nights rest and head out fresh in the morning."

"So what essentials did you pick up then?" Dorn asked with a beginning of respect in his voice. "That way we will know what else we need."

Griff nodded his understanding. Then he replied matter of factly. "After trading that obnoxious pony for a real horse, I picked up the items I would have brought from home had I the chance."

He used the table to pour out his pack. There was a shocked silence afterwards that Dorn finally broke. "What in the Dark Lord's Realm is that?"

"What do you mean? These are the essentials to traveling in proper style. I purchased silverware, proper drinking goblets, scented soaps, spices for cooking..."

Dorn interrupted by pushing back his chair. Standing up and leaning over the table, he selected a fork of dainty proportion. In his hand it looked like something you would use to serve a baby. "This is an essential?"

"Yes?" Griff replied uncertainly. Alimar figured that if the little silver utensil looked silly to him, Griff could probably see how impractical it would seem.

Alana picked up a bar of the scented soap and gave it a careful sniff. "It does smell good." She said doubtfully. Killian picked up a goblet and pretended to take a sip like he must have envisioned a fancy lord or lady.

Alimar started to laugh. He couldn't help it. The whole situation was just funny. Alana and Kilian joined in. Eventually, even Dorn and Griff saw the humor and all five of them shared a good laugh.

Finally, they settled down to make a list of the actual essentials. They had weeks to travel to meet the next person in the 'chain'. They wanted to be well prepared.

Alimar was so glad to have his secret known to all of these friends. Even Griff had proved himself in a small way. At that moment, he felt like anything was possible.

They spent the afternoon shopping. Griff introduced them to the two shopkeepers in town and pointed out the one that had belonged to his family. The shops were small and not very well stocked. They weren't able to get everything they wanted, but their basic needs were met.

It wasn't a rich town. The streets were rutted from wagon wheels and some of the buildings were in disrepair. Alimar could see that the state of the kingdom was reflected here in a smaller town. He mentioned to Dorn that he was happy to lighten his purse if it fed some of the hungry looking children they saw.

Looking around for Alimar at dinner that night, the group finally found him sitting on the front porch of the inn surrounded by children. He had taken a large plate of food out and told them all he was too full to eat. Could any of them help him finish it as not to offend the cook?

While the children gobbled up the food as though they hadn't eaten in a week, Alimar was telling them a story about dragons and knights. Alana joined him with another platter, and pretty soon they were all out on the porch sharing stories and food with the local children.

A full night's rest in real beds and meals taken that weren't made at campfire made all of their moods soar. Everyone was happy to be stocked up and rested. Loading up the horses that morning Griff showed off his new one to everyone.

"I will surely keep up better since she's bigger and better mannered. I got a great deal too. That pony is really pretty, but soon they will realize I got the better end of the bargain."

They all admired the new horse and it seemed true that while she wasn't as pretty as the pony, she did have a much better temperament. She was docile and cooperative. Maybe the pony would take better to her new owners and not be so difficult for them.

Then Dorn spoke up, "How do you plan on getting up onto her back? You better not be coming to me for a boost."

"Oh, didn't I tell you? That was one of the errands I ran yesterday. It was installed and waiting for me when we picked up the horses from the stable. See?"

Pulling a cord that was hidden under the saddle produced a rope ladder that unrolled almost to the ground. Griff climbed it and plopped down on the horse smiling at everyone as if to say, "Tada!"

Alimar was the first to recover enough to say, "Griff, you really are full of surprises!"

Everyone burst out laughing. Griff's crazy idea of essentials and Dorn's reaction to them had already had everyone in stitches off and on all the day before. Dorn walked around shaking his head muttering, "Essentials my ars!" Now add this rope ladder so that Griff could ascend in style and they couldn't help but start again.

Griff seemed confused by the laughter which only made everyone laugh harder. Finally, they finished packing all their gear and headed out of town. Griff seemed very tall on the new horse and he left town the same way he had come in, with his head held high and calling out greetings to everyone he saw.

This time, maybe in part to all the gold they had spent in the small town the day prior, some called greetings back. Children laughed happily and skipped along beside them. Some people actually called out to them with waves and invitations to come back soon.

Alimar thought that was just right. He was happy that their visit here had changed the way the town treated his new friend. He enjoyed watching the smile grow even bigger on Griff's face. There was no need to force a smile today. Alimar was more confident than ever that their strange group was going to work out just fine.

Chapter 30

An Interesting Pair

Looking over the map they realized that they had to travel over a mountain pass for the next part of their journey. Fall was coming and it would be cold up in the mountains. They would need some gear for cooler temperatures.

They spent the next weeks travelling and acclimating to their new companion. Dorn found Griff to be annoying most of the time. Secretly he was amused by him as well. The heat of summer cooled as they neared the mountains. It was a relief, but Dorn knew they were going to wish for the warmth of summer once in the pass.

Dorn had moved around a lot as a fighter, but he hadn't moved around this much. He was really wishing they could spend a little more time in the towns and cities they passed. Only going in for supplies and one quick night in a bed was making him a little grumpy. What he needed was a pint of ale or maybe several.

At the bottom of the mountain was a town that had sprung up as part of the trade route over the mountains. This pass was the only one that went over this mountain range that stretched across much of the northwest section of Asteria.

The only other way to get to the cities and towns further north was to go all the way around the mountains, so the little settlement prospered. While it was not yet big enough to call a city, it had several inns and taverns for weary travelers. They had even called the town Traders Haven.

Trader's Haven looked as though it sat on a section of rock that had been blasted right out of the side of the mountain. Most of the buildings were made of stone and the streets were stone as well. It seemed that Trader's Haven had more trading posts and inns than it had homes. Many of the shops were obviously temporary as the traders would set up shop and then move on when it suited them.

Some of them had carts with flip up windows to display their wares. The less experienced traders would use tents to set up in. They soon learned that in Trader's Haven a tent doesn't fare well due to the strong winds. Those traders would move on more quickly than those with carts.

Fall was in full swing with the leaves on the trees all oranges, reds and yellows. Many of the leaves had fallen already and the mountain winds blew them all through town like colorful little tornados. The wind was so strong everything was tied or chained.

The oil lamps hung on chains but were then attached to buildings with support chains as well so they wouldn't blow dangerously. The windows were thick leaded glass to keep them from breaking and many were shuttered also. The stone chimneys had iron supports and the doors did too.

Dorn had been in Trader's Haven a couple times years ago. It had grown and changed since then, but one thing he knew about these kinds of towns, there was always plenty of establishments that served ale.

Alimar and Kilian were figuring out what they needed in the town. Dorn realized that he needed to teach them that all work and no ale made Dorn a grumpy man. He figured he had earned a break. If there was a place Alimar would be safe without him for a few hours, this was the place.

They had agreed to stay at the inn right inside of town. It had an adjoining stable and was near many shops. Dorn saw his opportunity and took it.

"You two seem to have things figured out. I am going to find myself a stool to sit down in for several hours. I'll meet you outside the inn in the morning. Don't bother getting me a room. I'm not sure I'll need it. Alimar you'll be safe enough here. Nobody really knows anybody in a town like this."

"What? What do you mean, Dorn?" Alimar asked.

"He means he's going drinking and you young ones can look after yourselves. I wouldn't mind a pint. I think I'll go too." Griff added.

Dorn sighed loudly at that, but just said, "Suit yourself." Then he rode into town without another word.

Griff followed him while the other three looked curiously after. Then they shrugged and went to get the supplies. All they were interested in was a hot meal and some soap.

Dorn didn't like the looks of the first place he saw. The ceiling was too low and the bar was too crowded. There were a few tables available, but he and regular dinning chairs rarely got along.

"Hey where're you going? This place looks okay." Griff pointed out as Dorn got back on his horse.

"I'm going to keep looking. You like this place, you can stay here."

Griff put his hands on his hips and put on a stern expression that Dorn didn't even look back to see. Finally, Griff got on his horse before he lost sight of Dorn. Catching up he gave him a scowl. Dorn just ignored it.

The second place didn't interest Dorn enough to get him off of his horse. He paused for a moment seeing dirty windows and a roof he would easily take out if he stood upright in the place.

Griff just followed along this time. He obviously had gotten the hint that Dorn was on a mission. He was going to find a place he could drink the way he wanted.

Then they got to what might have been the last place in town. Dorn looked it over. It was built of log and had a high roofline. It would have fit right in if it had been in Strautin.

Around here, where most of the buildings were stone or more temporary, it stood out. The front was neat and the windows were clean.

He got off his horse and wondered over to the window. Looking through the thick leaded glass he could make out a respectable crowd, but the bar was long and had plenty of vacant seats. He tied his horse and went inside.

He would never admit this was a nicer establishment than The Gem, but it was roomy and a little rowdy. It was clean and he smelled the greasy food smell he liked so much. He went in and once he was through the door didn't even have to duck. Okay, it was nicer then The Gem, but he still missed Ruby.

He made a beeline for the corner of the bar. He set his pack and Axe down in the corner and looked over the stools. He decided the one three over was sturdier looking than the one in the corner. He switched them and moved the second stool over about a foot. Finally, having things how he wanted them, he settled down happily.

The barkeep had watched the whole thing and wondered over, "Are you comfortable now, my lordship?" He asked Dorn sarcastically.

He was a tall, thin man with a strange mustache. It looked waxed and curled up on the ends. His hair was long

and tied back in a ponytail. He wore a clean apron and wiped the bar with a clean rag and that was all that really mattered to Dorn. He definitely was no Ruby, though.

"Don't you worry about me taking up a little extra room. Take a look at me. Obviously, I'm going to drink more than any two men in here."

"In that case, two ales are coming right up."

"Make that three, please. Oh, and will you put mine in this. I like to provide my own clean glass." Griff climbed up on the stool next to Dorn and offered the barkeep a dainty silver stein out of his pack.

Dorn shook his head with embarrassment. Griff would have to pull out an "essential". The little man was going to drive him to drink. Actually, that was okay by him tonight. That is just what he was here for.

The barkeep took the stein carefully from Griff and laughed. "Oh, you two are an interesting pair. I get all kinds in here, from all over the Kingdom. Never have I seen a pair quite like you."

Shaking his head he poured the three ales and slid them in front of the two men. Dorn downed half of one of the two in front of him wiping his chin with a satisfied sigh. He watched as Griff picked up his shiny stein and took a sip.

"You drink ale like a little girl."

"Just because I don't chug it down while dribbling it like a baby doesn't mean I drink like a girl. They are called manners. You should see about getting yourself some."

Dorn took another pull hiding his satisfied smile. It had been a long time since he sat and drank with someone. He had only had Ruby to insult for so long. Griff annoyed him in so many ways. The little guy was really growing on him.

"Come on Griff, just this once, drink it down. Another round, barkeep!" Dorn Roared.

A couple of hours went by with Griff drinking one ale to every three of Dorn's. Dorn occasionally had to hurry Griff along at first, but soon he forgot at least some of his manners and loosened up. It seemed to work out about right, because they were both equally drunk by the time Dorn started teaching Griff his favorite drinking song.

It didn't take long before Griff had the song down enough to sing along. Soon they were singing full volume entertaining, or annoying everyone in the tavern. At some point, Dorn had slung his arm around Griff, which was a sight in itself due to their extraordinary height difference.

The song went like this:
I'll live my life,
In the service of our King.
We'll be joined by others,
For the battling.

Once the day is over,
And the victory is ours.
We'll celebrate our triumph,
Till the wee, wee hours.

By the light of day,
We'll all be free.
But we must remember,
Those that will not be.

It will be our burden,
We'll carry it with pride.
Until it all is over,
And the last of us has died.

They rocked wildly back and forth in their stools as they sang. Dorn sang in a deep baritone punctuating each line by punching his fist high into the air. Griff was too busy hanging on to Dorn fearful of losing his seat entirely.

A few voices had joined in the song. A few others had grumbled about it being sung. One of those spoke up, "I don't see why we have to hear that old song. The King is long dead. The only thing we battle for now is to keep our homes safe from thieves and scoundrels."

Dorn looked around to identify the speaker. Even drunk he didn't have a loose tongue, but he felt the need to respond anyway. "I've felt that same way for these long years. I believe things are changing. This kingdom will be a safe place again. I'm just sure of it."

"I'm glad the ale has made you feel so optimistic, friend. I can't seem to drink enough to get mine back. I used to be all about King and kingdom. Now it's every man for himself. We have to face reality.

Have you been traveling the kingdom much over the years since the King died? I have, and let me tell you everywhere I go I see the changes first hand. Power breeds greed. These city mayors and even maybe some of the governing parliament heads have grown greedy.

It's only a matter of time before we have civil war. I know of one army being amassed already that's not part of the regular army. I don't really know their intent, but they seem to be growing all the time. The kingdom is divided. Look around and you will see."

Dorn couldn't tell this man what he knew. He wished he could shout it out. These people needed to know that there was a King and he would make things better. The man's description of the kingdom was sobering. Many other people in the tavern agreed with this man with nods or words.

He thought of the way Griff had shared the corruption of the capital city with them. He had not wanted to believe. He hadn't trusted Griff at the time and that made it easy to tell himself it wasn't true. He had decided it had been an invention on Griff's part to cover why he was really in trouble.

Now that he was getting to know Griff more, he knew that the man didn't lie. He might twist the truth a bit to make his side of things sound better, but it was still a version of the truth. So, Dorn had come to believe the story Griff had told of corruption in Waterful.

He had lived all of these years in isolation. He had shut himself off from the outside world. Lumberjacking and sitting in the corner stool of The Gem had been his life for too long. He saw now that he could have been keeping his eyes open. He would be of so much more use to Alimar now if he had been paying attention.

Griff at twenty-four, and all of the other three especially, were too young to know what the kingdom had been like. He saw now what a difference not having a King had made in the last fifteen years. Dorn had to pay more attention and help Alimar see the troubles around them. The future of the Kingdom was in Alimar's hands, but he needed all the help he could get.

Chapter 31

Over the Pass

Going into the mountains was a major change in scenery. The trees thinned quickly. The trail had been carved out of the mountain so walls of rock climbed menacingly up towards the sky. There were fallen rocks lining the trail.

A wind beaten, old sign stated:

Beware Falling Rocks!

Another, obviously newer, sign read:

Watch Out for the Harpy Bats and Pass Lurkers Too!

"I sure hope none of those rocks come down on us." Alana said looking up.

"I'm more worried about the Harpy Bats and Pass Lurkers. What are they anyway?" Kilian wondered.

"Shhh please, no more talking this morning! My head feels it will crack open from the pounding." Griff groaned.

"If you two hadn't been out drinking all night you wouldn't be so miserable. It's your own fault." Alana answered in her sweetest voice. It was the voice their mother had used when she was really saying, "I told you so."

"Hey, don't lump me in with him. I was out of bed and ready to go, and you don't hear me complaining. I can't help it if the little man can't hold his liquor." Dorn rumbled. No one had missed him wincing from the headache he obviously had, though.

They all fell silent and rode on for some time. As they crested the rise, the trail leveled off. The rock face on one side receded too. A few crooked trees and shrubs decorated it.

The winds blowing through the dark tunnel-like path had been cold, mountain air. As the sky opened up again the sun warmed them. It was like that for several miles. Then as the afternoon sun was fading they came to another rise that was again closed in on both sides.

It was darker now with the sun lost to the sheer rocks surrounding them. They all pulled the furs they had picked up in Trader's Haven around themselves. The wind got much colder as night approached.

"When we get out the other side of this, we can find a place to camp. There are some clearings up ahead." Dorn let everyone know.

Griff's pack had been making an awful racket every time the horses went up a steep rise. Another rise came up and the clattering of his silver began again. Dorn grumbled under his breath about the noise.

Then they heard a loud shrill screech from above. It made everyone's ears ring. It was joined by another and then a whole chorus of them started. By the time the first one began swooping down towards them, their ears felt as though they might explode from the pressure. The horses were obviously suffering too and were hard to handle.

The quarters were too tight to swing his giant axe, so Dorn pulled his smaller axe instead. The others took this to mean they needed to arm themselves too. They had picked up a small short sword for Griff so he pulled that instead of needing to make use of his shovel again.

"Kilian, you asked about the creatures on the sign this morning. I think we might be about to meet some of those harpy bats it mentioned." Dorn warned.

Then there were wings and talons coming down from the rocks above. They were large bat like birds or maybe bird like bats. They were jet black and had a wingspan that would rival that of an eagle. The wings were leathery like a bat and were claw tipped. Instead of beaks they had sharp teeth. They had three talons on each of their four legs two front and two back. The talons were long and wickedly sharp.

Everyone was swinging wildly with sword and axe. It was pretty ineffective against the winged creatures. They only managed to hold them back for the most part. Between being confined by the rock walls and the horses in a panic, it was a wonder that they managed to hold the creatures off at all.

Dorn finally caught one in the wing and it flopped to the ground. It might have done some damage to a horse from there. Fortunately, Alimar's horse was very well trained, because he was able to lean over and hack it with his sword from his saddle till it stopped thrashing around.

Then after a couple close calls, Kilian thrust his sword away and pulled his bow from his back. He had killed two of the creatures before anyone even realized he was shooting. Alana saw him and pulled her blowgun out of her tunic and was able to hurt one enough to stun it, allowing Griff to get in a solid blow and kill it.

Two swooped down side by side, talons extended and ready. Kilian notched two arrows at once and let them fly. Both creatures crashed into the side of the rock and almost knocked Alimar from his horse. It was soon over with only minor cuts on Griff and Alimar.

"I've seen you carrying that bow around for all these months. I know you use it for hunting all the time, but I had no idea of your skill. Why have you never thought to pull it in a fight before?" Dorn asked of Kilian.

"It's something I only used for hunting. I thought of it as a tool really, not so much as a weapon. I prefer the sword."

"You're not bad with the sword, my young friend. I have to tell you though; you are truly skilled with that bow. I recommend you use it more often."

Soon they found a campsite and bedded down in a small grove of trees that offered them some protection from the wind. They were tired and cold. They established the watch rotation, of which Griff was now included. It was an uneventful night after that.

A few more days went by in the pass. They found it was difficult to hunt and only managed to have fresh meat one night. Their dried supplies were running very low and they all yearned for a nice hot stew.

They soon realized they were lucky to be getting over the pass as early as they were before a major snowfall. A couple more weeks and the pass would have been much colder and covered in snow and ice. As it was, they had endured a couple of light snowfalls and that was treacherous enough since the horses had not been shod for such conditions.

Rocks had occasionally tumbled down the mountain. Fortunately, they had not been hit by anything but a shower of pebbles. Alana had a good size bump on her head from a larger one that had hit her, but she was okay.

The trail was starting to descend instead of climb. They were all glad to be coming to the other side. There had been few areas to camp and they were all tired of the cold wind and other conditions they had been enduring.

Dorn predicted it was the last night in the pass as they settled down in a poor campsite. There was barely room to tuck the horses under an outcropping of rock. They had to lay out their bedrolls closely. A light snow was falling and the fire was not giving off much heat.

Griff was on watch and bundled up trying to stay warm. He heard a noise that didn't register at first. He looked around and saw it. His eyes got wide at the sight of it. It stood near the rocks blending in with the snow that was falling. If it had been a little later in the season and more snow had fallen it would probably not have been visible in the darkness at all.

It was twenty feet away standing on the other side of the trail, but it had well muscled legs and looked as though it could leap across the distance without much effort. Another dropped from the rocks and joined the first.

They stood upright, like a man, but had wide feet that looked a bit like claw tipped snowshoes. They had sharp claws instead of fingers at the end of their four arms. They had the beak like mouths he had expected to see on the Harpy bats a few days back. Only these beaks were serrated like a knife.

They had short white fur that matched the color of the snow perfectly. Their eyes were ice blue. These must be the Pass Lurkers the signs had warned of.

He spoke softly and didn't move at all. "Wake up. Something is here."

Dorn was a light sleeper and woke first, sitting up with axe in hand. Seeing where Griff was looking he spoke louder as he climbed to his feet, "Everybody up and to arms!"

Then the Pass lurkers came at a full run. Alimar somehow got free of his bedding and to his feet, but Alana and Kilian were still only sitting up when the things were upon them. One came to a sudden stop, tumbling right over them both. As it got quickly to its feet and turned, it swiped its claws towards Alana's face. She threw her bedding up in front of her since that was all she had and the Pass Lurker shredded it.

Kilian had managed to pull his sword free and hacked off one of the creature's arms before it tried for Alana again. It howled in pain. Alimar leapt towards it and swung his sword too, another arm fell the ground. The thing jumped away in the direction of the horses.

In the meantime, the other one had gotten to Griff. Griff had stabbed the Pass Lurker but had then lost his grip on the small sword. It had grabbed him and was attempting to haul him away for a warm meal elsewhere. Dorn was trying to get to it with his axe but Griff was in the way. Finally, he threw down his axe and grabbed the thing by the neck.

One of the horses screamed. Alimar got over to the horses with Kilian and Alana both armed and behind him. It was Alimar's horse that had screamed and the creature was already crouched over it enjoying a meal when Alimar took off its head. Unfortunately, it was too late for his horse.

The remaining Pass Lurker was as big as Dorn and its neck was thick and strong. It had its arms full of a wiggling Griff and a sword in its side. Dorn was able to get a headlock on it and finish it off by snapping the creature's neck with a vicious crack.

Cleaning up the mess wasn't easy in the cold dark of night. They were down one horse and one bedroll. As Alimar stripped his things off of his horse he realized that he had lost more than just a ride.

He had gotten this horse as a colt for his eighth birthday. He and his uncle had trained it together. He felt as though he had lost a friend. He was very sad, but kept it to himself.

Alana had lost her bedroll. Not only was it pretty well shredded, it was covered in the Pass Lurkers blood. The blood seemed to be all over camp and it was an ice blue that matched the color of the now dead creatures' eyes.

Everyone cleaned up their belongings the best they could. The strange blood was freezing on everything as cold as the air was. They all gave up on sleeping any more. They unanimously wanted out of this pass.

By early morning they were loaded up with Alimar's belongings spread out amongst the other horses. Dorn had told Griff to ride with him since he was the lightest. Griff had grumbled but complied. Alimar rode Griff's horse feeling melancholy.

Everyone was relieved to leave the pass later that day. The air warmed considerably though it still felt like winter was setting in. On this side of the pass was another town. This one was a mining town that backed up to the side of the mountain.

The wind was not so strong on this side of the mountain. This town was newer than Trader's Haven and Dorn hadn't been here before. They saw a tin sign swinging on chain outside of town that read:

ORESRUS
POP. 482

They saw a very different sort of town than that of Trader's Haven. While it had been almost all rock on the other side, almost everything here was tin and metal. The buildings were tin roofed and metal sided. Even the hitching posts for the horses were made of iron instead of wood.

It was a sooty town too. The smoke coming from the chimneys told why. They obviously burned coal instead of wood for heat. The streets, buildings, and even the people seemed to be dusted with the soot.

Alimar wasn't looking forward to replacing his horse but it had to be done. They found a stable and after getting the remaining horses situated he asked about where to buy a horse. The stable keeper told him there were two available for sale that were there at the stable.

Kilian and Alana had been wondering over the name on the sign. They couldn't figure out how to pronounce it. Alana had to ask the stable keeper.

"How do you say the name of your town? Is it Oresrus?" She had decided it must be pronounced so it rhymed with rhinoceros, but it still didn't quite sound right when she said it.

"Nobody gets the name right. The man that named the town several years ago has a strange sense of humor. See, we mine all kind of ore here. He called the town Ores R Us. I wish we could change it, but he owns the mines, so he pretty much owns the town." He answered.

Alimar looked both horses available for sale over carefully. One was older and only had a few years of good riding left. The other was young and full of spirit. He knew the better choice was probably the younger of the two, but he chose the older one. Its temperament reminded him of his old one.

Once that was taken care of, they went into town. They found an inn and while Dorn and Alimar stayed there to get cleaned up, the others offered to pick up supplies. They all wanted to get to bed early and get to their next destination. It was about another weeks ride maybe a little more. They wanted to arrive during the day as not to knock on another door in the middle of the night.

They were glad to be heading away from the pass. The mountains had been hard on them and they didn't want to linger by them longer than necessary. Alana and Griff were still complaining that it was going to take forever to get all of the smelly blue blood off of their clothes and other belongings.

While they were shopping, Griff overheard talk about someone in town offering a reward for information about a giant man traveling with a young man and possibly two others. He knew then that if Dorn was spotted, there would be trouble. He went and warned the others and they decided to leave even earlier than they had planned, when most everyone else would still be in bed.

Before the sun rose the next day they were already on their way out of town. Dorn stuck to the shadows and avoided the two people they saw that were already up. A young boy was tending the stable and Dorn crept ahead while the others collected the horses so he could avoid being seen. They would surely make the next stop in the next several days and everyone was curious about what they would learn next.

They spotted a camp in the distance and Dorn spied a familiar horse. He thought it might be Dal's. Dal was the man who had come to Strautin to let Vorgen's crew know that Alimar was coming. Dal hadn't been one of the men they had killed in the fight at the mill. Dorn held up a hand to signal everyone to stop.

Dorn slipped off of his horse and quietly crept up to the camp. The entire camp was asleep, including the man that was surely supposed to be on guard. He saw Dal and knew that these were the men looking for them. He counted eight of them. He hoped to get by without a fight. Eight to five weren't very good odds and they were all still weary from the pass.

He snuck back and got on his horse. He held up a finger to his lips to signal for quiet. Then he slowly rode up towards the camp. It was on a hill and the incline was a bit steep.

Griff was pulling up the rear. Dorn had made the top of the hill when Griff started up. Dorn looked back sharply when Griff's pack started its familiar clanking.

Dorn held up a hand again. He slid from his horse for a second time. He walked down the hill and grabbed Griff's pack. He whispered angrily, "You and your damn essentials!"

He walked back to his horse holding the heavy pack carefully as not to make any noise. Afraid to get back in the saddle holding the pack he walked his horse on passed the camp and out of hearing range. Then he turned and waited for Griff to catch up to him.

As Griff reached out for his pack Dorn lit into him. "That's twice now we have been in danger over this junk you call your essentials. Are you trying to get us all killed? Repack this thing so I don't hear that clanking again or I swear I will throw the whole pack over the side of a cliff!"

Dorn gave back the pack briskly and got back on his horse. Griff shook his fist at Dorn's back, but didn't argue. Griff had figured out that when Dorn got like this it was best to keep quiet.

They had made it passed the men. It was a relief after all they had gone through in the mountains not to have to fight again so soon. There was only one problem and they all knew it. Eventually, these men or some like them would catch up with them.

Chapter 32

Just Max

"**H**ello, we're here to see Maximilian Pratt."

They had traveled for weeks to get here. They had fought their way over a dangerous mountain pass and snuck by sleeping men that were trying to kill them. Another week later, finally standing at their goal, they all waited with anticipation for the reply to Alimar's greeting.

It had been an uneventful week of travel since passing the men. They hadn't come across any other beasts. The mountain was well behind them now and the wind was gone. They were all happy and warm.

This area was populated by farms and ranches. There was plenty of open space on this side of the mountains. Small groves of trees punctuated the rolling fields of grass and crops. Finding the home they were looking for was not hard. There was a simple wooden sign on the main trail pointing the way, in fact.

It said:

Dr. Max Pratt

House Calls by Request

A stone lined path led them to a little cottage. The yard was dotted with trees and filled with wildflowers. There were two doors. One had the name over it and was off to the side.

That must be where he saw his patients. The other looked like a standard front door. Alimar had knocked on the latter.

The man who had answered appeared to be in his late twenties. He looked the group over with interest then said simply, "Max."

"I beg your pardon?"

"Max, he was just Max. He couldn't stand to be called Maximilian."

Alimar had a sinking feeling. This didn't sound good. "Couldn't? Has something happened to him? Who are you by the way?"

"He got old. He's dead, died about two years ago now. Who's asking?"

Alimar was stunned. They had come all of this way for nothing. The man he needed to see was gone. One whole link in his father's carefully built chain, missing. They would have to go almost all the way back to Strautin to find out the identity of the next link as Shari had explained it.

"Thanks anyway. It's been a long time. I guess this was bound to happen. Sorry to have disturbed you." Alimar turned to go.

"Wait, are you him?"

Alimar turned back, feeling a glimmer of hope return. "Him who?"

"Well, I can't really say. If you aren't him then I've already said too much."

"We're having a lot of issues with strangers. I can't trust you if you won't tell me who you are or who you think I am."

"You're having trouble with strangers? Let me tell you something. Over the years my father was watched, questioned, and even beaten up once. Our family had issues with strangers. I have every reason to be careful."

"You're his son then, I take it?"

Realizing his mistake the young man swore, "Yes, I am. Now it's your turn."

"My father's dead too. He died right after I was born."

That earned Alimar a thoughtful look. "Come in. Who knows, someone could still be keeping an eye on this place. We may as well talk inside."

They stepped into a comfortable sitting room. It had chairs and padded benches around the perimeter of it. There was a fireplace in the corner with a warm fire burning. There was room for everyone to sit, though Dorn eyed the chairs with dismay.

Through a doorway they could make out an office with an oil lamp lit. There was parchment on the desk and a wet quill on the blotter. It seemed that the man had been working there when they had come to the door.

Once they were all inside, with Dorn perched carefully on the edge of a chair, the man looked around at the four traveling with Alimar. "Is it okay to talk freely in front of all of them?"

"They know everything about my situation."

"I'll start with the common knowledge anyway. My father was the royal family doctor. He delivered the King himself. He was very proud of that. We lived in a grand home. It wasn't in the castle grounds, but it was the first house on the level below it.

Now, before I talk about things that aren't common knowledge, I need to know you are the right person for me to share this information with. I really do need to be careful. My father went through a lot to keep the things I am about to say from getting into the wrong hands."

Alimar thought for a moment. "I bet your father delivered me. I met the woman that was to be my nanny. Her name is Shari. Then I traveled to find this."

Alimar pulled the bloodstone amulet from under his shirt. "I didn't even know what a bloodstone was before I found this. Did you know that a bloodstone can identify its rightful owner by taking a small drop of their blood? It isn't wearable by anyone but me now. You might have seen this on my father."

The man nodded and had to swallow twice before he could seem to form words. "Yes, I did. I wonder if you know the history behind that amulet. Generations ago, not long after all of this trouble stared, the King wanted to have a way to clearly identify the rightful heir to the throne. There was talk even then of hiding the prince from danger until he came of age.

He asked his mage to work on the project to the exclusion of all else. He worked night and day on it and had it ready except for one problem. He couldn't figure out a way to make it only recognize the heir. It recognized anyone in the royal family, at first.

Then my great, great...Well, my grandfather back four or five generations anyway, offered a suggestion. He said that everyone's blood is unique. If the amulet was designed to recognize that uniqueness and was offered a sample of the heir's blood upon his birth, it would always recognize that blood to the exclusion of all others.

So, my ancestor the doctor, working with the mage, completed the bloodstone. The King has worn it on the day he is crowned ever since. Your father wore it during times of great ceremony and so I did see him in it. Upon your birth it must have been made ready for you.

You said you didn't know what a bloodstone was before you found that? That is the only bloodstone. There is no other. You wear the most significant item your father could have given you.

He was a great and noble King. I hope you know that. I was lucky to have grown up in such a different time and remember the glory of the kingdom with your father as our King.

Well, enough of the history lesson. You are here for something. Excuse me for just a moment, and I will retrieve it for you. I'll be right back."

He left the room coming back with a book. He sat down again and spoke. "My father did deliver you. He was starting to teach me by then. I was about your age. I wanted to help with the delivery. He told me I couldn't and to never speak of the Queen's pregnancy. I didn't understand. I pointed out that everyone knew she was pregnant.

I will never forget his response. He said, "It is not for us to question the will of the King. If he asks us for our service or even our silence, it matters not what others do, we will obey." That day, I thought I understood loyalty. Then the King died and we left the city. My father became a country doctor and I followed in his footsteps.

As the years went by, I saw my father's loyalty tested in many ways. He never wavered. He would have given both our lives to fulfill his duty to the King. I don't resent the fact. He taught me what loyalty really was.

The fact that he was the one that delivered you, that he could confirm your existence, was the very reason he was watched and beaten. They tortured him in this very room. They probably would have killed him, but I snuck out and got some of the men nearby to come and chase them away.

I didn't know what information he was hiding for sure. I guessed at it, but my father didn't want me to even think about it for fear someone would try to get the information from me. Finally, two years ago now, he called me in to his bedside.

We were both doctors. We knew he was not likely to last the night. He pulled this book from beneath his pillow. He told me you would come for it one day. He told me to tell you that your father may have been born to be King, but that he earned his place on the throne every day. He wanted me to tell you to be that kind of King."

He didn't seem sure how to go on, so he gave the book to Alimar. It looked old and worn. It was leather but the title was worn off. As it turned out, it didn't matter what the book was called.

Alimar opened it up. The book had been hollowed out

and inside it there were two items. The first was Alimar's birth certificate. Alimar saw that his name was listed as Alimar Devlin Aster. The second was a letter from Doctor Maximilian Pratt certifying identifying marks on the newborn. The main one he mentioned was a birthmark Alimar had on the bottom of his right foot.

Alimar was starting to see what his father had been doing. He had left different types of proof with the people he trusted most. Alimar would have a whole arsenal of items that would show, without leaving any doubt, that he was the true and rightful heir to the throne. In the process it was being confirmed in his own mind as well.

"Oh, and one other thing, I guess you need to know where to go next. Just outside of the city of Point Crossing on a cliff by the ocean is a cemetery. Two graves over and three up is the one you want."

He went on to tell Alimar of the person to find next and where they should be. Also he gave him the hiding place of the information for the next person in the chain if that person couldn't be found. Alimar and the others got up to leave.

Alimar felt he owed this man a huge debt of gratitude. He had nothing but words to offer him. "Thank you so much for keeping this for me. I am so grateful to have these items and the information your father had to give me. Thank you, also for putting your self at risk for me. I wish you hadn't had to.

I regret that your father was treated badly because of what he knew. I wish there was a way I could apologize to him in person, too. Since that is not possible, please accept my sincerest apology. I am very sorry for what your family had to endure to keep me safe."

"I told you that my father showed me the meaning of loyalty. I see the way the kingdom is deteriorating and I understand more every day why the kingdom needs its king. I accept your apology wholeheartedly. Now that I have met you and understand the importance of you finding your way to the throne, it is all worth it.

My father would have loved to be here to see you. I am proud to have been able to fill in for him. Go, and be safe my King." The man bowed as if in court instead of standing in his sitting room.

As they all filed out and got ready to head back out, Alimar turned and said to the man, "I'm sorry, I never got your name."

"It's a tradition in my family to pass on the father's name to his first born son. My father was Maximilian Pratt the eighth. My father so despised his full name he just named me Max. Doctor Max Pratt the first, that's me."

Chapter 33

A Dream Come True

A lana was still reeling. She hadn't heard a single thing since the doctor had said they were to go to the cemetery. Even the cliff side location fit her dream.

She had been thinking a lot about her dream since Alimar had talked about his. His first had shown the past, but the one he had had just before meeting them seemed to show the future. Was hers like that, she wondered?

She also wondered if it was the future she was seeing then couldn't it be changed. Why would she have a dream like that if she couldn't do anything about it? She had mostly dismissed these thoughts as silly, but now they were going to a cemetery that sounded just like the one in her dream.

"Alana, you're falling behind. What is with you? I have been calling your name and you haven't heard me. Have you been daydreaming or something?"

Alana looked at Kilian and then she noticed that he was right, she had fallen behind. The others were still visible, but they were quite a ways ahead. She decided she needed to use this opportunity to talk to Kilian alone.

"Do you remember the night I had that awful nightmare and I wouldn't talk about it? I want to talk about it now. I need you to listen and have an open mind."

She told Kilian the details of the dream. She explained how real it all had seemed. She told him that her dreams had that feeling of being there that Alimar described from his dreams. Then she reminded him of the description of the cemetery they were on their way to visit.

"That can't be a coincidence, right?" She needed him to tell her she wasn't crazy. She was practically holding her breath in anticipation of his response.

"Alana, do you remember the time Da sent us on a scavenger hunt to help us learn the woods by noticing landmarks? Remember we were getting tired at the end and that last clue had us so stumped because we kept seeing the tree in the description but it was never the right one. We wanted it to be, because we were ready to be done.

I think your dream may be like that. I think any cemetery would sound like the one in your dream because you fear it so much. I think that's the only explanation possible.

Alimar is the King. He had the dreams he did because it was part of his heritage. His dreams really are supposed to be prophetic. We have dreams, but no matter how real they may seem at the time, they're just dreams."

Alana let out a breath of disappointment. He didn't believe her. She was right not to have told him about the dream when she first had it. She should have just kept this to herself.

Thinking over what Kilian had said did make her doubt herself. He made some valid points. Dreams were just dreams for normal people. He was right, Alimar was King and he was special. Who was she to think that her dream could really mean anything the way his did?

"Just forget I said anything. You're probably right. It was just so real and when the doctor described that place, I was so sure it was the same. My imagination must just be adding the details so it seems the same. I feel so silly."

"Maybe when we get into camp tonight you should tell the others about it, anyway. I could be wrong. It wouldn't hurt to get some other opinions."

Alana imagined the responses she would get from the others. She was not going to humiliate herself anymore. "No, I don't want to tell them. I don't want you to either. This was just between us, got it?"

They caught up to the others then, and even though she didn't think she would, she felt a little better. Dorn and Griff were up to their now familiar banter. She smiled in spite of herself when Griff got in another insult.

"Every time we do go to town, everyone stares all right. They stare and whisper to each other, "Look at that, those travelers have their very own giant."

"No, little man, it's you they are staring at, I say. The whispers are more to the tune of, "Look at the half dwarf those people are riding in with. Look at his little legs flopping about on the full size horse. How ever does he get up there? Oh, he has a cute little ladder, isn't that delightful. He's so neat and tidy too, just like a little doll." Dorn spoke in a high pitched sing song voice when imitating the whispering locals.

"I just wonder if you have a shirt that actually fits and isn't food stained, you big oaf. Dwarf you say. There's no dwarf in my family at all, perhaps I heard of a Halfling back some generations. It's getting dark. I think I'll ride ahead a bit and scout out campsites."

After he was out of earshot Dorn complained, "He loves to get the last word. Runs off every time he runs out of hot air or I start to get the upper hand. The man is frustrating!

It reminds me of Ruby back at The Gem. How I could use a few pints of her ale right about now. I wouldn't mind getting put in my place with some ale to wash it down with."

Kilian had to ask, "Are you fond of this Ruby, Dorn?"

"What? Well, no. I mean, I like her place. She's got a fiery tongue, and I liked talking with her some. It wasn't like that, really." He ended in a thoughtful way that made Alana think maybe he had feelings for Ruby he hadn't considered he had. She learned something new about at least one of these men she traveled with all the time.

She had to call them all men now, too. Kilian was filling out a little more. The big changes were in Alimar though. He was not the skinny little boy of fourteen that they had originally met.

They all practiced sparring most every night at camp. They rode all day, hunted a few nights a week, and had a diet that was rich in meat. All of them had gotten more fit and lean, except maybe Dorn who had already been fit. Griff had lost the belly he had grown accustomed to from city life. He actually wasn't happy about it. He muttered about only the poor being so thin.

In some ways it seemed like they had all been together for much longer than it had actually been. Since leaving home, months had passed as they traveled through the Kingdom. Most of that time had been spent with Alimar. Dorn had joined up with them only a couple weeks after they had found Alimar, with Griff being the newest addition.

Alimar was showing the passage of time. He was more muscular and was filled out almost as much as Kilian. He had aged in other ways too. He was not an innocent any more. He seemed wiser and more like the King he was to become every day that went by.

Since leaving Dr. Pratt's their journey had been mostly uneventful. Four more weeks had passed. If it hadn't been for her dream and the growing dread she felt, she might have been more relaxed.

Winter was coming and the further north they rode the more snow they could see in the mountains and hills around them. In higher elevations the snow occasionally fell along the trail, but it was still warm enough that it melted quickly and didn't affect the horses pace much.

Several more days passed like this until they were almost to Point Crossing and the cemetery on the cliff. Perhaps it was for this reason that she was thinking so much about her dream. That night she had the dream again. This time she heard the man who grabbed her called by his name, Marick.

Kilian woke her again. This time she wasn't quite so overwhelmed by it. She was at least able to hold her stomach. She repeated the name to herself, "Marick."

"What's that?" Kilian asked.

"The name of the man that took me in my dream, it was Marick."

"Maybe we should tell the others. It worries me that you've had it again."

Alana thought that over, but wasn't comfortable with the possibility that they would not consider her dream important like Kilian had originally. "It's just that I have been thinking about the dream since we are getting so close. That's why I had it, I'm sure. Anyway, you have my back, right?"

As they traveled that day she almost changed her mind several times. She took turns doubting the validity of the dream to doubting the wisdom of keeping it to herself. Night began to fall and the others discussed the need to go in under cover of darkness. That is when her terror rekindled. Night was when her dream took place.

"We can't go in the middle of the day. We'll look like some sort of grave robbers." Griff pointed out.

"Oh and going at night won't seem that way at all. Dorn replied sarcastically.

"What would you suggest, asking permission from the locals? "Hello there. We just need to dig up one of the graves in the cemetery." They wouldn't mind that at all." Griff responded just as sarcastically.

In the end, the decision was made to ride right through and get the work done by cover of darkness. Then they could go into the city to get rooms and supplies. They rode on with Alana numb with fear.

Arriving at the cemetery really confirmed Alana's concerns. It was the graveyard from her dream. It wasn't just similar, it was the very one.

She noticed that the trees were twisted and were shedding bark strangely. The branches hung down as if they were too heavy for the trees. They were leafless now that it was winter which made them seem lifeless and creepy.

It was a large cemetery that looked very old. There was a wrought iron fence around the whole thing that was decorative more than to keep anyone out. The tombstones were lined up like obedient soldiers. Some of them were very old, some were newer. There were many, maybe a hundred or more.

Her limbs seemed leaden. She got off of her horse and heard the sound of the waves and could smell the salt in the air. It was all happening.

The cliff called to her somehow. She wanted to look over the edge to see if it was also the same. She had never seen the ocean before in her life. That was where the difference would be. How could she accurately dream something she had never seen before?

The men were gathered around the grave at the spot where the doctor had told them to dig. She had time to take a quick look over the edge. She had to see the difference. That would prove this was all going to be okay.

Nothing had happened in her dream until they had the item out of the ground. It would be a while before they got the digging done. She stepped towards the fence almost without deciding to do it. It seemed she was just suddenly looking down at the waves crashing up onto the rocks.

She was transfixed by the sight. Everything was just as it had been in her dream. She turned to shout a warning. She should have told them all when she first had the dream with all of them in it.

Then it hit her. Griff had been in her dream. She hadn't made the connection with things being so crazy when they had met him, but he had been in her dream before she had ever laid eyes on him. She should have remembered that. She would have told everyone about her dream with confidence if she had only remembered that Griff had been in it.

She saw them then. All three were circled around Alimar who stood in the hole holding something. How had they gotten the hole dug so quickly? She had been looking at the ocean below for only a moment, hadn't she?

Kilian turned then with wonder on his face. He searched her out with his eyes. He motioned to her to come and see. Then he saw her face, in the glow of the moon, frozen in terror.

A noise then alerted them both to the danger. Kilian stepped towards her. He pulled his sword and warned the others, but it was too late. Dark hooded figures stepped out of the shadows.

She stepped towards Kilian as he moved towards her. Then the men swarmed around him and she couldn't see him anymore. She knew what was coming next. She couldn't even pull her sword or turn to see him coming. She heard the voice call out, "Marick take her. We've got this."

Then the steely grip wrapped around her. How could she have let this happen? She had had the warning. She could have stopped it. If only she had told everyone. If only she had believed in herself.

She struggled and she screamed, but to no avail. She heard the man muttering under his breath as she fought. Suddenly the air seemed electrified. The ground started to quake. She watched as the bodies began clawing their way to the surface.

Some of them were almost fresh. Some were merely bones staying together by magical means. The worst were the ones somewhere in between. Eyes rotted in their sockets, skin green with mold, lips peeled back revealing grotesque smiles of the decaying dead. Their clothes were decaying too, and the flesh revealed beneath was sometimes sagging, sometimes bloated, but in the dim light cast by the moon it was a disturbing sight.

Then the smell was upon her and she gagged. The rotting smell was overpowering. It wasn't just the smell, either. It was so thick; to breathe it in was like tasting the decay. The screams continued as the corpses seemed to be everywhere.

They were ripping, biting, and grabbing anyone in their path. They were jerky and uncoordinated, but the damage was still being done by the sheer number of them. She saw one man go down under five of them screaming and thrashing. She hadn't been able to catch sight of Kilian or any of her friends.

She was desperate to know they were okay. She knew that she couldn't stop the dream from coming true, but what of her brother and the others. Would they be okay?

Finally, Marick dragged her out of the cemetery. She had to get away. She lashed out the only way she could think of. She rose up her knee and kicked back towards him as hard as she could. She made contact with his shin solidly. He swore and before she got the chance to try again, he hit her over the head with something very hard and Alana knew no more.

Chapter 34

Divided

Kilian was excited to see what they were going to dig up. Upon reaching the cemetery they quickly found the marker to dig at. Dorn dug for a few minutes and then Kilian offered to spell him.

As he took a turn at digging he wondered, as he often did, what it must be like for Alimar. To find out you are King after living almost fifteen years of a regular life must have been overwhelming. He was not envious of Alimar. He was glad to be a part of his adventure though.

Look at all the places they were seeing. Look at the creatures they had fought. Fighting the men didn't bother him too much either knowing they were fighting on the right side. That was what he wished he could share with his parents. He wished he could tell them that they were okay and fighting for the kingdom. His father would be proud.

Griff offered to take a turn and Kilian climbed out. He stood with Dorn and faced the city then to make sure no one had been alerted to their presence and was coming to investigate. Looking at the city made him wonder about the people that lived here. They hadn't really had many opportunities to see the cities and get to know any people in them.

A hit on something hard alerted them to Griff's making the bottom of the hole. He reluctantly climbed out but watched Alimar carefully as he brushed off the sides of a plain box that was much smaller than a coffin. Dorn and Kilian turned to look curiously down into the hole as Alimar opened the lid.

He reached down and pulled out a purse full of coin from the sound of it. Alimar slipped that away in his pack. Then he pulled out a small piece of parchment and added that to his pack as well for further examination in better light later.

Then Alimar pulled out a ring and two bracers. It was hard to make out any details here at night. They hadn't lit any lamps not wanting to draw unwanted attention. Griff squinted and leaned closer to try to see in the dim light of the moon. "What is it? What is it? Don't keep us in suspense, Alimar."

Alimar looked them over and as he slipped the ring in his pack he answered. "The ring is the seal of the King. I recognize it from the wax seal on the letter my father left for me. He must have used this very one to seal the letter he wrote to me. The bracers must have been his too. The King's crest is branded into them. They look very fine." He moved to add the bracers to his pack also.

Kilian realized Alana wasn't beside him. He looked around curiously. Then he spotted her on the far side of the cemetery by the fence. He motioned her over. She was standing very still. Looking more carefully, he saw the look on her face and he realized something was wrong.

Dorn spoke then. "Alimar, you may as well wear those. Your sleeves will hide them and there's no reason to carry around what you can safely wear."

Alimar slipped them on, pulling his sleeves down over them. "They tingle a bit."

"Hmm, must be some magic in them then." Griff responded thoughtfully.

"Something is wrong." Kilian started. He pulled his sword and stepped towards Alana. Then the men emerged from the shadows. There were at least twenty of them. It was a trap. They must have known they would be coming here. Then it hit him, it was just like Alana had described.

His heart began to beat furiously in his chest. He hadn't listened and now it was happening. He had to get to her. There were too many men. Dorn jumped right in front of Alimar swinging his axe in its giant arc. Men closed in on him from the side. He was soon fighting for his life.

Alimar stepped in beside him just as he was about to be overwhelmed. The men soon had them all surrounded. Alimar turned with his back to Kilian. Dorn and Griff stepped back to join them. They had formed a loose circle that protected their backs. It was all the four could do to keep the men back.

Then the ground began to rumble and shake. Kilian knew what would happen next. While everyone one else looked around in surprise, he took two of their assailants down. He braced himself and pulled Alimar away from one grave that was opening up beneath his feet.

Dorn had recovered enough to have killed two men that were thrown into them as the ground shifted. Griff took a sword from the man in front of him and killed him with his own weapon. They used the confusion to even up the odds.

The dead rose. Kilian had to get to Alana. He knew for sure now that she was in danger. Her nightmare was coming true around them and there was no way for him to get to her. How could he have ignored her warning? He could hear her screaming, but couldn't see her through the crowd.

In desperation he dove through an opening in the men. Behind them were corpses that continued rising from the earth. He crawled through them. One bit him on the arm. He took its head. It went down after that and didn't move again.

Then one got him around the ankle in a bony grip. He tried to shake it free and another grabbed his arm. He was being bitten again, this time on the calf. As he tried to free himself, he saw one of their previous assailants next to him getting torn limb from limb as he screamed.

He could hear screaming all around the cemetery. He listened hard, but realized that he couldn't make out Alana's voice anymore. Did that mean he was too late? He struggled to get free of all the corpses that had him now.

He rolled onto his back. He felt a hand at his throat and looked to see a grotesque sight. The corpse that had him by the throat was a woman. Her skin was rotted away from her mouth and eye sockets. Her eyes were filmed over white and maggots wiggled out of her dress.

Everything was growing dark. He couldn't move at all now. The pressure on his throat was so that he couldn't get any air. His arms and legs were being pulled at ferociously. He felt one shoulder come free of its socket. His scream joined the chorus of others.

Suddenly the pressure was gone. He opened his eyes and looked around. There was a glowing light coming from behind Alimar and Dorn. The corpses shied away from it. He crawled towards the source of the light.

There was a young woman standing there he had never seen before. She held a glowing staff. The jewel on the top radiated a circle of blue light. In her other hand she held some sort of holy symbol while chanting in a language Kilian had never heard before.

Nothing mattered but getting to Alana, he had to find a way to where she was. He climbed carefully to his feet. Everything hurt. He had been bitten and torn at and was bleeding from many small wounds. His arm hung uselessly down at his side. He looked around. The fighting continued with the corpses outside the blue light's power.

Dorn was the only other person on his feet besides the woman and Kilian inside the light. Alimar was under several corpses that didn't make it out of the blue light's power. As the few men that had been attacking them that were left inside the blue lit circle rose to their feet, they took one look at Dorn and ran away.

Kilian looked at Dorn. He saw that the big man was covered in blood. He bled from multiple wounds. He had a cut on his scalp that was bleeding into his eyes. He had a cut high on his chest that had bled enough to cover the front of his shirt. It looked as though he had been bitten and scratched at too. Yet, he held his axe high with a menacing expression for all of those that rose.

Alimar was tucked behind Dorn. Dorn had obviously shielded him the best he could. Alimar had sat up and had his sword held out in front of him as if it was a ward. He was looking around for more assailants as he finally freed himself from the pile of bodies and climbed to his feet. Alimar had some wounds too. It seemed as though most of them had come from the corpses like Kilian's had.

Kilian still couldn't see a way through to the other side of the cemetery. He saw Griff in the hole they had dug. He had fared the best out of all of them. While the corpses were coming out of the ground, he hid under it.

He started towards the edge of the light. He had to get to Alana. It was probably too late already. Then the corpses fell. Not one by one, but all at once. Just like that the way was clear.

He ran as fast as he could to the last place he had seen Alana. He looked briefly down at the rocks below. They were just as she had described them. He saw where she had been standing and examined the ground. He could see where her small feet had been. Then he saw the larger impressions of boot clad feet that were right behind hers.

He could tell that she had kicked and fought. He followed the prints as quickly as he could out of the graveyard and down around a path that led to the ocean. He could see where there had been horses hidden. Some of them were still tied near a small outcropping of rock. He looked and he saw where Alana had stood too. Then he saw drag marks from where she had been standing to the area the horses had been tied.

The other three caught up to him. They all were bloody and weary from the fight. They looked at Kilian and then taking in his despairing look Alimar asked, "Where's Alana?"

Kilian didn't know whether to cry or yell. He had to go find Alana. "She's gone. They took her. I'm going after her."

"I hate to say it, Kilian but she may already be dead. She could still be in the graveyard." Dorn said not without caring in his voice.

"Okay, let's not think like that just yet. We'll look around and find her and then we need to get moving. Some of those guys could regroup and come back at any time." Griff pointed out.

"No, I tracked her here. See the drag marks? She was forced down here and then taken away on a horse. We have to follow the tracks. See them? They headed down the beach this way." Kilian pointed frantically.

They rushed back to their horses and came back to the spot where Kilian had seen the drag marks in the sand. He started carefully tracking from there. The lone horse had gone down the beach for a couple miles then the trail just vanished.

Kilian went back and forth looking at the end of the trail. It was easy to read. The tide had left a clean slate. The trail was there, and then it just wasn't.

"Are you sure this was the right trail?" Dorn asked.

"Yes, I'm positive. This is it." Kilian pulled at his hair as he continued looking at the dead end.

"What do we do now?" Alimar asked.

"You get out of here as fast as you can," Answered a female voice from the darkness. Then she stepped closer. It was the young woman with the staff.

"I'm not going anywhere without my sister." Kilian replied.

"If you stay here you're all going to die. They know you're here and they will not stop until every last one of you is dead." The woman said all of this matter-of-factly.

"Who are you? What do you know of all of this?" Alimar asked.

"My name is Cheresa. I am a priestess, or will be when my training is complete. My mentor has been hearing very alarming rumors of travelers that are trying to ruin the kingdom. I am guessing the travelers are supposed to be you?

He sent another apprentice to look into it some weeks ago and he didn't make it back. I was sent here to observe and collect information to take back to him. I have learned only a little, so far.

Here is what I do know, in the simplest terms. The people that are after you are very bad people. You all seem to be okay. Reading people's auras is one of my personal skills, that's how I know for sure.

The ones you ran into tonight were just the ones that got here first. There are more coming, and soon. You need to get out of the area right away. They have very accurate descriptions of some of you." She looked at Dorn meaningfully with the last sentence.

"Do you know where they took my sister?" Kilian asked desperately.

"No, I'm sure that was just an opportunity they saw. These people know how to take advantage of a situation. She must have gotten separated somehow? They probably took her to get information from her about all of you." Cheresa looked around curiously.

Kilian shook his head in frustration. He should have listened to Alana when she told him about the dream. At the very least he should have made sure she was by his side when they came here so he could have kept her safe. He had been too busy thinking about what they would find to realize she hadn't been with them.

He had failed her. He had failed their parents. He had promised to keep her safe and instead put her right in harm's way. Instead of making sure to keep her safe he had been thinking about the great adventure they were on. Now, he had lost his sister.

He had no idea where to go from here. His tracking skills wouldn't do him any good since the trail had vanished. He had to come up with another way to figure out where she was.

Then he realized the only way to find her was to find the men that took her. The only way to do that was to leave Alimar. Alimar couldn't risk himself like Kilian would have to do.

"I have to find the man that took her. I know his name. That might help me." Kilian said.

"How do you know his name? She was all the way across the cemetery from us?" Dorn asked.

"She told me before. I don't have time to explain right now. I am already falling too far behind, wherever they went."

"What was his name? That way we can all keep our ears open." Alimar pointed out.

"Marick, his name is Marick."

Griff's eyes got wide, "I know that name! That's the dirty, rotten constable of Waterful. They could have come right up the coast and beat us here. He would probably take her back there."

"We can't go to Waterful. Griff would be thrown right back in jail, and who knows what would happen to Alimar." Dorn pointed out.

"Go on without me. I will find Alana and catch up to you later. Tell me where you're going next and I will find you." Kilian said.

"No, we can find her together Kilian. We all can work as a team just like we have been. This doesn't change that. We need to stick together." Alimar stepped towards him beseechingly.

"I have to go where it won't be safe for you. I have to figure out where they have taken her. Don't you see? I have to find them to have a chance of finding her. My only choice is to go after them and get the information on where she is somehow. I may even have to pretend to join them."

Dorn was nodding at this. "Alimar, he's right. There is really no other way. It is how I found you, after all. Infiltrate and listen, that's what I'd do if I were Kilian.

He might even learn more about what they know. It would also help if he were to be able to figure out what their numbers are. He could also find out who is leading this opposition and what they're after."

Kilian nodded too, though all he cared about at the moment was getting Alana back. He had to go on his own. He had already put Alana in harm's way. He wasn't sure he would be able to get her back safely, but he had to try. He wouldn't risk Alimar as well. He was already in jeopardy every day.

"Yes, you go on. Tell me where to find you and I will be there. I've got to go now. There is nothing more to say. I have to hurry and get to Alana. We will all be safer the farther from here we can get, anyway. Separating for just a little while will confuse them too."

Alimar looked torn. Then with a glance at the woman, stepped forward and whispered the next destination into Kilian's ear. Then suddenly he was hugging him fiercely.

"If I had a brother, I would want him to be you. I am so sorry this has happened. I will wait for you for as long as I can. Please find us. I don't have any idea where we are going after that. I don't know what I would do without you and Alana." Alimar added quietly in his ear.

Griff stepped forward and gave him a careful hug. "You take care of yourself. Find Alana and catch up to us. We will miss your hunting and her singing."

Dorn stepped up too. He put his arms around Kilian also. Then he said, "This will only hurt for a minute." Then he quickly popped Kilian's shoulder back in place. To Kilian's credit, he only let out a painful hiss.

Dorn only added, "Be safe."

With that, Kilian got back on his horse and began riding away. He looked back once to see them all staring after him. Alimar looked close to tears watching him leave. He turned away not able to bare the sight.

Then the tears were streaming down his face as the reality of the situation really hit him. Where was his sister? Was she alright? He didn't know what he would do if something had happened to her. Somehow he had to find Alana. He would find her. He focused on that and rode on alone for the first time ever.

Chapter 35

Devotion

A limar was done. He wanted to tell someone, anyone that he didn't want to be the King anyway and to forget this whole thing. He wanted his family, Louis and Jana. He wanted his friends, Kilian and Alana. Why did he have to be the one to give up everything for a kingdom that didn't want him anyway?

He explained all of this to Dorn and Griff. They were his friends too and needed to understand that he couldn't bear to risk their lives anymore either. He hadn't understood all of the risks when his uncle had sent him off with Fogerden.

Being sent off to risk his own life was one thing. Thinking of Fogerden reminded him that he had almost lost his life protecting Alimar. Then he thought of all of the times that they had been in danger since. He had lost his horse and now Alana and Kilian were gone too.

Thinking about everything, he had lost someone else also. The Alimar he had been was no longer. He was changed irrevocably. Nothing he did could ever give him back his innocence and youthful joy.

He, Dorn and Griff had left Point Crossing not long after Kilian had disappeared from sight. Watching him go had been one of the most difficult things Alimar had ever had to do. He could tell it hadn't been easy for Dorn or Griff either.

Cheresa, the priestess in training, had given them the name and location of her mentor so they could follow up with him later if they chose too. Alimar was too distraught to be able to think about that, but he had remembered his manors long enough to thank her for her help in the cemetery. He knew if it hadn't been for her they would all most likely be dead.

They had purposely started off in the wrong direction since someone seemed to know at least some of the locations they would be heading to. If they continued they were going to have to figure out how they were being tracked. They sat around a campfire far off the road as Alimar told Griff and Dorn all the reasons they should not continue.

"I think I need to go home. I have to go talk to my Uncle Louis about all of this. I'm sure he didn't think it would get this bad. He'll know what to do."

Dorn and Griff looked at each other sadly. Griff shrugged his shoulders and Dorn finally turned to Alimar. "Alimar, I'm going to say some things now that you might not want to hear. I think some of it may even hurt your feelings. There is no help for it, though. You need some raw truth right about now.

You don't get the option of quitting! Sure you can just give up. You could run on home and put those you love in danger. You could decide that you're so noble that you'll just surrender rather than risk another life for this cause. You can do any of those things, but you aren't going to.

All of the rest of us volunteered for this. The risk was always there. It might have been Nocturals or it might have been bandits, but something could have gotten any one of us killed at any time.

Things haven't been easy. They are going to get a lot harder too. Kilian may come back without Alana. He may not make it back at all. Griff or I or even you could be killed. All of that is true.

Can we quit on you? Yes, we can. We aren't going to though. Why, you might ask, we believe, that's why. This kingdom can be great again, but it needs its King. Sorry if you didn't get to volunteer, but that King is you. Like it or not, you can't make it go away.

Griff, you want to add anything to that?" Dorn looked at the little man with fire in his eyes. It was clear he felt every word he had said.

Griff swallowed hard and replied with a shrug, "No, um, nothing I can think of to add to that. That's about it, in a nutshell. I couldn't have said it better."

"One other thing while I have a good rant going, when we were in the tavern on the other side of the mountains we got into a conversation with a man about the corruption in the kingdom. I have been meaning to talk to you about that Alimar. You have a lot to think on already, but you're smart and can think on this too.

We've been going about this the wrong way. See, the way I figure it, you are supposed to go to all these places all over the kingdom right? I get that leaving all of this stuff in one place might not have been safe. Why did your father want you to go so far and to so many places, though?

I think he wanted you to see the state things were in. Here you are roaming the kingdom, incognito or at least that was the idea. Since we have been having problems we have been rushing through all these cities and towns along the way. I think we have to be smarter instead of faster from now on.

We have to get information as we go. That is the real treasure hunt, don't you see? You have a chance to learn what's going on. For example, who's in charge in Point

Crossing? Are they good people? Are they corrupt like Deputy Mayor Little back in Strautin? How about the constable in Waterful, Griff? What is his story anyway?"

"I don't really know much. A few years after the King died he was promoted to constable by the mayor. He got so much power over the years since then that he started telling the guard what to do. That's when Kamaron finally got fed up.

He told the mayor he was leaving if Marick kept it up. I guess he didn't like the mayor's response. The next thing I heard, he and a third of the guard just rode out of the city one day. Marick runs the city now, as far as the residents can tell. The guard and the militia are both run by him now." Griff explained.

"Do you see, Alimar? This quest is about rebuilding the kingdom. When you take the throne you have to be able to decide what changes need to take place. That is why you're out here. Your father knew that all these years would change things. He couldn't know how they would change. He knew that you would have to figure that out."

Alimar sat with his head in his hands. He listened to everything Dorn and Griff had said. Dorn had been right; some of it was hard to hear. His head felt like it was spinning with all the different thoughts fighting for a chance to crystallize. He felt on the verge of something. He just couldn't process everything to figure it out.

"Can we go to sleep now? I just need some time to think." He finally said. Both men had been looking at him with concern in their eyes.

He lay down and rolled away from them. He pretended to sleep. He listened as Griff offered to take first watch and Dorn agreed. As it grew quiet, he thought about the day they had had. It wasn't just about this day, though. It was about all the days. He had to go back to the beginning and think it all through.

First, the dream was what started it all. No, that wasn't right. It was the prophecy or curse as he thought of it. So many generations of the same royal bloodline doomed to fight. Why couldn't they choose not to? Who made them battle to the death, anyway?

Then his part in that same old story began with the dream. So, the dream tells him that somewhere out there is a man that is destined to be his enemy. He still didn't understand why that couldn't be changed. He would have to come back to that later.

Then he leaves home with Fogerden who gets hurt keeping him safe. He definitely had some guilt about that. The question was did Alimar do all he could? The answer, he had to admit to himself, was yes. He had to let go of that guilt.

Kilian and Alana came along then. He was so grateful that they had. He'd needed them in so many ways. They had helped him with Fogerden. They had become him friends. They had chosen to stay with him month after month. They hadn't even known the truth about him for a long time, but they still stayed with him. Did they regret that now?

He didn't think so. They had wanted to stay with him. Even Alana, in the end hadn't needed to be convinced. Alimar was glad of that. Alana got taken. Kilian went after her the only way that he could. Alimar needed to let go of that guilt too.

Even Dorn and then Griff, still with him right now, had joined willingly, Dorn for a good cause, and Griff for a way back to Waterful, eventually. They were aware of the risks. So that guilt too, was useless.

His real issue wasn't the past, or the present. His real issue was the future and what it held. Was he really brave and selfless enough to be the King? That was his real problem. He didn't feel worthy of the kingdom. He didn't even understand how things worked.

He wondered about all the power Griff had said Marick had in Waterful. He was right in the capital city and it sounded like he was pretty much running things. Was he the one he was going to have to fight? If so, the man already controlled the very army Alimar would need. He didn't see how he would be able to take the throne as long as Marick was running Waterful. He was going to have to get more information about what was happening there.

That had been Dorn's point. They had to start paying attention to the workings of the cities and areas they were going through. He had missed so many opportunities to do that already. He should have figured that out for himself. The fact that Dorn had made that connection for him only proved that Alimar's concerns were valid.

Griff had woken Dorn for his shift at watch some time ago. Alimar could hear Griff's quiet snoring as he lay there thinking. He rolled over and looked at Dorn through the flickering firelight.

"Dorn, will you answer me something honestly?" Alimar asked quietly as not to disturb Griff's slumber.

"Always," Was Dorn's simple answer.

"After all of these months of traveling with me, do you really think I'm cut out to be the King?"

"Alimar, after all of these months of traveling with you I know you are cut out to be King. The fact that you even ask proves it better than any words I can say. You see, the best Kings in history are the ones that ask the questions.

If you assumed you knew everything just because your blood says you are King, then that would be a whole different story. Don't you wonder why I protected you before I even knew you were King?

I did it because if someone really has that nobility in them, anyone who looks closely will see it. I didn't have to know you were the King to see you were good and that whatever was after you had to be bad. It started out just that simple for me.

Realizing you were King only made me see that my choice was even easier to make. To fight for a good man is enough for me. To fight for a good man who will take the throne and give that goodness to his people, well that is the greatest man I could ever fight for."

"I wouldn't even have made it this far if it wasn't for all of you though. You even think of things I should have, like the fact that I should be getting to know the kingdom as I go. Let's face it; I am not the bravest or the smartest. Doesn't that change your mind at all?"

"Did you think a King did everything? Who are these people your father sent you through the kingdom to see? They were his advisors and closest friends. Isn't that what we are? No man can stand alone. Your father didn't. You can't be expected to either.

Once again you prove your worthiness to me. Expecting yourself to be better than you are is a good quality for a King. Keep striving towards that man you know is in you. He will be a great and mighty King. You wait and see."

At that, Alimar rolled back over a little overwhelmed by Dorn's responses. He knew he had more thinking to do, but his questions had been answered. It gave him clarity of mind that allowed him to drift off to sleep.

He dreamed not of the battle where his father died. He didn't dream the dream with Kilian fighting at his back, either. He dreamed instead, a new dream. It was peaceful and beautiful.

He rode his horse through a majestic city that had amazing waterfalls like he had never seen as its backdrop. He knew it was Waterful from the descriptions he had heard. The streets glistened like jewels in the sun from the beads of water on the cobbles. People he didn't know lined the streets clapping and waving. Children ran ahead of him throwing flowers along his path.

He rode like this for a while moving up through the levels of the city. Finally, he reached the castle. It was an awesome sight. He had had a picture in his mind of a beautiful castle. This was so much more then he could have imagined.

He sat on his horse looking up at it. He was too stunned by the view to move his horse through the gate.

Then a voice spoke to him from atop the wall, "You wonder if you belong here, don't you?"

He nodded to the beautiful woman who stood there. He had never seen her before. Then his father, whose face he had seen so many times in his dreams, appeared beside her and put his arm around her shoulders. The woman must be his mother then. How good it was to see her face and to have heard her voice.

Then his father spoke in a great booming voice, "Let's ask the people if you belong here Alimar. People of Asteria, I ask you to step forward and tell us, does this King belong on our beloved throne?"

Then there on the wall, Alimar saw them step forward one by one.

There was Louis joined by Jana, "Yes!"

There was Fogerden joined by Shari, "Yes!"

There was Dorn joined by Griff, "Yes!"

Then up stepped Kilian who was joined by Alana, "Yes!"

From behind him he heard as one the citizens of the great capital city of Asteria join in as his family and his friends shouted together, "Yes!" They all agreed as one.

Alimar woke to sounds of breakfast being made by Griff. He sat up and rubbed the sleep from his eyes, looking around as if for the first time. The dream had seemed just as real as his others though he knew it wasn't the same. It hadn't and wouldn't happen, yet it was real. It showed him what he needed to do.

Dorn and Griff both looked at him questioningly, maybe trying to gauge his mood in the new day's light. Alimar remembered their faces in the dream as they shouted out on his behalf. He saw that same devotion in their eyes. He realized now it had been there for months. He just hadn't been looking.

"We have a lot to do and still far to go. Dorn, you were right. We need to find a way to collect information as we continue. I need both of you to be committed to getting to the end of this quest. I do need your help. I want to assure you both, I am ready now."

The End of Book One of Alimar's Quest

Look for
Alimar's Quest
Book 2
A Kingdom Divided

Here is a sneak peek at the next book in the series

Chapter 1

Rajon

The boat rocked. Dorn groaned from his perch by the railing and retched into the sea. He hadn't moved from that spot since they had come aboard. His reaction to the movement of the boat had been almost instantaneous. Griff looked at him with some sympathy but mostly glee.

"Dorn, you're missing the best adventure yet! Poor Dorn, look at how the simple motion of the sea can take such a big strong man down. Let's hope we don't get attacked while we are on this boat. Dorn wouldn't be able to lift his axe, much less swing it, eh Alimar?"

Alimar looked at the giant of a man. He was green with motion sickness. Alimar had never thought he would see Dorn look weak but, Griff was right, Dorn probably wouldn't have been able to lift his axe if his life depended on it.

"Well Griff, I feel a little queasy from time to time too. You're the only one that seems made for sea life. Dorn would probably say it's because you're so short you don't feel the motion as badly."

That earned a momentary chuckle from Dorn, but that was all he seemed able to manage. Griff crossed his arms and grumbled. "So now you're going to gang up on me, is that it?

I'll have you know that I have always liked being out on the water. I am a very good swimmer too.

Did you hear Dorn asking the Captain how safe the boat was? He was pretty nervous long before we boarded. He hasn't moved since. I don't think he can swim."

Alimar looked back at Dorn who looked chagrined. Griff must have guessed right. Now, Alimar really felt bad for him. Being prone to sea sickness was one thing, going out in a boat that was barely bigger than you and not being able to swim must be horrible. It showed Dorn's dedication that he was even here on the boat with him.

Griff was right up front by the bow. He was standing with his feet spread and looked natural and happy with the wind blowing through his hair. He was bending his knees slightly to compensate for the movement of the boat like it was the most natural thing in the world.

When Dorn had carefully boarded the boat back at the dock, the whole thing had listed to the side he was on. The small crew had had to adjust the cargo to compensate for his weight. The captain had told him to stay put. Dorn didn't look like he could have moved even if he had wanted to.

Alimar had been queasy off and on as he had told Griff, but he could see the appeal of sailing. It was invigorating and he thought he could get used to it with a few trips. Of course, he wasn't sure he would sail again after this round trip was done.

The captain's name was Jared Highmast. He had told Alimar he came from a long line of sea captains. Captain Highmast had estimated that it would take about two weeks to sail to the island if the weather held out and they didn't lose the wind.

He told everyone to call him Jared. "No point in formality when we'll be shoulder to shoulder on a ship for two weeks."

The ship was called The Wayward Woman. Jared pointed out that she was a single mast vessel with fore and aft rigging. She was small and maneuverable which was extremely important with the mostly reef locked bay they travelled in. There were two small cabins below deck. One was the captain's quarters and the other a cabin with four very small bunk beds in it. There was also the galley, a cargo hold, and a head below deck.

The boat was full of strange noises. There was a constant creaking of wood as people moved around on deck and the boat shifted in the water. The sails snapped and rippled in the wind. Being that winter was setting in, the wind was usually cold, but occasionally it would change direction and a warm breeze would sweep over the deck.

The two deckhands were twins by the name of Rik and Rok. They were strong and quick though not the smartest. Rik and Rok did their jobs efficiently enough and seemed a good natured duo. There would be periods of inactivity and then they would scurry around quickly when a course change was needed or the wind changed direction.

The Wayward Woman was not made for carrying passengers. It was a small cargo vessel. The crew was small this trip and only two crewmembers besides the captain were on board. Jared had told Griff and Alimar that if they wanted to use two of the bunks in the crew quarters they were welcome to it, but that Dorn was too big and would have to make due up here.

They were a few hours from the dock in Point Crossing when Alimar heard a noise from the water. He looked over the side expecting to see a school of fish jumping or maybe one of the seals the captain had said they might catch sight of. Instead, he saw what looked kind of like a dolphin's dorsal fin, but there were two of them.

He leaned over to look closer and suddenly whatever it was disappeared from view. Just as he was about to straighten, something shot out of the water. It was bigger than he was and heading right for him.

Before he had a chance to move out of the way, it rocketed right over him and onto the deck. He turned with a gasp of surprise. He received a face full of sea water as whatever it was shook. He wiped his eyes and couldn't believe what he saw.

It stood taller than he did on powerful legs that ended in flipper like feet. Its arms were long and muscled with very long fingers. Its eyes were not in front of its head, but not completely on the sides either. It had the ridge of a nose, but no nostrils. Its skin was very smooth and grey.

It examined him as he examined it. He saw Griff staring too, but the crew went about its business like this was nothing new to them. Then the creature did something Alimar wouldn't have thought it could, it spoke.

"I Rajon, you name?"

Alimar was so surprised it took him a minute to figure out what it had said. Then he answered, "My name is Alimar."

The creatures face changed a little and Alimar thought it might be trying to mimic a human smile. He smiled in return. Rajon started garbling excitedly then. Alimar thought it sounded like rhythmic squeaks and whistles. He didn't understand any of it.

Jared came over and joined them. "He gets pretty excited about meeting new people. He only comes on the ship after we're well away from the shoreline. They are very social, but extremely careful."

"What is he?" Alimar had to ask. He had never seen anything like it. He couldn't even tell it was a he though it wore no clothing.

"He's a Cetacean. They live in the sea. There aren't many of them. Hmm, what are you going on about, Rajon? I can't figure out what you mean."

"You understand him? Those sounds he's making are words?" Alimar asked in amazement.

"I have learned their language a bit over the years, just like they learned some of ours. I think he keeps saying you smell of King. I guess I don't understand him as well as I thought. Calm down Rajon, I don't understand what you're saying."

Alimar was stunned. He smelled of King? What did that mean? Finally, Rajon quieted, shook his head, and blinked several times with strange translucent eyelids.

"I've heard rumors of the Cetaceans. I always thought they were just a myth. Wow, can I feel its skin?" Griff came over and reached towards it carefully.

Griff stepped forward and Rajon let out a howl. "Oww, you step me fluke!"

Griff stepped back looking down to see the huge flipper like feet. "Sorry, I didn't notice the size of your-flukes, did you say?"

"I okay. You name?" He replied.

"I'm Griff."

Rajon turned to the captain. One eye still looked at them with interest. He seemed to know to face the person he was talking to. His strange hands were in motion all the time. Gesturing must have been a big part of learning to communicate, at first. It seemed he had kept the habit and every phrase seemed to come with a different gesture.

Alimar noticed that the back of his arms and calves had finlike protrusions. The dorsal fins he saw in the water extended down Rajon's back from his shoulder blade almost to his hip. He also saw why Rajon didn't have a nose. He had an opening on the back of his neck that occasionally would open and close.

"I reef, you fruit?" He asked the captain, gesturing to himself and then holding out his hands as if to receive the fruit in question.

"Sorry Rajon, no fruit today."

Seeing the curious looks from Alimar and Griff he added, "They love fruit. They help us navigate the reefs as we get closer to the island, and we give them fruit. From time to time, I find something else he doesn't mind taking instead, but usually they just want fruit. I can't seem to make him understand that fruit is seasonal. I offered him dried fruit once, and he was not impressed."

"Okay, okay. I reef, you fruit next. Yes?" Rajon seemed unconcerned with the idea that he might receive no payment. He reached over and grabbed a net that was nearby. Then, just like that, he leapt up and back into the sea.

Alimar stood there thinking about the amazing creature, man, or whatever. He wasn't sure what to call it. He wished Kilian and Alana were here. He was sure they would be just as fascinated by it as he was. He hoped they were both alright.

He looked ahead into the deep blue sea. The coastline was far behind them now and he could make out no details. The island they were headed towards wouldn't come into view for many days, he assumed.

They had been lucky, Jared had said, that the weather was so nice. In the winter, storms could sweep in and make sailing more difficult and less comfortable. Alimar was especially glad it seemed to be blue skies in all directions for Dorn's sake. A rough sea would not bode well for him. Alimar might have to join him if it got rough. It wouldn't take much for him to lose what little equilibrium he had gained after coming aboard.

Only a few minutes had elapsed when Rajon landed effortlessly back on the deck again. This time he had the net and it bulged with wiggling fish as he stood there. Then he dumped the net out and the fish flopped about.

"I fish, you eat Alimar King Smell." He gracefully dove back into the water without waiting for any kind of response.

"I guess he likes you. I wonder why he thinks you smell like the King. It's been years since he saw, or smelled him for that matter." The captain wondered.

"The King knew him?" Alimar asked anxiously.

"The King would visit the island from time to time back when I captained his ship. They met on more than one occasion. Rajon's people are not exactly subject to our laws and kingdom etiquette, but they have always seemed to understand who the King was. They always offered him gifts and fulfilled any request he had that they could."

Alimar marveled at the idea that he would somehow smell like his father. How could Rajon remember a smell after all of these years and then associate it with Alimar? Maybe Rajon didn't even mean smell. He could be trying to say he looked like his father or reminded him of the King in some way, for all Alimar knew.

No matter how many new things happened to him since he left home he never seemed fully prepared for the next surprise that was coming. As he had so many times in the months since he left home, he wondered what the future held. He knew now that he couldn't guess at what waited for him. All he could do was be ready, as ready as he could be, for anything. He wondered, as he had so many times in the past months, what kind of crazy adventure his father had sent him on. What could possibly happen next?

Chapter 2

Dry Land

everal hours had passed since Rajon had leapt back into the sea. They were having a simple lunch of dried meat and the dehydrated fruit that Rajon's people had no interest in. Dorn was lying face down on the deck. Alimar had offered him some of the food telling him he needed to eat, but he didn't look up or move at all. He replied with a groan.

"Don't show me food, please. I just found a nice cold spot of deck to lay my head on and I am not throwing up at the moment. If you get me started again, I think I may die. Do you want that on your conscience?"

Alimar shook his head and went to join Griff. The queasiness he had felt earlier had passed and he was able to enjoy the fresh sea air. Soon it was dark and after getting Dorn as comfortable as he could be, sick and stuck on deck, Alimar went below to find a bunk.

It was a relief not to worry about posting a guard or sleeping with his sword drawn in case they were ambushed in the night. Being on a boat was peaceful. He felt more relaxed than he had in a long time. He slept, and he dreamed.

Kilian was with him on the knoll. This time he knew who he was looking for and there, too was Dorn and Griff. He was so relieved. Then he looked for Alana. She must be here too. He was frustrated when he couldn't see her. Looking back, he searched Kilian's face. He ignored the sound of the army moving towards them and just focused on Kilian.

Kilian looked grim and determined. As he shouted orders back towards the army waiting with them, Alimar saw it. The sadness of a great loss filled his eyes. The twinkle of merriment Kilian had always had with his sister around was missing.

Alimar woke and just looked at the ceiling above him. Two things struck him as he lay there thinking about the dream. He was learning to direct the dream to be able to observe details. He had always just been pulled along by the dream before.

The second thing was that he didn't think Alana was coming back. It hurt him deeply to think it and he feared that Kilian would be changed forever if he lost his sister this way. He just felt sure that if Alana had been there, he would have been able to see her this time.

At the same time, Alimar guessed by the look of everyone that maybe a year or closer to two would pass before this dream became reality. Maybe Alana was just not with them. She could be okay but doing something different. Alimar didn't think Kilian would have had the look he did if everything was okay with Alana, though. He couldn't think of anything else that would have made him look so sad.

He watched the sun come up through the small porthole in the crew quarters. Once the others woke, he slipped out to check on Dorn. He was worried about him getting through two weeks of travel. He found Dorn right where he had left him the night before, but was happy to see him propped up, pale but eating some porridge.

That week and the following were pretty uneventful. Alimar learned more about nautical terms and the workings of the sails. The wind had stayed pretty steady through the night and they were making good time. The morning of the fifteenth day he came up on deck to find Rajon standing there with the captain.

He looked out and realized the island was in view. It was still a ways off, but they would surely arrive there sometime later in the day. Rajon was pointing with his long index finger out into the water. Alimar noticed that while his first two fingers were extremely long, his ring finger and pinky weren't much longer than that of a human.

He was still in awe of the man-creature. Even though his language skills seemed rudimentary Alimar wondered at his intelligence. Something in Rajon's eyes made Alimar think that there was more to this race then at first met the eye.

Rajon had been looking at Alimar through one eye as he finished talking with the captain. Now he turned to him and with a small bow spoke, "Fish good Alimar King Smell?"

They had cooked the fish Rajon had brought on board in a fire kettle they used on deck. It had been delicious and very fresh. Alimar wished he could ask about the King smell thing, but there were always too many ears around.

"Yes Rajon, the fish was very good. Thank you so much." Glancing at Dorn, Alimar thought he might be up to meeting Rajon today. "Have you met my friend Dorn?" He gestured towards the big man sitting on the deck.

Rajon went over and spoke to Dorn in the simple way he did. Alimar was so curious about him and his people. He decided to find out what the captain knew.

Jared rubbed his stubble for a moment as he thought about it. "Cetaceans are peaceful and simple. You saw how he reacted to us not having the fruit he hoped for. They are not worried about things. Easy come easy go seems to be their philosophy.

Only one thing really upsets them, violence. I have a story you surely will not have heard that will demonstrate. It will give you a much better understanding of Rajon and his people.

The King a few generations ago had a dream to sail out beyond the reefs and see what else was in the world beyond Asteria. The reefs are treacherous and surround the kingdom on all sides. Even navigating to the island can be dangerous.

So, he asked the Cetaceans to go outside the reefs and see what the ocean was like. His idea was to build a fleet and get it out beyond the reefs somehow to explore. He just wanted the Cetaceans to scout for him a bit first.

They are easy going, as you can tell, and agreed to help. They sent four of their men out to look around and report back to the King. Weeks passed and then only one returned.

The lone survivor told the King that there had been much open ocean past the reefs, but there was a terrible creature they said was called the Raiknadiel that ruled the ocean. It had killed the other three and gave a warning to the last before letting him go.

He continued by telling the King it was a giant beast. He described it as being bigger than forty of those Yegoxen we use to load the bigger cargo going across the bay. It had tentacles and claws and sounded like a truly horrific beast.

The King still wanted to know more. Did they see any land or ships? Was there only the one Raiknadiel or more of them?

The Cetacean told the King that there was nothing out there but the Raiknadiel. A ship would be crushed effortlessly if it ventured into the ocean. That was the warning the monster had given. No one was to come into the ocean on pain of death. He knew no more than that.

The Cetaceans vowed never to venture beyond the reefs again. Losing three of their community was devastating for them. They didn't come to the surface again when boats were out for many years after that. The King gave up the idea of building a fleet and moved on to more obtainable goals, so the story goes.

The Cetaceans call their community a pod, and I understand it is very small. They mate for life. They have very few females and each female only has one mating cycle. They must live a long time. I can't even guess at Rajon's age, but he hasn't changed a bit in all of the years I have known him. I don't know for sure how many Cetaceans there are, but I don't get the impression there are more than 50 or 60 of them altogether.

So, they are careful. They don't go to the mainland. They fear the violence there. Only unmated males are allowed to come into contact with us at all. Even then, they are careful to get to know you for years before coming aboard.

Rajon and I have known each other for twenty five years or so. I give him lots of fruit when it's in season, and he helps us safely navigate the reef so we can travel more quickly to the island and the other coastal cities of the mainland.

I'll tell you one more thing about Rajon and his people. I think they have it right, you know? I've often thought over the years that they have the answer to the meaning of life. They just don't quite know how to tell us simple races what it is." The captain laughed then and, with a look at Rajon, they got back to work planning the passage through the reef.

Alimar understood Rajon a little better now. He had seen more than his fare share of bloodshed in the past several months and expected to see more. He wished it wasn't the way of things, but it was. Alimar could see what the captain meant. He didn't like the violence and greed he had seen in the kingdom so far.

Rajon dove gracefully back into the sea. Soon Alimar saw his dorsal fins break the surface of the water. The captain called out instructions to the crewmember working the tiller. Rajon made his movements very clear so as to guide the ship safely.

Several hours went by like this, Rajon not needing to surface since he was able to breath with his blowhole in the back of his neck. Then they were clear of the reefs and Rajon disappeared before they came too far into the small inlet of the island.

It seemed like they had landed on a totally different world when they reached the dock. The beach was sand as Alimar had expected, but it was red, as was a mountain in the distance. There must be a lot of iron on this island.

He took a closer look at the island. The half farthest from them seemed to be covered by the mountain. The red rocks ran around the outside edge of the island except on this short stretch of beach where the dock had been built. Nestled against the mountain was a small forest. Between the forest and the beach lay the village.

The village had a variety of construction techniques. The simplest buildings were clay huts, but in contrast they had brick buildings too. Some of those were even two stories and quite grand looking. Here and there, Alimar could see a few wooden structures as well. Mostly, it seemed that wood was used carefully. He could understand why. This island wouldn't be able to trade large items like lumber as easily as on the mainland of Asteria.

The people that obviously lived in the village were as varied as the construction techniques. Many were dark skinned and long limbed. Others were lighter of skin and very small. The adults of the smallest of them were the size of human children. Some ranged in between the two.

Some wore simple frocks or loose fitting pants and shirts. Others wore more fitted city style clothing. Alimar saw that there were those that wore a little of both. Many wore colorful sashes around their waist or woven in their hair.

A tall dark skinned man came to the front of the crowd waiting to greet them. He was well dressed and spoke in an educated voice. "My friends, it is so good to see you! I see you have new crew members. That is unusual for you. Come, let's have a cold drink and talk about what you brought for us."

He embraced the captain warmly as he stepped off of the boat. Dorn was right behind Jared and with a brief, "Excuse me," ran down the dock to the beach where he collapsed in relief.

Jared laughed and explained to the curious locals around him, "No, these aren't crewmembers, but passengers. They have someone to see here. I know it's not like me to have passengers, or for you to have visitors for that matter. This was a very old favor I owed someone.

I'll pick them up and take them back on my next trip. I figure their business here will be concluded by then. I'm not sure the big one there will want to leave. He's not a sailor, that's for sure!"

The captain introduced them to the man. His name was Glavin. It turned out he was the elder of the village. It sounded like it was similar to being the mayor of a town. He explained that he didn't like titles any more than Jared did and they should just call him Glavin.

Glavin then looked over his visitors carefully. Seeing Griff he smiled, "Welcome to Tranquility. I hope you find comfort and joy in our peaceful village. You must be the one that has someone to see here. Which of the Halfling families are you from? You're more human, but I certainly see the Halfling in you. Are you a quarter then?"

Griff looked around and seemed to notice the smaller residents Glavin was referring to. His face colored and his expression grew defiant. He looked back at the tall smiling man and shook his head. "I think not. There was a rumor of Halfling on my father's side, but I am surely only human. We run small is all."

Glavin laughed loudly at that and the locals around him joined in. The captain chuckled a bit too. Griff didn't seem to get the joke and frowned. Noticing his distress, Glavin quit laughing and spoke to him in a fatherly manner.

"Sorry my young friend, I didn't realize you would be sensitive about it. My grandbabies are a quarter Halfling. We are proud of it. No point in being ashamed of where you come from. Your father must have taught you that, huh?

It's okay, really. I've seen that attitude before. You'll find none of that here, though. We love our differences, but see more of ourselves in each other. The tallest or darkest of us is very like the smallest or the fairest.

All of you come, and once Jared and I have taken care of our business we can get acquainted and you can tell me what brings you to our humble village. You will find we don't have many visitors, as the captain said. So be ready to be looked over and whispered about as new faces. It won't be long, if you stay for a while, before the people here will want to ask you all about yourselves."

It looked like a parade going down the dock. Glavin, as the Elder, took the lead with Jared, Rik, Rok, Alimar and Griff behind him. The locals that had joined them on the dock followed behind them and it seemed the rest of the village lined the beach as they passed by. As warned, there was whispering about them, but it was harmless speculation from everything Alimar could hear.

Alimar realized that other than theirs, not a weapon was in sight. There were no guard towers or uniformed men to be seen. There was no wall or defenses that he could see at all. Everyone was smiling and pointing. No one looked at them with suspicion, only with curiosity. Every face he saw was open and welcoming.

His sword slung across his back seemed heavier than ever. He wished he could hide it away. It made him feel like an invader bringing his weapon and his troubles to this simple island village. It seemed aptly named as it was tranquil and apparently untouched by the trouble of the mainland. He didn't like the idea of bringing any harm or disillusionment to these happy carefree people.

Alimar was more curious than ever about whom he was to see here. Who here would be involved in the things going on back on the mainland of the kingdom? No one here looked capable of secrets or hidden agendas. What could be waiting for him here, he wondered again.

LaVergne, TN USA
09 June 2010
185611LV00001B/5/P